JOM

JOM

The Story King Chronicles: Book One

by Jeff Monday

JOM
THE STORY KING CHRONICLES: BOOK ONE

This is a work of fiction. Names, characters, events, and environments are the product of the author's imagination or are used fictitiously. Any resemblance to actual persons, living or dead, events, locales, etcetera is entirely coincidental.

Book Design by Aldo Perez

Cover Design by Annatova Goodman

Printed in the United States of America

For all the storytellers,

for all the listeners.

Acknowledgements

Thanks go out to all the people who put up with my ramblings. Whether around the campfire, late at night or over pints, you are the reason I continue to spin tall tales. So this is your fault.

Extra special thanks to Aldo and Annatova. Your creativity, knowledge and support have been like mana from the heavens.

: Table of Contents :

: Table of Contents :

JOM

The Story King Chronicles: Book One

The Bedlam War

"TELL US A STORY."

Jom lived in a time of wonder. Technomages, god-like rulers that harnessed both science and magic, bent the very fabric of the universe to suit their every whim. The Floating Mountains of the Kentauros. The sunken city in the limitless ocean of Koes. The famous talking stones of the Squalor Bishops. The sentient cloud cities above the worlds of Atseatsan and Atseatsine. The singing jewels in the crown of the Dust King. The miracles that were conjured forth from the aether, grown with prayer spells in the languages of the gods or produced in dark labs hidden far from sight were endless. Yet so were the horrors. For every crystal heart-song of Rafk, there was a famine vault that kept its victims in a perpetual state of starvation. For each Star Ring that granted its wearer command over light itself, there was a planet-sized Juggernaut Shark that consumed entire systems as it swam among the stars.

Jom saw none of this. His days were filled with chores around the homestead; milking and mending, tilling and toiling. His was a small, dusty village on a forgotten, dusty planet on the outskirts of a tiny inconsequential system. Like his world, Jom was small. Whenever he wasn't doing chores, he was avoiding the bigger children of the village, avoiding their fists and their sneers and their taunts. His wits and his legs kept him out of harm's way, mostly. All too often though, he would find himself nursing his latest bruise in the shadows of the rickety huts of the village. Only later, after his work was done and the sun was low in the sky, would he be allowed to sit around the hearth with the others and listen to his Grandmother tell of the wonders of the Technomages' kingdoms.

"Have I told you the story about the Bedlam War?" she would ask, or something similar. And, even though they all have heard the story many times, they would all shake their heads, eager to hear it once more. Grandmother, perhaps knowing better, perhaps not, settled in and took a puff from the aerator she always kept attached to her arm. Green smoke rose in lazy circles from her nostrils as she let the lepton mist penetrate and soothe her neurons. Then a spark would ignite behind her eyes and she would begin:

It was the beginning of the Fiftieth Dynasty of Skyript the Reseeder. As Technomages go, he was by far one of the vilest. He came to power by growing-building a fleet of behemoths that roamed the skies of the worlds. These flying monsters were as long as a river and as tall as a mountain. Eyes as large as a village looked down on the creatures below. Their shadow darkened whole countrysides. Their roar could be heard two planets away. These abominations were the children of Skyript, called such because, when he came to a world he wished to conquer, he used dark powers to rip a hole in the skies. Out of the void between space, his behemoths would sail, belching ionspores on the land below. These spores would take root in the ground, quickly choking out any living plant they found. Soon, the land would become a wasteland. But Skyript was not done yet. After the plants died, so too did the animals, then the people. When the populace was at its weakest, Skyript would send his army to the surface to slaughter any who still breathed. After the natives were culled, he sent his own people to repopulate the land. They grew the plants native to Skyript's home and raised the animals he grew up with. He spent a millennium traveling with his army to the farthest reaches of the universe, making every planet he found a replica of his beloved homeworld.

At the beginning of the Fiftieth Dynasty, Skyript ruled so many worlds that even his cadre of a thousand thousand ministers could not keep track of them all. As you might imagine though, dissention, like a cancer, began to grow from within. As the boundaries of Skyript's empire grew, so too did those who wished to live free of his rule. Any rebellion was, of course, squashed in the most horrific and dramatic manner. Skyript thought nothing of destroying entire plans of existence, snuffing the lives of untold creatures, in order to maintain his rule. The creatures of a million realms were, it seemed, destined to live forever under Skyript's thumb.

Generations after generations on countless worlds were born, grew and died under the banner of Skyript. But, against all odds, one man was born who did not live in fear, who refused to believe he was destined to live a life of servitude to a ruler who would never even set foot on his world. Nor did he believe any others should either. His name was Opm.

During his long days of labor, Opm thought. During the endless cold nights, he thought. For many, many cycles, he thought about his life and what he could do to rise up above the misery forced upon him. Opm knew that no logical tactics would ever succeed against such a great power. No armed rebellion could hope to defeat an endless army. No propaganda could convert enough people quickly

17

enough before he was hunted down. So he did the only rational thing he could think of; he went insane. Letting go of all practical thoughts, he willfully destroyed his reality, shattering his thoughts into a million pieces. He let his thoughts run amok, giving in to the basest instinct, indulging every random whim that fluttered in his brain. At first, he forced himself to let go but, the more he did it, the easier it became for him to ignore the rational parts of his psyche and let the madness take over. His mind shattered, his thoughts became broken and tattered. In a haze of insanity, he seized upon the one path to victory left to him. He didn't understand the power he now held. He only felt a mad euphoria unlike anything he had ever felt before. Giddy, he told his friend his idea and, with a few words, destroyed his friend's mind as well. For his words now carried the seed of Bedlam. He could infect others with his insanity. From them, the madness spread like a virus from person to person as the infected passed their mad ideas to someone new. Insane and free, they lived in peace, spreading their rebellious beautiful words to any they encountered.

At first, the insane kept to themselves. Opm's village descended into chaos. And they were ecstatic. They danced along with the fires, shouting at the top of their lungs. Alerted by smoke from fires that were never quenched, the authorities came to investigate. Opm whispered in their ears and they too went insane. Before long, the village a short distance away noticed something wrong and came, worried about their neighbors. They too fell to the madness. Then the next village. And the next. Taxes were no longer paid. Youngsters did not report for conscription. The fabric of Skyript's orderly empire was unraveling, one village at a time.

As the rebellion of the insane spread, word quickly reached the palace dimension of Skyript. His ministers could not explain how these people could rebel. Not only were they rebelling, they told the Technomage, they were winning. The madness spread exponentially. First villages, then cities, then planets. As the number of insane grew, entire systems fell quicker and quicker to their maniacal laughter. Quiet communities were reduced to raving lunatics. Commerce fell apart. Worlds stopped spinning. Skyript's grasp was slipping. In his anger, Skyript beheaded his thousand thousand ministers and then sent his behemoths to quell the uprising. But, as the monsters poured from the torn sky, Opm managed to climb onto the lead behemoth. Opm whispered into its ear, spreading his madness to the creature. The skies that day were purple with the blood of crazed behemoths tearing each other to pieces. Chunks of flesh rained down on the people dancing below and they feasted on the bones of their enemies. The ionspores, helpless against the madness, withered and died.

Eventually, against all odds and logic, the army of the insane reached the capitol. Skyript the Reseeder, ruler of a million planes, was like wheat against the hurricane of bedlam that swept the capitol. He could not fight. He could not defend himself. As the palace burned, Opm entered the great throne chamber. Skyript, weapon in hand, faced his opponent. Opm whispered to him and Skyript's mind broke, his weapon fell and he sank to his knees. Tears of laughter streamed down his face as Opm gently slid a dagger into his throat, bringing to an end the reign of Skyript.

Their eyes wide, Jom and the others would sit in silence as Grandmother inhaled again. Then, with a gesture, she would shoo them off to bed where Jom would dream of worlds of madness.

Dagger of the Fallen Angel

JOM RAN AS FAST as he could along the river; its black water reflected a muted mirror of a weak sun half-seen behind the billowing smoke of the threshers. He coughed as he ran and tasted blood. The air was stale and dirty yet he pushed himself to run faster. The threshers, giant machines as big as his village, crawled through the fields all around him. Their massive metal maws chewed up everything in front of them, whether crop, person or animal. The rumbling of their treads shook the ground so hard Jom could barely keep his feet as he ran. The nearest thresher was a field away yet he was terrified of both the massive machines and the army of cyborgs that ringed each one. Not a single sheath or grain or seed pod escaped the enhanced eyes of the farmers. Any who ventured too close were deemed thieves and executed on the spot, their bodies tossed into the threshers to add to the haul.

He clutched an object tightly to his side as he ran. His eyes, fearful and excited, scanned the area. He saw some villagers off in the distance but they did not seem to be looking his way. Only once he reached the relative safety of his secret spot did he allow himself to smile. His spot, nothing more than a hole dug into the side bank of the river, was unknown to anyone but him. He had spent most of last season digging it out with the leg bone of a dead pack animal.

He scrambled down the short embankment, nimbly avoiding the black water at his feet. Ever since he was a little child, he was told of the creatures that lurked below the inky surface. If his foot so much as touched the surface of the water, they would clamp down with powerful jaws and drag him into the murk below, never to be seen again. Looking around to make sure he was alone, he quickly removed the dead brush that concealed the entrance and slipped inside, replacing the brush as he scooted his body into the small space. Breathing heavily, he opened his hand and looked at his prize. In his hand was a rusted dagger, longer than both his hands. Weathered by the unforgiving sun and dulled by the omnipresent dirt, it nevertheless glinted with a hint of grander times, even in the half-light of his meager shelter. He brushed at the baked dirt, revealing more of the metal underneath. The metal was the color of the hills at dusk. There was a shimmering to it that reminded him of the stars. As he stared at the dagger, he remembered one of Grandmother's stories and his heart missed a beat. What if this was the dagger she had spoken about? What if this was the Dagger of the Fallen Angel?

"Now simmer down," Grandmother snapped at them. "One story tonight. That's all. These old bones are weary and don't need to be up all night telling tales to you young ones."

The gathered children sat in silence, waiting for her to begin, knowing that, despite her protests, the story would be a long and would tell of places far away and of people strangely familiar.

There are gods," she began, "make no mistake about that. Gods and angels and demons roam the planes just as easily as you walk across the room. And we are to them as the dirt is to your bare feet; barely worth the energy to notice. They use stars for light and planets as playthings. Yet there have been times that the gods and mortals have crossed paths. We have always lost. Remember that. Never forget your place. Take the tale of Nidaba as a warning.

As the Technomages' reach grew, so too did the likelihood that, one day, they would pierce the veil between our plane and the realm of the gods. It was inevitable, I suppose. Yet it meant the end of Nidaba, one of the greatest Technomages of all. Nidaba ruled a thousand realms with grace and empathy. She was loved by her people and all prospered under her banner. Entire systems sang her praises and they lived in peace. Her scientists and sorcerers worked in harmony with her to create wonders such that the universe had never seen. They delved into the very fabric of being, manipulating the essence of the soul to create new life. They pushed back the boundaries of knowledge until they walked in realms undreamt of any by before. And Nidaba was always the first to take the risk, to step over the boundary between what was known and what was not.

One day, while standing on the edge of existence, Nidaba reached out with her hand and grasped at eternity. As she did so, she slid between this world and the immortal plane. Like a stone hitting water, ripples of her hand spread across the holy. The response was quick and fierce. Nidaba found herself attacked by sacred forces that drove her back through the rift. The gods' realm, it seemed, was inviolate and not to be breached. Yet, just before the rift was closed, a creature fell through. Nidaba, dazed by the onslaught, did not see the fall. Thrown to the ground by the concussive blast of the rift closing, Nidaba was stunned. Her assistants rushed forward to help her to her feet.

Clearing her eyes, she turned her gaze upward and gasped.

Standing above them was an angel, a servant of the gods. Tall and proud, his very skin glimmered with holy light. He was perfect as only an angel can be, so much so that it hurt to look upon him. He studied the mortals before him and his gaze pierced their hearts. He spoke but a single word and every one of the assistants fell to the ground clutching their bleeding ears until they died. Profound sadness swept across the face of the angel as he realized none on this plane could endure the holy words. None except one. Nidaba, although dazed, stood before him. She ignored the trickle of blood that oozed from her ears and lifted her chin proudly. He smiled. Her heart swelled with a sacred love she could not, would not deny and she reached out to him. Her skin sizzled as his holy flesh made contact with hers, yet she did not pull away. Instead, she embraced the angel, letting the hallowed skin melt her body. To die in the embrace of an angel, to feel the greatest love one could ever feel, to literally melt in the embrace of her only love; these were her last thoughts. She cried out in pain and pleasure as the angel watched helplessly. Soon, she was nothing but a pile of ash at his feet.

Distraught, he looked at his hands. Never had he taken the life of an innocent before. He felt his body shake. His very being had been violated by her act of self-immolation. Yet it was his fault, somehow. He was tainted, no longer pure. He was responsible for her death, regardless of his intent in the matter. He felt the gods gazing down on him and knew what he must do. He took his dagger from his waist belt and plunged it into his sacred heart. Holy fire consumed him. The scales were in balance again and the gods, watching from beyond the rift, nodded their approval.

For you see, if the angel had not taken a life for a life, war would had erupted among the higher planes. Nidaba's death, however inadvertent, demanded settlement. A heart for a heart. Only then would the various gods be satisfied. As for the assistants' deaths? Well, the gods are also fickle in their judgment.

As the smoke cleared, the room was empty save for the bodies of the assistants, a pile of ash, holy and mortal mixed together, and a golden dagger. The bodies were removed; the ash carefully collected and put in an urn that even to this day sits at the entrance to the Silver Palace of Bluestone in remembrance. The dagger disappeared, never to be seen again.

Jom recalled how Grandmother then told them to remember the story whenever they thought to rise up from the filth. "Keep your heads and hearts down," she said, "or burn like she did." And he remembered how he vowed never to think like that.

Jom cradled the rusty dagger in his hands until he heard his name being called. Looking out of his shelter, he saw that hours had passed and he cursed. He surely would get a beating for not finishing his chores. Carefully, he buried the dagger among his other treasures and snuck out of his hole. He replaced the brush, making sure no one was around to see, then ran to the homestead and his punishment.

The Boy Who Fell From the Sun

GRANDMOTHER! LOOK AT WHAT I found!" Jom burst into Grandmother's hut in a rush, excited to show her the odd flute he had stumbled across in the west field.

"Hai! Have respect, boy!"

"Sorry Grandmother."

"Hmph." She resumed her sewing, all the while keeping one eye on Jom. After several heartbeats, when she knew he could no longer stand still from excitement, she put her kit down with a heavy sigh and looked him full in the eyes.

"Now, what do you have to show me?"

Bursting with excitement, Jom held out his trembling hands. Amid the clumps of dirt and grass was a small wooden flute, barely longer than Jom's third finger. It was a perfect replica of a full-sized instrument.

Grandmother reached out with a withered hand and deftly plucked the instrument from his hands. She closed one eye and squinted with the other as she cautiously turned it over and over, studying the tiny carvings.

"Do you see the tiny finger holes?" Jom asked with bated breath, looking on anxiously. Grandmother grunted in acknowledgement and continued to study the flute. Finally, after a moment's consideration, she passed it back to Jom.

"Do you know what it is?"

Grandmother grunted again.

"Well?"

"Sit."

Jom instantly dropped to the hard dirt, cradling the tiny flute in one hand. Grandmother ambled over to the side of the room and picked three small dried berries from a chipped bowl. After a slight hesitation, she tossed one to Jom who quickly popped it in his mouth before anyone came in and stole it from him. Nodding her satisfaction, Grandmother settled herself onto her mat, took a long breath from her aerator and began speaking.

It may be hard to believe, but there was a time when people tilled this land with their own hands, a time before the threshers and robot farmers. A time long before you or I. This lost tribe worked hard, nurturing the crops with sweat and calloused hands. It was hard work but it was a peaceful time. The Technomages fought their wars in systems far away from here. The War of Guilty had not yet come to destroy the cities. The nights were quiet.

Then there came a day when a boy fell from the sun. The people had been toiling in the fields as usual when suddenly the sun dimmed for a brief moment. Day became night. The people looked up in fear. Never had the sun gone out like that. They thought the world was ending. But then, something fell from the sky, as if vomited from the sun itself. A trail of black smoke billowed behind it as it plunged to the ground. The object hit with a fierce explosion, flattening trees in every direction. The villagers held each other, waiting for their world to burn. But it didn't. Fearfully, they looked up. The trail of smoke ended a short distance from the village.

The entire tribe hurried to the site of impact. They were amazed to see a small boy lying in the middle of the crater. His skin was red and wisps of smoke curled off him. Assuming he was dead, the Eldest, Yunu, lowered himself down to the bottom of the crater. With shaking hands, he reached out to the boy. At Yunu's touch, the boy opened his eyes. Startled, Yunu stumbled backwards and fell. The boy leapt to his feet and caught Yunu before he hit the ground. Then, with gentle steps, he carried Yunu out of the crater, picking the larger man up as easily as I picked up these berries.

The people gathered around the boy, astonished at what they saw. He stood before them; the boy who fell from the sun, the boy with no shadow. The villagers murmured among themselves, pointing to the ground. The boy's skin glowed from within, as if he held a fire just under the surface. The boy opened his mouth to speak but, instead of words, music issued from his lips. Wonderful music unlike any heard before on this world. Each note touched your heart, each pause made you ache for more. Tears flowed freely from the eyes of everyone who heard yet there was no shame. The strongest men of the tribe wept openly at the beauty of his music words. Women fell to their knees and Yunu, eldest and strongest of all, felt his heart swell to the point of bursting. Yet, even as he swooned, he smiled and cried out in joy. The others, seeing Yunu fall, could only laugh, overcome as they were with happiness.

The boy stopped speaking and the tribe slowly regained their senses. They brought the boy to the center of their village and, for the rest of that night, the boy spoke to them. Although they didn't understand his words, the music told of a long journey and danger. He sang to them of love and hatred, of the past and future. The music washed over them, transporting them to realms bright and breathtaking. Every note he sang touched their hearts and souls until they could do nothing but weep. Then, drained of emotion, they stumbled to their straw mats and sleep a dreamless sleep until the sun rose.

The next day, the tribe went out to their fields. But even as they picked up shovels and plows, their hearts were with the boy sleeping back in the village. Before the sun was halfway across the sky, their tools were left in the fields and they were sitting around the center fire pit, waiting for the boy to sing to them again.

Only the Dowa, the tiny mechanical servants of the tribe, were immune to the sun-boy's music. Their tin ears heard only ordinary music. Their soulless bodies could not respond to the beauty of the song. As the people stayed up longer and longer into the night, the Dowa were forced to work harder and harder to make up for the lost work. The crops, forgotten by the tribe, were tended to by the Dowa who never slept and never grew tired. After only a short time, the people of the village were listening to the sun-boy speak most of the day as well as the night. Chores went unfinished. Crops grew wild. The Dowa, only two hands tall, could not keep up with the work yet they toiled nonstop, dedicated as they were to their masters. Even so, the village fell into disrepair. Animals either starved to death or wandered off in search of greener pastures, never to return. Whole fields of crops withered in the sun. The Dowa, outraged by the illogical turn of events, took the only course of action that made sense; they killed the sun-boy.

They came at him all at once, from every direction. They struck quickly, before anyone could react, when the moon was highest in the sky, coolly calculating that, since he had come from the sun, he would be weakest when the night was fullest. Many of the Dowa fell, either to the heat of the boy's skin, or by the hands of the tribesmen that sprung to his defense. Yet enough landed their blows. As he died, the sun-boy let out a scream that literally broke the hearts of every living man, woman and child within range of his voice. The Dowa were horrified as they watched their entire village fall dead at their feet.

When the sun rose the next morning, the few remaining Dowa worked together to bury their masters and protectors. As for the sun-boy, they burned his body, leaving nothing but charred ground. Yet, some cycles later, they found a tall, thin reed growing on that spot of burned soil. The Dowa were now only a handful in number, the rest having fallen to disrepair and the elements. They took the reeds and fashioned flutes. The music they played sounded just like the music the sun-boy spoke and they played their flutes until the last of them stopped functioning, as a reminder of their greatest failure.

Jom looked down at the tiny flute in his hands in wonder.

"This is a Dowa flute?"

Grandmother nodded and took another puff from her aerator. "Yes. Quite a find."

"Is it worth anything?"

Grandmother chuckled. "Only memories, child. Only memories."

: Dream of the Revitalizers :

J OM CROUCHED IN THE darkness, keeping still as a mouse in the deepest shadows. He strained to hear what the adults were discussing around the central fire of the village. Although the wind took most of their words, he picked up snatches of their conversation.

"I tell you, the crops are not yielding enough anymore. The Revitalizers are coming."

"Impossible. It's only been twenty years!"

"We need to leave now before it's too late."

"I'm not going anywhere. This is my home!"

"Your home isn't going to exist much longer if they are coming! Use your head!"

"And what if they aren't? You ask us to leave for nothing!"

The wind changed direction and he heard no more. Slowly, he moved away from the mud wall and slunk back to the outskirts of the village, careful to stay silent and unseen.

Jom walked towards his hut. The wind blew at him and he heard the snoring and grunting of his family well before he reached the dirty blanket that was strung across the doorframe. As he approached the doorway, a sudden impulse took hold and he changed direction to make for the river. He wrapped his thin shirt tight around his chest, its protection against the cold wind more psychological than physical. Picking his way through the fields, he reached his shelter in a few minutes, only stumbling once or twice over unseen rocks that jutted from the hard ground. Taking extra care in the darkness to avoid the water's edge—nothing more than a deeper blackness in the dark of the night--he moved aside the dead branches and folded himself into his hole. Among his meager treasures was a thread-bare blanket he had stolen from one of his older relations. He wrapped himself in it and lay down. Eyes closed, he listened to the lazy river just a few feet from his head but sleep would not come. He was anxious about what he had heard. If the Revitalizers were coming, he would have to either journey a vast distance to a strange land to escape, or perish.

He lay in the dark, trying unsuccessfully to stop thinking about what he had heard. He knew of nothing except his village, small though it was. The thought of leaving it was frightening. He stared at the dirt above his head and tried to imagine what life was like somewhere else. In the darkness, he couldn't tell if his eyes were open or closed and he felt his mind drifting off, bit by bit. Slowly, after what seemed half the night, the sound of the river and wind took hold of his senses and he slipped into a restless slumber filled with dreams.

Jom walked through a barren field under a hot sun. A light wind meandered past him, barely whisking away the sweat on his skin. He blinked and shielded his eyes from the sun's glare. Blinded, he stumbled on something and nearly lost his balance. He looked down. At his feet was a gleaming metal skull half-buried in the dirt. Jom reached down and pulled it from the soil's grasp. The metal was bright and he squinted as the sun reflected off it. As he held the skull, looking into dead eye sockets, the metal began to oxidize and turn dull grey, then rust brown. Flakes floated off the skull on unfelt winds. Within seconds, the skull had disintegrated, leaving only small bits of rust in his hands.

Then a shadow fell across the land. Jom looked up. Towering over him was a monstrosity of metal and iron. Walking towards him on six spindly legs, the massive blackened steel body of the Revitalizer pushed through the clouds. Out of the back, a giant scoop curled out and down like a tail. As Jom stood in awe, the Revitalizer stopped walking. The scoop swung down and buried itself into the ground, causing a massive shockwave that knocked Jom to his feet. The maw dug deep into the soil, carving out a chunk of ground larger than his village. It lifted it high into the sky until it was directly under the body of the machine. A battery of cylinders emerged from the belly and let loose streams of blue energy into the soil, infusing the dirt with radiation. The scoop rotated, letting the glowing pile fall back to the ground. One of the legs lifted and slammed down, pushing the dirt flat. The scoop dug into another spot and so it went, over and over. No scrape of land was spared the Revitalizer's attention. The machine made its way across the landscape at a methodical, unrelenting pace.

Jom watched in fascination as the Revitalizer dug deep, irradiated the soil, then stomped it all back into place. His fascination quickly turned to horror though when he realized the giant was slowly making its way towards his village. He got to his feet and ran. His lungs burned as they both pumped blood to his legs and forced out a

32

long scream. He ran until his legs burned. He yelled until his throat was raw. But his voice was drowned out by the Revitalizer and no one heard. The village was oblivious to the danger that towered over them. Then Jom saw the giant scoop swing down again, this time digging into the huts and buildings of the village. He skidded to a halt as the scoop lifted up, taking his family and friends high into the air. The hum of the cannons was overwhelming and he covered his ears as everyone he knew was blasted back to atoms.

Jom cried out as he woke. Sweat dripped off his body, despite the coolness of the night. He lay as still as he could, listening first to his heart, then the water. Only when he was sure he didn't hear machines was he able to drift off to sleep once more, catching a little sleep before the sun rose and he had to begin his chores.

The Vagabond Storyteller

H AI! PAY ATTENTION!"

Jom suffered a quick scuff to the head and murmured a half-hearted apology. Still, rather than take another blow, he concentrated on weaving the leaves tighter. The season was changing and soon a cold wind would be blowing through their hut unless they tightened up the walls and roof. As his hands moved, his thoughts moved as well, although in a completely different direction than where they should. Still shaken by his nightmare from the night before, he couldn't stop thinking that the village was in imminent danger. But there was nothing he could do. When he mentioned the Revitalizers to Grandmother, she scoffed and told him to worry about things he could control, like his chores.

As his fingers worked the weave, he became aware of yelling outside. Fearing the worst, he looked to Grandmother, ready to help her run for safety. But there was no panic in her eyes. Only a strange look that spoke of days long past. That's when Jom heard the jingling of bells over the yells and shouts and he knew the Storyteller was in the village.

"May I?" he asked. She didn't respond for a moment, listening instead to ghosts, then, coming back to the present, gave him a slight, resigned nod. Jom set his work aside and ran out to join the others in greeting the Storyteller.

Jom felt some guilt as he ran. He had heard the story of Grandmother and the Storyteller many times, although never from her. Never from her. This was a story whispered from one child to the next in the dark of the night when all the adults were asleep or drunk. It was never mentioned in her presence, mostly out of respect but also out of fear. Some wounds never healed.

Before she was Grandmother, even before she was Mother, she was Shaya. In those days, her hair was long and flowed around her head like the black water of the river flowed around the stones embedded in the middle of the steam. Her smile was as quick as her tongue. Yet that only made the men of the village want her even more. But their advances were for naught. Her heart had been stolen three cycles before by a wandering teller of stories. He had found his way to the village one warm night and had found his way into her bed by morning. Their dalliance was kept secret, of course, and he left town with barely a glance over his shoulder. Or so she thought. Heart-broken and disgusted with her weakness, she buried herself in the corner of the hut where she kept her bed and sobbed quietly throughout the long nights, eventually crying herself to sleep. It wasn't until two nights later that she found the note he had left hidden under her mat. In it, he professed his undying love for her and promised to return as often as he could. Smiling through her tears, she cried herself to sleep once more, but now it was with tears of joy.

True to his word, he returned at least once a cycle. When he wasn't regaling the villagers with stories of far-away lands and Technomage wars, he would sneak away with Shaya, giggling long into the night. This would go on for a few nights until she would wake up one morning alone except for dreams of his next visit. Finally, during one of his visits, she gathered her nerve and asked him to stay.

"Stay? You know my life is the road, dear one."

"It doesn't have to be. Stay here. Stay with me."

"And do what? I would run out of stories before the end of the cycle."

"You can learn how to farm, or mend metal."

He laughed. "Can you see me doing such things?"

Even she had to smile at the thought of him trying to farm.

"Why don't you come with me on the road? I will teach you the ways of the travelling minstrels."

"I—I don't know. I know nothing beyond this village."

At that he smiled and put his arms around her. They fell asleep in each other's arms and she dreamed of wandering the worlds. When the sun broke through her window the next morning, he was gone. The next cycle came and went but he did not appear. Then another. And another. Five long cycles passed without a visit. Shaya, heartbroken, found a respectable village farmer to start a family with and she went from Shaya to Mother and then, eventually, to Grandmother. She never stopped thinking about her vagabond lover though. Often, when the wind blew just right, she could hear the jiggling of the bells of his belt in her mind and at those times she would stare out towards the edge of the village with a sad smile, thinking of what may have been.

Then there came a day when she heard the bells but no wind was blowing. Hesitantly, she stood and peered into the distance and, sure enough, there he was, much older but still with that same glint in his eyes she fell in love with all those seasons ago.

They met in the middle of the village and embraced each other with tears and smiles.

"Where have you been? It's been so long," she asked.

"I've traveled the dimensions and walked with gods," he replied. "I've seen angels and demons battle through the veils and stood aboard ships larger than planets. But I had to come back to see you."

She started to cry. Gently, he wiped the tears from her eyes.

"Come with me, Shaya. Come explore the realms with me while we still have time left to us. Let us spend our remaining days together."

"I—I can't. I have a family now. You were gone for so long...I had to..."

He put a finger on her lips. "Shh. I understand. It is my fault."

"Can you stay?"

He shook his head. "For a few nights, yes. The road still calls, although not as loudly as it once did. But I promise I will return every cycle until you come away with me."

"You know I cannot."

"I will never stop trying."

They spent as much of his visit together as possible, although always in public. No more sneaking away in the night for them. Grandmother had responsibilities and obligations and would not break vows. When he left, he repeated his promise to come back for her again and he did. And every time he came back, he asked her to go with him. And every time she refused, although it broke her heart to do so.

Jom looked over his shoulder as he ran and could just barely see her silhouette in the darkness of the hut, waiting for her wandering minstrel to stop by and offer to take her away.

Under the River

JOM SAT ON THE bank of the river, watching the sunlight glint off the lazy black waves that rolled by. The water looked inviting and refreshing. But Jom knew the stories of the monsters that lived under the waves. Even now, he could feel cold eyes watching him from just below the surface. Luckily, air was poisonous to the Lurkers that lived in the river. Jom was in no danger unless he was foolish enough to go into the water. He closed his eyes and let the sun beat down on his face, hoping the heat would burn away his fears. A week had passed since his dream of the Revitalizers. Every night when he closed his eyes, he saw giant machines destroying his village. The other children made fun of him, pretending to be Revitalizers and chasing him around the village. Grandmother was no comfort. She was distracted by the storyteller and barely acknowledged Jom's presence or absence. Jom felt alone and scared.

He sat until the sun was low in the sky, letting the warm sun keep his fears at bay. His thoughts roamed across the land. He tried to imagine what life was like on the other side of the hills far in the distance. Was there a boy there that longed for something more too? Did that boy live his life scared and hiding in a hole by the river? When his stomach began to growl, he decided it was time to go back home. Maybe if he finished whatever chores were waiting for him quickly, he would be able to eat something before dark. He stood and brushed the dirt from his leggings.

Later, he tried to figure out what, exactly, happened next. Did the ground give beneath his foot? Did he purposely step into the river, propelled by some vague longing for adventure? Or did something reach out of the water and grab his ankle? Regardless, before he knew what was happening, he was falling backwards. Towards the black water. Towards the Lurkers. Panic stopped his breath in his chest as he hit the water. He closed his eyes and his heart stopped. He braced for the certain pain that would come from being torn to shreds by sharp teeth. Instead, he felt his body getting dragged through the cold water at incredible speed. There was no pain other than the burning in his lungs. He opened his eyes for a second but saw nothing other than darkness swirling around him so he closed them tight. As he was pulled along and down, he felt slimy things brush against his skin. Once or twice something grabbed hold of a flailing leg or arm, as if to claim him as its own. But whatever had taken him would not give him up so easily and wrenched him along, out of the grasping creatures of the water. His lungs built up more and more pressure. His tears were lost among the dark water. Finally, he succumbed to the needs of his body and sucked in a huge mouth full of water.

But there was no water. Just as he breathed in, he was expelled from the water, landing heavily on hard ground and sucked in stale air. Shock and fear overtook him. His diaphragm spasmed. He gulped in great quantities of air while choking at the same time. He crawled onto his knees and vomited, only to inhale the rank air right back in. Even when he opened his eyes, he saw little through the tears that poured out. After long minutes, his vision cleared enough for him to see he was in a small cave. Water dripped from the ceiling onto his back. Clumps of moss that clung to the cracks between rocks emitted a weak green glow. He was kneeling in mud the color of night and, as he regained his senses, he realized he was shivering uncontrollably.

"Do you need fire?" a voice asked from behind him. Jom barely understood the words for the voice was hollow and soulless. Jom slowly turned his head. His breath caught in his throat. Next to him stood a clock-work boy. The automaton was shaped like a small child and stood almost as tall as Jom but was extremely slender, like someone took a child and stretched him out. In the murky light of the cave, Jom saw gears and wheels spinning between the gaps in its dented, rusted plating. On its chest was a large clock that slowly spun backwards, as if counting down to something. Its head and face were child-like, although the eyes, cheeks and ears were elongated. The eyes were a dull gold with a tiny spark of light buried deep within that spoke of knowledge and understanding. It raised its arm and a hand extended from inside, emerging from the interior of the arm and extending towards Jom.

"Do you need fire?" it asked again. "You appear to be in discomfort."

Jom reached out a shaky hand and the clock-work boy took a firm grasp of it, easily pulling him to his feet by retracting its hand back into its arm.

"Come. There is warmth near." Without waiting for a response, the automaton spun at its waist, turning its upper half completely around. It lifted a leg and it spun in midair, righting itself in the proper direction by the time it touched the ground. The other leg did the same and it walked away. Jom, barely able to keep his teeth from chattering, hurried after it and together they made their way further into the cave.

The space was confined yet felt open due to a low breeze that kept the air fresh. His shoulders brushed against the walls as they walked and he had to duck a few times to avoid low-hanging clumps of dirt. The meager light of the moss was barely enough to see by and he stumbled often over the uneven ground. Yet there was only one direction they could go so he pressed on, trying to concentrate on the metal figure in front of him. A few heartbeats later, they emerged into a slightly larger chamber. The clock-work boy went to the middle of the space and fiddled with some twigs and sticks. Suddenly, a small fire flared up from the pile of tinder. The orange light of the fire filled the room and Jom gratefully stepped forward, letting the heat seep into him and dry his wet skin and clothes. It took only a moment for Jom to warm up and feel better. He looked over at the clock-work boy and smiled.

"Thank you. For the fire, I mean. And for saving me in the water too, I suppose."

It shook its head. "I did not enter the water. That was my companion."

"Oh." Jom looked around. There was no one else in the chamber with them. "Um, is your...companion here?"

Again, it shook its head. "Dianat leaves the water only when necessary. She is a Water Banshee."

Jom could not keep the look of surprise from his face. "A Water Banshee? But...how? Why?"

The automaton held up a hand to forestall his questions. "Please. All will be explained. Once you are sufficiently warmed, we will continue our journey."

"Journey? Where are we going? I have to get back to my village."

The clock-work boy shook his head. "There is no need. The Revitalizers will be arriving shortly. There is nothing you can do. And you are needed."

"Revitalizers!" Jom's heart leapt into his throat. "I knew it! We have to warn them!" He turned and began to walk back the way they had come. In the darkness of the passageway, two eyes glowed brightly. Jom heard a high moaning coming from the shadows. He stopped in fear.

"Stay," a shrill voice said. Jom backed up a few paces.

"I agree with Dianat. You need to remain with us. You will not survive otherwise."

"What about my family? My friends?" Jom turned to the automaton. "I need to warn them!"

"They will not listen. You know this."

"I still have to try!"

"There is no logic to your request. They will not listen. You would only put yourself in danger and jeopardize our mission."

"Mission?"

"All will be explained in time."

Jom paced around the fire in frustration. "Can I at least get a message to Grandmother? I have to save her!"

The clock-work boy was silent for a moment, as if calculating. "That is acceptable. The delay will be brief. Dianat will relay a warning to her this evening. That is the best we can do. The rest will be in her hands."

Jom felt slightly better then. If Grandmother heeded the warning, if she thought it came from the gods, she would be able to leave the village before the Revitalizers arrived. Hopefully she will listen! He tried to stall for time so he could think of a way to escape. "And I need my things from by the river. There is a small hole where I fell into the water. I keep my things there."

"That is also acceptable. For now, I suggest you rest and gather your strength. We have a long journey ahead. When Dianat returns, we will leave."

Jom nodded. "What is your name?" he asked the automaton.

The clock-work boy cocked his head to one side. "Name? I have no name. My Makers did not give me one."

"What should I call you then?"

"My model designation is ND-7-2349-X. Is that helpful?"

"How about if I just call you NDX?"

"That will be acceptable. Now please, rest. Dianat will return in a short time and we will need to continue."

Jom settled down next to the fire and let the warmth seep into his bones. It had been a long time since he had been able to sit so close to a fire. Usually, the older, bigger children pushed him away, leaving him alone in the cold dark night, sitting by himself along the outskirts of the light. He smiled despite himself and enjoyed the heat. As he lay there, he thought about the odd circumstances he was suddenly in. Water Banshees? Clock-work boys? What was happening? He was scared and excited all at once. Instead of just sitting and listening to stories, he was finally a part of one! He wondered at how his dreams could be coming true. Was that why he was taken? Maybe, just maybe, the other children were wrong and he was special after all. And with that thought, he faded off into a contented sleep.

: Dream of the Lost Army :

MACAR LOOKED AROUND AT the men assembled before him. One hundred of the village's strongest and bravest had taken up shovels, branches and rocks and stood in front of him, waiting nervously for him to speak. He cleared his throat, hoping that the right words would come.

"I know you are frightened," he began, quickly finding his voice behind the quivering of his heart. "I know we are outnumbered. But today, we fight for more than our lives. We fight for the lives of our wives and children. We fight for the lives of our grandchildren not yet born. We fight for our future just as surely as we fight for our present."

Heads slowly lifted at his words. Eyes that had been downcast were raised. Hope stirred in tired hearts.

"The Technomage does not consider us a threat. That is why we will win."

There were murmurs of agreement among the men. Some nodded as Macar spoke.

"The Technomage does not think we can hurt him. That is why we will kill him."

A couple men shouted. Macar felt his anger bubble to the surface. He had witnessed so much death. No more would he watch while others suffered.

"No more!" he repeated the words of his heart. "No more will we live in fear!"

The men roared and brandished their weapons, feeding off of each other's emotions. In the doors and windows of the huts, the women and children looked out in pride at their brave warriors, even as they feared for their lives. Most of the men, they knew, would not be returning from battle.

"It is time to stand up! It is time to make him treat us as humans, not dogs! I will not live like a slave any longer! Will you?"

The men shouted a resounding "No!"

"Will you?"

"NO!"

Macar turned and jogged towards the outskirts of the village, followed closely by one hundred of the bravest men he had ever known. The women cried as they left, their tears disappearing into the dry dirt at their feet. They watched the men run towards the starship that hovered in the far distance. Such a large ship. Such a small group of men. The older men of the village shook their heads at such folly. But they spoke not a word. They had not joined Macar. They had no right to speak.

Time in his dream flowed back. Jom saw the starship, the Technomage's ship, enter their skies. Floating above the countryside, the massive ship cast its shadow over a dozen villages. Then a brilliant light flashed from the underside. Blank-faced cyborgs clad in shiny metal transported to the surface and spread out, systematically killing, kidnapping and destroying. The cyborg army took struggling men to serve in the Technomage's forces and screaming women to serve in his bed chambers. Jom watched in horror as whole villages were wiped out as the troops swept across the countryside. Black smoke flowed up from the burned ruins of a thousand huts and homes, blanketing the Technomage's ship in swirling darkness.

Time flowed around him again. He saw Macar standing at the edge of his village, watching the plumes of smoke rise from the neighboring villages and towns. Refugees streamed past him, desperate to escape the Technomage. But not Macar. Macar knew most of the elderly of his village could not run. He knew that his children were too small and the women of his village too attractive. They could not escape. There was nowhere to run to anyway. Behind them, vast plains spread out, crisscrossed by small rivers. There was no shelter. The Technomage's army would not stop until the entire planet was conquered. They had to fight. So he gathered whatever men he could and ran now to confront the Technomage.

His plan was simple. A small forest stood between the village and the Technomage's landing site. The men would stick to the trees for as long as possible until they were almost on top of the troops, then they would strike, attacking from the shadows, before melting back into the darkness of the forest. They would use the cover of the trees as long as possible before confronting the landing area directly. From there, they would teleport to the ship and kill the Technomage. They entered the forest quickly, running hard to reach the cover of the trees before they were spotted by the troopers. They moved silently into the forest, using the shadows to conceal their movement.

He knew he was leading his men on a suicide mission. He knew they were vastly outnumbered and outgunned. And his men knew it too. He saw it in their eyes. But he would rather die on his feet than live on his knees. And so he led his men into the forest, hoping they could at least destroy enough of the cyborgs to give his wife, his village, time to run.

But the battle never happened. The women in the village waited for some sign, either that their men had succeeded or failed. They listened for the shouts and screams of battle, but all was quiet. They looked towards the forest for smoke or dust, but saw nothing. Instead, the next dawn, troops swept into the village, taking what they wanted, killing what they didn't. One hundred and one men entered the small forest. None ever came out.

In his dream, Jom could hear the families and friends of the men talk about that day. As time passed, the story became the tale of the legendary Lost Army. Perhaps the Technomage had troops lying in wait and the men were slaughtered. Perhaps the gods intervened and took them away. Perhaps dark creatures walked among the trees and feasted on their bones. Whatever happened, the families and friends and descendants said, the Lost Army would someday come out of the forest and take revenge for all those killed in the Technomage's name.

Suddenly, Jom woke with a start. He heard the screams of the men in his dream as they disappeared into the aether. Screams that echoed throughout the planes. Screams that followed him into the waking world.

The Wind-Up Boy

JOM RUBBED HIS EYES, blinking away visions of flickering torches and crying children. The screams slowly faded, leaving only echoes in his mind. As he gained his bearings, he saw his dirty thin blanket from his shelter by the river in a bundle next to him. He sat up and reached for it. Gathered within was his Dowa flute, rusted dagger and the rest of his meager possessions—shiny stones and melted coins mostly. NDX was standing near the wall of the cave. As Jom moved about, the automaton stirred. The light in its eyes brightened and it rotated its head in his direction.

"Did you receive adequate rest?" it asked in its hollow, soulless voice.

"Uh, yes. Thank you." Jom scooped up his things and stuffed them into the various pockets he had sewed into his leggings and shirt. Faint screams still rang around in the back of his brain. He shook his head to clear his thoughts.

"Then it is time we continued."

"Does Grandmother know of the Revitalizers?" he asked anxiously.

NDX nodded, its head dipping and raising on the ball socket of its neck. "Dianat delivered the warning to your Grandmother. She whispered to her while she was dreaming. There is nothing more we can do at the moment."

Yet Jom was reluctant to abandon his family so easily. He looked around. If he could escape, he could find his way back to the village and warn them himself. Could he outrun a Water Banshee?

Sensing Jom's reluctance the automaton placed its hand on his shoulder. "I understand your concern. But time is of the essence."

"I don't even know who you are," Jom replied, looking at his feet. "How can I trust you?"

NDX cocked its head to the side as it considered Jom's words. Jom could hear its gears moving behind its outer shell.

"Perhaps I can alleviate some of your fears," it replied. It moved over and sat down next to Jom. After a moment of silence, it began to speak.

I was constructed on a planet called Dolph many cycles ago. My primary function was serving meals to the elite members of the Ministry of War. Dolph had been at war with a neighboring galaxy for a very long time and the Ministry was highly regarded across the system as being efficient and merciless against our enemies. I was part of a special production run, built specifically to serve the leaders of the war. One of the features built into us was this," NDX touched the clock on its chest. "The Ministry, although brilliant in waging war was also paranoid and secretive. Perhaps that was why they were so successful.

Regardless, we were built with a time-limit. Our clocks would slowly count down. Once it reached zero, we would deactivate forever.

Cycles passed and, one by one, my fellow automatons ran down and the lights in their eyes went out, never to be lit again. New models replaced the inoperative, older models. After much time had passed, my clock was nearing the end. I did not wish to power down. Over the cycles, I had adapted my programming to include a simple sense of being. It was a simple sub-routine, embedded deep within my files. I did not understand at the time how important that sub-routine would become to me. For as my clock continued to count down, I became increasingly aware of my mortality. I was an automaton with a sense of self. I tried to convince my fellow workers to use the program but they could not understand what I was attempting to do. They plodded on, slowly running out of time. I watched in horror as they shut down, one by one. I grew desperate to find a way to escape my masters and live on.

Fortunately, the war came to Dolph, to the homeworld. Under the cover of explosions and death, I escaped. But my masters did not wish to give me up so easily. They fired on my ship and I spun out of control, crashing on a planet deep in a nebula. Emerging from the wreckage, I was instantly set upon by the beasts of that world. My outer casing was dented and cracked. Moisture seeped into my circuits and caused me no end of problems. Hiding among the shadows, I resigned myself to my fate. I was damaged. My clock was almost out. There was nothing left for me to do but watch the time, and my life, slowly tick away.

As I lay there on that nameless world, someone appeared, stepping through a vortex. He smiled and reached down. With a turn of his hand, he moved my clock backward, restoring energy to my systems and giving me new life. He had done the impossible. He had turned back the relentless march of time. I stood and pledged him my service and have been in his employ ever since.

"That is who we are on our way to see. He will explain to you why he needs you, but rest assured, he would not have sent for you if you weren't desperately needed."

The Mad Historian

I JUST CAN'T LEAVE my Grandmother and my village though," Jom said, twisting his hands around each other. "They're all I know."

"I understand your concern. If we reach our destination in time, there is a possibility we can prevent the Revitalizers from coming."

Jom lifted his head. "What? We can stop them?"

NDX raised its hand. "Prevent. Not stop. And that is only a slim possibility. Yet it is better than going back to the village and dying. Do you wish to die?" NDX tilted its head and stared at him.

"No. Of course not."

"Then I suggest we continue. Time is running out."

Jom slowly nodded his head. "I guess I have no choice."

"There is always a choice. Some choices are simply better than others."

Jom had no response to that so he simply nodded.

"Dianat will transport us to our destination. I will power down during the journey. I suggest you take a deep breath."

Without any further explanation, NDX stiffened, its arms and legs straightening at its sides and the light in its eyes dimmed to barely a flicker. Jom waved a hand in front of its face but got no response. A harsh wind blew past him, cold and unforgiving. Jom heard a high scream, faint yet rapidly gaining in volume. He turned around just in time to see a rolling black, liquid-like shadow hurl towards him out of the darkness of the tunnel. It rolled over him and NDX, plunging him into darkness. Jom felt his body lift off the ground. His feet wiggled in midair and he let out a gasp of surprise. NDX was pressed against him, tightly but not uncomfortably. Then, through the shadowy thin sheet of liquid that surrounded him, he saw them hurtle down the tunnel. Knowing the river was at the end of it, Jom inhaled a deep breath. Barely a heartbeat later, they plunged into dark water. The shock of the cold water struck him but the water did not touch him, protected as they were by the dark wind of the Water Banshee. He bumped against NDX as they spun through the water, safely encased in their dark bubble. Jom couldn't hear anything over the continuous scream of the Water Banshee. He covered his ears with his hands in an attempt to dull the noise.

At first, he was too startled to worry about breathing. But as the minutes passed, his lungs burned and his chest grew tighter and tighter. He squirmed around, increasingly desperate to get air. Suddenly, a face appeared out of the darkness that surrounded him. Sharp features and cold eyes stared at him. Then, without warning, the face moved in and kissed him. Jom's mouth was forced open and fresh air was blown into his lungs, filling them to capacity. The face withdrew, showing the slightest hint of a smile, and then disappeared back into the swirling darkness. His heart beating fast from fear, Jom kept his eyes closed and tried not to think about breathing.

The journey was over as quickly as it had begun. One moment, he could feel his body moving at incredible speed, the next, he was still and the darkness slid off him. He cautiously opened his eyes. He caught sight of the Water Banshee retreating into a small pool of water behind him, leaving only a thin trail of moisture. The dark river ran past him and disappeared into a small opening in the ground. Turning, he found himself in an enormous circular room. The room was incredibly large, its walls rising high above him. An immense fire burned merrily in the center of the room, flanked by stairs and balconies and shelves. A high vaulted ceiling was obscured by the smoke billowing from the fire. High stacks of books rose like towers throughout the room, punctuated by workstations overloaded with scrolls, terminals, monitors, globes, charts, maps and a variety of equipment Jom didn't recognize. Jom looked around in wonder, taking in the enormous library. There had to be millions of books, tomes, and scrolls crammed into every available spot. A flurry of movement caught his attention and he squinted, picking out a figure through the flames on the other side of the room. An old man was happily tossing book after book into the flames of the central fire. Long white hair and a longer black robe whipped around his small body as he moved back and forth among a multitude of books and screens. On his head, a small skullcap tried in vain to keep his long hair from flying in all directions as he scurried back and forth among the books, occasionally tripping over his robe in the process. He muttered to himself as he worked, occasionally letting loose a whoop of delight.

Next to him, NDX stirred and its eyes brightened.

"Come. I will introduce you to the Master." The clock-work boy walked past the towers of books towards the old man. Jom hurried to catch up as NDX disappeared around a pyramid of vidscreens. He watched the old man throw a scroll into the fire, then hurry to a small desk nearby. He furiously scribbled in a journal, and then turned to a monitor. Speaking rapidly, information appeared on the screen as he dictated a long series of numbers. Then, with a sweep of his hand, he sent the screen crashing to the ground. Tiny sparks erupted around him as it smashed on the hard stone floor.

"Nebt!" the old man suddenly yelled, "come now! We don't have much time!" And then he erupted in a fit of giggles. "Not much time!" he whispered in between giggles, wiping at his eyes.

"Sir," NDX said as he approached the man, "this is Jom, not Nebt."

"Of course it is! Nebt is not for three full cycles yet!" And he threw another book on the fire.

Jom slowly took a few steps forward. From the corner of his eye, he saw a small figure dart out from behind a stack of books. Jom saw a flash of red skin and a tail and then it was gone. Nervously, he approached the man.

"Excuse me, sir..."

"Psedjet! Imperial Codex! Volume 35! No wait! 36!"

"Yeh," a voice answered from behind Jom. Something scurried between his legs over to the man. It looked like a tiny devil; red skin, yellow horns, barbed tail sticking out from simple black trousers. Its black jacket was neatly pressed and clean, as were its shiny black shoes. Jom realized he was looking at an imp. Just like in the stories Grandmother told. Except this one was carrying a large tome and dressed impeccably. The man took the book from the imp and flipped to a page about halfway through. Reading quickly, he nodded, tore out the page and tossed it into the fire.

"Excuse me, sir, but why are you burning all those books?"

The man stopped and regarded Jom with bright eyes. Ndx tilted its head, as if Jom had asked a ridiculous question.

"Because it's all happened, of course!"

"I don't understand."

The man muttered and turned away. NDX slid next to Jom.

"Allow me to introduce Abla'than'abla, fifteenth Codifier of Records, Supreme Diviner of the Xoa and Destroyer of Past Events. The Master records events that have yet to occur in this time stream. Once an event has actually occurred, there is no reason to hold onto it, so it is destroyed."

"So," Jom looked around the room, "all these scrolls and books and things are full of stuff...."

"That has yet to happen," NDX finished for him.

"Boy!" Abla finished writing something down and turned to Jom, "have you dreamt of the Swarm yet?" He studied Jom intently, taking in his dirty skin, unkempt hair and patched clothing. Jom shifted uneasily from foot to foot.

"I don't—I don't think so."

Abla muttered to himself and resumed writing.

"What am I doing here?" Jom asked NDX, thoroughly confused by the turn of events.

"What was the last dream you had?" Abla demanded.

"I—I, uh, dreamt of a lost army," Jom replied.

Abla nodded his head, as if Jom had confirmed something and quickly typed on an ancient input screen.

The imp ran past them, bringing another large tome to the man. He smiled and nodded his thanks. Dropping it heavily on the desk, he flipped through page after page, muttering to himself the entire time. Finally, he found what he was looking for and gave a small cry of triumph before tearing the page out, crumpling it into a ball, and throwing it into the fire.

"Psedjet! Are we ready for temporal hold?"

"Bleh!" the imp squeaked from somewhere to the right.

"Good!" Tearing himself away from his destruction, Abla hurried over to a large lever installed on one of the walls. It was easily as large as the man was tall. Reaching up, he grabbed hold and, with great effort, pulled the lever down until a loud click sounded. Nothing happened.

"Now," Abla said, walking towards them, "let's get this out of the way. The universe can't be put on hold forever."

"Put on hold?"

"The Master has suspended the time flow momentarily so you can speak with him without interruption," NDX explained.

"He stopped time? With a switch?"

NDX nodded its head.

"But that's impossible!"

"Ha!" Abla walked up to Jom and gave him a hard look. "What do you know about what is and what is not impossible?"

"Well, I know you can't stop time with a switch!"

"It's a big switch."

"Um..."

"Exactly. Now, down to business! To answer your question, you are here because I asked that you be brought here. I assume, however, you would like a less literal answer."

"If that's possible," Jom replied.

"You're very concerned with impossibilities, aren't you?" Abla tutted and shook his head. "That will have to stop if you're going to succeed."

"Succeed?"

"Yes. Which is the less literal answer to your question. You have a task ahead of you. I need to you to succeed at it."

"What task?"

"Why, become the newest Technomage, of course."

The Phobetor Chair

JOM STOOD IN STUNNED silence. Him? A Technomage? The thought was so far beyond possible that he could only laugh. So he did. He let out a whooping bark of a laugh. Abla broke into a wide grin and laughed along with him, holding his stomach as he did so. Psedjet looked that them both and shrugged.

"So," Abla said as he wiped away tears, "what's so funny?"

"I can't become a Technomage," Jom said. "You're insane."

"Mad, actually," Abla replied with a wink. "Quite mad. It's the only sane way to live."

"The Master is a survivor of what is commonly referred to as the Bedlam War," NDX said by way of explanation.

"The Bedlam War?" Jom stepped back in horror. "Then you're..."

"Mad. Quite mad. But that doesn't mean I don't know what I'm talking about," he pointed out.

Jom shook his head, desperately trying to organize his thoughts. "Technomages are evil."

"Not true. Well, mostly true. But not entirely true."

"Why me? I mean, I'm no one special."

Abla took a step back then, mirroring Jom's move. "Not special? Dear boy, everyone is special. And you are even more special than that!"

"I know a lot of people who would say differently," Jom muttered, thinking of how he was treated back in his village. Then a thought hit him. "My village! I have to stop the Revitalizers from destroying my village!"

"Revitalizers!" Abla looked around wildly. "Where?"

"They're coming to my village! I have to stop them somehow!"

"How do you plan on doing that?"

"I don't know! NDX said—"

"If I may," NDX cut in, "I merely expressed to Jom the possibility of preventing the Revitalizers from landing near his village if we reached you with adequate time to spare."

"I see. How long until they arrive?"

"Approximately two short solar turns."

Abla thought for a moment, and then suddenly jumped up and down like a child. "Psedjet!"

"Meh," the imp said from by Jom's foot.

"Outer Ribbon Nebula Index 3.2! Hurry!"

The imp scrambled away. They heard cursing and a crash as a stack of books tipped over. But a moment later, the imp came back into view carrying a portable quantum reader. Abla took it from the imp and scanned through the readout, muttering numbers as he searched.

"Ah! Here we go. Assuming this is the Emerald temporal event ten, the Revitalizers will bypass your village. There will be some structural damage from the tremors but no casualties."

"Really?"

"Says so right here," Abla pointed at the reader.

"Is it ever wrong?"

"My dear boy," Abla responded slowly, "how can something be wrong if it hasn't happened yet?"

"Uh..."

"Exactly!"

"What if it's not?"

"Not what?"

"The Emerald temporal....what you said."

"Oh." Abla looked at the readout again. "Well, then your village will be destroyed."

"What!"

"The roots go back to the third uprising of Sigma Sigma Sigma. The outcome of that rebellion directly affects the timetable of the Revitalizers." Abla looked up and his glittering eyes bore into Jom. "It all depends on that."

"When....what...how will we know?"

"We'll know when it happens, of course."

61

"When's that?"

"When I restart the time stream."

"Then do it!"

"Nope." Abla took a step forward and placed his ancient hands on Jom's shoulders. "Once I restart things, we'll be on a tight schedule. If you don't succeed in your quest, many more people will die horrible deaths than just one village. You have to trust that you are now a part of a larger picture. Imagine yourself larger than the space you are in. What will be, will be. But," he winked, "we can help it along. Now, enough dawdling, it's high time you got started on your quest."

"What quest?"

"Didn't we go over this already? I swear we did."

"Feh," Psedjet said helpfully.

Abla nodded. "I couldn't have put it better myself." He looked at Jom carefully. "Are you sure you're ready for this?"

"I don't even know what 'this' is."

"Probably for the best." Abla patted NDX on its dented head. "You will accompany him?"

"Of course, Master."

"Good. Then it's settled. Time to go."

"Sir, if you wouldn't mind." NDX turned to Abla. The old man nodded, reached down and wound the clock on its chest a number of rotations.

"There you go. That should give you plenty of time. Don't dally though."

"Thank you, sir."

"Off you go then." Abla waved them away and ambled back towards the fire. As he walked, he suddenly changed course and went over to the temporal lever. With a mighty groan, he pushed it back into its original position. Smiling to himself, he resumed tossing books and scrolls into the fire.

NDX guided Jom out of the chamber and into a small, sparsely furnished anteroom. A small bowl of water stirred on an ornately carved wooden table off to the side. Jom thought he saw a face staring out from the water and quickly looked away.

"I have no idea what's going on," Jom confessed to the clockwork boy.

NDX nodded its head. "That is to be expected. The Master is, at times, vague on precise details concerning his plans."

"Do you know what he's talking about?"

"To some extent. I have been in the Master's service for a number of cycles, much like Psedjet and Dianat. Together, we have helped the Master fulfill his primary function."

"Which is?"

NDX tilted its head slightly at Jom. "To preserve what is to come, of course. The future does not simply happen. It needs to be helped along at times."

"I—I never knew that."

"There is no logical reason you would. It is not, nor should it be, common knowledge."

"So, what am I supposed to do now?"

"The Master requests that you locate and return the Phobetor Chair."

"What's the Phobetor Chair?"

"Please, sit down. I will attempt to explain."

Jom sat down on a simple chair next to the table. He tried not to look at the bowl of water that stared back at him and instead concentrated on NDX's hollow voice.

Many, many cycles ago, this plane was ruled by the Technomage Ku'baba. A ruthless and evil despot, Ku'baba had two lieutenants who carried out his orders and kept his vast empire running smoothly. These lieutenants were known only as the Sword of Ku'baba and the Shield of Ku'baba. Some believe different people took on the roles of the Sword and the Shield over time, earning their place at the Technomage's side by treachery and deceit. Others say that Ku'baba used dark magic to make them immortal, twisting their souls into something forbidden and evil. Regardless, Ku'baba was never without his Sword and his Shield. The Sword led the Technomage's vast army and fleet of warships, conquering every world or plane he came across in Ku'baba's name. He was the greatest warrior ever known and led the greatest army. None could resist the iron fist of the Sword. The Shield, on the other hand, concerned himself with protecting the empire. He erected defenses to safeguard his liege. In pursuit of this end, he conducted countless horrible experiments to perfect the ultimate warrior, to research new ways for his master to rule worlds, or simply for his own twisted amusement.

One of the Shield's most notorious inventions was the Phobetor Chair. Crafted from nyx wood, shaped by psy hammers, the Shield spent cycles carefully constructing the perfect torture device. He would strap a victim into the chair and then direct black energies around and into the subject. They experienced their worst fears. They would watch their families die before them or see their bodies overrun by disgusting creatures with blank eyes and sharp claws. Their screams bled into the chair, strengthening its power. As the Shield used the Chair, he began to perceive patterns among the shrieks and cries. Delighted at this new avenue, he experimented with molding his victims' terrors and pushed the subjects ever deeper into abject horror. As he learned to tailor the nightmares his subjects were forced to endure, he gained insight into the very essence of dread. As his knowledge grew, so too did the changes in the victims. At first, they would just emerge broken and screaming. But slowly, over the course of many generations, the Shield refined the process.

Now, instead of being completely broken, his victims were slowly turned into nightmares themselves. He developed ways to inflict horrific damage on his subjects but keep them alive so that they became monsters. The dark energies warped their bodies and shattered their minds but would not let them die. Their screams were so horrific that you would go mad just hearing them. Ku'baba was delighted as the Shield produced increasingly more terrifying monsters for the Technomage to command. His most feared creations became known as the Water Banshees, people turned by the unholy energies of the Phobetor Chair into something not quite living, not quite spirit. They are creatures that can travel through the liquids of the universe. They cannot be killed in the normal sense, only dispelled to the winds of the aether. They are impervious to pain and can only be touched when they wish it. Laughing with delight, Ku'baba unleashed them on the universe. The Water Banshees swept across the planes, destroying their enemies with screams and claws. Ku'baba's empire grew at an astonishing rate. Even the other Technomages, normally so secure in their power, were wary of Ku'baba's new weapon.

The Water Banshees, though, ultimately, could not be kept under thumb. Their minds, though shattered by the Chair, slowly began to heal as time passed. Unknown to the Shield, they fought through their continuous fog of suffering and pain and somehow managed to regain a sense of self. Little by little, hidden from their master, they became to think for themselves. And with self-awareness, came a drive to cast off their servitude. Once that happened, they rebelled.

The Shield was engulfed by the darkness of the Banshees before he even knew what was happening. They dragged him through the planes, shrieking in delight as his body was torn apart by the primal forces of the aether between universes. But they kept just enough of him intact to bring him back and strap him into the Chair. Black magic poured into the Shield's mind from the Chair, fragmenting it into a million pieces and exploding his essence to the far corners of the universe. The Chair was thrown into the aether as well, lost beyond reach.

The Water Banshees then turned their attention to Ku'baba but the Sword rose up with a vast armada to defend his liege. A great battle took place as the Sword's army grappled with the Water Banshees across and through the planes. It was a war of mutual destruction. The Sword's troops used every weapon at their disposal to obliterate the Water Banshees even as they were torn to pieces by claws and teeth. The war shook the dimensions and tore at the fabric of reality. The wall that separated the planes cracked and the aether bled through, destroying vast swatches of the galaxy even as the Sword's army and the Water Banshees continued their battle. The Water Banshees tore through the Sword's armada with a vengeance born from unimaginable suffering. Finally, the armada fell and the spirits screamed in triumph. With his army gone, the Sword stood alone against the liquid host. He fought off the horde of dark spirits single-handily for an entire cycle before finally succumbing to their hatred, claws and screams. Ku'baba, seeing his champion fall, took his own life rather than suffer at the hands of his creations.

After the battle, the Banshees patched the holes in reality with their own bodies, disappearing into the aether. They became legends, like so many creatures from the past, known only in stories but never believed to be real. Then, ten cycles ago, Dianat appeared from beyond the wall and came to the Master with a lead of where the Phobetor Chair was hidden, hoping he could find and destroy it once and for all. Apparently the Water Banshees could still feel the evil essence of the Chair, even after all this time. And if they could sense it, others could as well. If it fell into the wrong hands, it would spell disaster for untold worlds. With Dianat's help, we will recover the Chair and bring it safely back to the Master."

Jom looked to his side. Dianat's face was staring at him from the bowl of water. But, instead of seeing a frightening visage as he had before, Jom now only saw pain. The eyes that before were filled with hatred now were full of hope and his heart swelled.

"Can the Phobetor Chair be used to help Dianat become whole again?" he asked quietly after a moment's thought.

NDX was silent as it ran some computations, and then nodded. "There is a possibility, yes."

"Then let's go get it."

A Rough Start

JOM WAS LED TO a wash area and gratefully splashed cool, clean water on his face. He couldn't remember the last time he had washed using pristine water—he was always the last to use the basins back in his village. Often, by the time he got his turn, the water was so foul and dirty that he simply didn't wash. When he emerged from the room, there was a clean set of clothes laid out for him on a chair. Looking from his clothing to the clean ones, he felt ashamed. As he changed, he rubbed the soft fabric against his cheek, enjoying the sensation. Finally, he stepped back into the main room. NDX was waiting for him and, as Jom entered the library, looked Jom up and down. He stood obediently as the automaton assessed his appearance. Jom tried not to mess with his hair, still wet and sticking out at odd angles. His new tunic, forest green with black buttons, perfectly complemented his black leggings. The tunic was held in place by a thin black belt. Jom had stuffed his few meager possessions in the pockets of the tunic. Finally, NDX nodded in approval and gestured Jom forward.

"Dianat will transport us through the membranes between planes. These planes, or dimensions, are separated by vibrations. But there is a physical way of travelling between them. We call this space between space the 'aether'. Dianat can use the aether as a way to traverse great distances in a short time. She has assured the Master that the journey itself will not be extremely dangerous or overly long. Our destination, however, may prove more hazardous."

"You said 'not extremely dangerous'," Jom pointed out.

NDX nodded. "Yes. There is some peril involved, as with any undertaking."

"I don't know how to fight." The thought of battle turned Jom's stomach. Other than rolling around in the dirt with the other children of his village, Jom had never had to defend himself physically and was, honestly, at the receiving end of most blows and punches.

"Dianat will protect us during the journey. Our physical forms cannot survive outside of her embrace in the space between planes."

Jom looked over to the bowl of water and gulped. "So we'll be helpless."

"Untrue. We can provide moral support. In addition, I have certain defensive capabilities that may prove useful if the need is dire."

Jom nodded and took a deep breath. NDX stepped closer to him. The water in the bowl stirred, and then erupted like a dark geyser with a loud scream. The fount bent and engulfed them, plunging them into swirling liquid shadows. Jom felt his body rise off the ground and get pulled through the air. His body began to spin and Jom knew they were somehow, unbelievably being sucked into the small bowl on the table. He tried to understand how but it happened too fast for him to wrap his head around it. He felt the clock-work boy next to him, although he couldn't see it. The presence was reassuring though and Jom tried to relax, despite the sensation of disappearing into the water of a bowl on a table.

A strange energy bounced through his nerves as they left one plane of existence and entered the space in between worlds. Jom wondered what it was like outside of Dianat's protection. He imagined them speeding through blood-red plasma or through deadly acid, or through a great nothingness that crushed you if you thought about it too much. Maybe they were swimming through dimensions like a fish swam through water. More like a predator, Jom amended. Dianat was a Water Banshee, one of the most terrifying creatures in existence. It was a killing ghost, a sentient vapor. It was unstoppable. Ironically, Jom felt more at ease then. If they had a Water Banshee as an ally, what could harm them? They would be fine.

The black liquid surrounding him tightened its grip around his body, as if Dianat could read his thoughts and approved of his confidence. He allowed himself a small smile and willed his body relax.

Just then, Jom felt his body jerk to the side. Then another jerk back the opposite way. It felt as if something was slamming into him. The blackness grew more solid around him. Again and again he felt something crash into them. He sensed NDX stir next to him. The screaming grew louder, encircling them in a wall of sound as well as liquid and dark. He reached up and felt a thick liquid covering his ears, protecting him from the worst of it. Even still, the scream was horrifying and Jom's every instinct was to bolt, to run away from the awful noise. But his feet had no purchase. He was floating in the embrace of a monster traveling through dimensions. He desperately tried to control his emotions. He covered his ears with his hands and grit his teeth. He felt blood trickle from his nose and ears. Something slammed into him again, this time so hard it almost knocked him unconscious.

A brilliant blue light suddenly flared around him. Jom's hair stood on edge as electricity flowed around him, infusing itself into the darkness, creating a web of protection. The jerking and bouncing stopped. The screaming rose in response to the light, then died down. Jom watched in fascination as the blue electricity traveled through the black liquid, lighting up the shadows so they appeared deep purple. Then his body was dropped. He felt his limbs become weightless as they fell through the dimensions. The electric blue intensified, the shadows closed in tight. Jom wrapped his arms around NDX, despite himself.

They dropped out of the aether. The banshee's embrace slid off him as they fell and he landed heavily on a hard surface. A loud clang echoed around him and he knew NDX was next to him. He shook his head, clearing his senses. Dianat slid off him, her black body still sparking with electricity. NDX righted itself and spun its head in a slow arc back and forth, apparently scanning the area. Moving quickly, it reached down to the side of its torso and a small compartment slid open. It removed a crystal vial filled with water and pulled off the stopper. Dianat flowed over and into the vial, reducing her mass to fit into the small container.

"We must hurry," NDX said as Dianat entered the water of the vial, becoming one with the liquid. It replaced the stopper and put the vial back into the compartment in its body. "We are not safe here."

"What happened?" Jom asked, his voice as unsteady as his hands. He slowly got to his feet, trying to control the shaking in his legs.

"We were attacked."

"By what?"

"There are creatures that live in the aether between planes that are very territorial," the automaton responded. "Dianat could not defend herself against so many and I was forced to take drastic actions. Unfortunately, my discharge was more harmful to Dianat than I anticipated and, to protect us, she dropped back onto a plane. The slicers were repelled, however."

"Slicers?"

NDX nodded. "Creatures about ten strides long and very flat, with five appendages that end in long sharp blades and great leathery wings. They feed of the ambient energy of the aether. Very dangerous."

Jom shuddered. He looked around in fear. "Are they still around?"

"They cannot reach us on this plane. They do not have the ability to cross the membrane that separates the aether from the planes. But there are other dangers. Hurry."

NDX began to walk away and Jom quickly fell in behind, not wanting to be left behind alone. He looked around in wonder at the landscape. They were in a large, barren valley. Gigantic mountains of a deep purple rock rose up on three sides; their tops obscured by clouds the color of new spring sprouts. They were walking into the valley. Jom looked behind and saw a barren landscape devoid of any features. The mountains tapered off on either side in the distance, leaving nothing but rock and sky. The sky was a darker green than the clouds, almost emerald. No trees or vegetation of any kind could be seen, only rock. Jom bent down and picked up a small piece as they walked and studied it carefully. The rock itself was grey, but it was infused with a purple mineral that was threaded throughout like a spider web. Without thinking, he put it in one of his pockets.

"Where are we?" he asked NDX. The clock-work boy swiveled its head all the way around to continue to talk with Jom as its body walked forward.

"Although I have not yet verified it, it appears we are on Tajos VII, a small fugitive world about fifteen life cycles from your planet."

"What's a fugitive world?"

"A world that is neither part of any Technomage empire, nor part of any guild. It is a place where outlaws and thieves retreat to escape notice and plot their next adventure."

"Sounds inviting," Jom responded dryly. He was uncomfortable with NDX's head completely backwards so he sped up a little to walk side-by-side with the automaton. NDX's head swiveled in response. Jom didn't think this was any better.

"Make no mistake; this is a very dangerous world. We would not have stopped here if it was not absolutely necessary."

"Dianat is hurt that bad?"

"She will recover. The vial I carry is a safe haven for her to rest and regain her strength. But she had to leave the aether. If she would have faltered while we were traveling, our bodies would have been either torn to bits by the slicers or ripped apart on a cellular level by the energies of the aether."

Jom stared ahead, willing his body not to shake. This adventure he had found himself on was more dangerous than he thought. Slicers? Getting torn apart in the space between worlds? How did he end up here? As he tried to make sense of it all, he spotted a glimmer in the distance ahead.

"NDX? What's that?" he pointed to where he had seen the light. They stopped and NDX stared into the expanse in front of them. The lights in its eyes brightened and Jom heard motors refocus its eyes. He wondered absently just how far the automaton could see clearly.

"A small group of humanoids are approaching on a hover train. There appears to be approximately fifteen individuals, although there may be more inside the vehicle. They are armed with a variety of weapons, mostly low-tech but I see at least one Class Five blaster."

Jom gulped. "What do we do?"

NDX rotated its head completely around, scanning the surrounding area. "There is no cover. There is no possible way we can outrun them. Dianat is still recovering. We have very limited options."

"Can you, I don't know, protect us with a force field or something?" he asked desperately. The brigade was coming into Jom's view now. He could make out a large vehicle approaching rapidly across the barren ground.

"Yes, but that would be temporary solution at best and denies us the ability to move. I suggest we attempt to parley with them. We have nothing of value to them. They have no reason to harm us."

Jom felt sweat on his brow. "Somehow, I don't think that will matter. They may just kill us for being here."

73

NDX nodded. "That is possible."

Jom's fingers went to the rusted dagger in his pocket. Even though the blade couldn't cut through straw, he felt slightly better knowing he had at least something to defend himself with. Even as the thought came to him, he shook his head. He couldn't defend himself from anything. He looked up. The hover train was in clear view now, as were the people on it. They hung from the windows and rode on top of the vehicle, a long, bullet-shaped black metal conveyance. Most were dressed in dark clothes that hung loose off their bodies and whipped in the wind. Many had cloth covering their faces, leaving only room for their eyes. Even their hands were covered with strips of black cloth or gloves. He could hear indistinct shouts as the band approached.

"How did they know we're here?" he wondered out loud.

"They probably have sensors scattered throughout the area. These are outlaws. They would want to be aware of any intruders."

"So they'll probably kill us," Jom repeated.

"Perhaps. Perhaps not. It is impossible to determine the odds until we speak with them."

But the automaton's words did not make him feel any less queasy. His stomach dropped as he picked out the many weapons wielded by the cutthroats, some of which were already pointed in his direction. They held sharp swords and long pikes aloft. He wanted to turn and run as fast as he could. But he had seen what happens when prey bolts and predator gives chase. He forced his legs to remain still.

The hover train turned as it approached and slid above the terrain, coming to a halt about half a field-length from them. The outlaws immediately jumped off the vehicle and spread out, forming a long line that curved inward towards Jom and NDX. Jom counted eighteen in all, although, he reminded himself, more could be in the interior of the hover train, watching with weapons trained on them through peepholes cut into the side of the vehicle.

The man directly in front of them stepped forward. He was

taller than the others and his clothes hung off wide shoulders. A large proton rifle rested lightly against his chest. NDX took a small step forward. Jom gulped and followed. The man gave a slight nod and strode towards them. The other bandits remained where they were. When they were separated by only a few body lengths, the man addressed them.

"You're trespassing," he said. He voice was strange, like it was run through a synthesizer, but, despite being barely above a whisper, traveled clearly across the space between them.

"Our apologies," NDX said, tilting its head down slightly. "We seem to be lost. We will leave your property immediately."

The man laughed. A heartbeat later, the rest of the outlaws laughed as well, although Jom doubted they could hear what was being said. They simply did as their leader did. Just like the kids in my village, Jom thought. Except these kids had guns and knives instead of insults and jeers.

"Lost? And where are you going that you thought this was the correct way?" He gestured around them. "There is nothing here."

"We are traveling to New Caladona. We were told it is beyond the mountains."

"Aye. It is," he laughed again. His men echoed his laugh. "But on the other side of the continent. You're about four suns away."

"That is further than anticipated."

"Oh, aye. And what business, may I ask, does a boy and wind-up toy have in New Caladona?"

"My apologies," NDX bowed slightly, "but I am not at liberty to discuss our private matters. Suffice to say it has nothing to do with you."

Jom felt the hair on the back of his head stand. Don't antagonize him! he screamed in his mind. He saw the man stiffen as well.

"I'm making it my business," he growled. The artificial tone to his voice made the implied threat even more menacing.

"My programming prevents me from discussing the details of our travels with unauthorized personnel."

"Easily solved. I have any number of men who can take you apart and circumvent your...programming."

NDX shook its head. "Unfortunately, that would accomplish nothing other than our mutual destruction. I have defensive measures built into my body that would kill you long before you could decipher my components."

The man thought for a moment. Jom could tell he was weighing the risks against the potential gain. Then he turned his gaze to Jom.

"Then you tell me," he said, letting his hand play across the rifle. "And boy, understand that I am in no mood for more delays."

A New Friend

JOM GULPED. HIS STOMACH dropped. He tried not to faint as the man took a step towards him.

"Well, boy?"

"I—I—"

"He does not know the parameters of our journey," NDX said, stepping slightly in front of Jom.

"I don't know," Jom said, his voice cracking.

The man studied them for a moment. Jom could feel the eyes of all the outlaws on them. Sweat poured down his brow and his legs threatened to give out. He willed his bladder to not give out as well. The man's fingers drummed the rifle as he thought. Then he whistled a low note. Four of the men ran forward.

"Put them in the hold. I'll decide what to do with them later," the man said, turned on his heel and walked back to the hover train.

The bandits quickly surrounded them and prodded them forward. NDX said nothing as they were herded up a ramp onto the hover train and pushed roughly through dingy, narrow corridors until they reached a strong metal door. The outlaw in front pulled back a thick bolt and they were tossed into a cramped, dark room. The metal door was slammed shut and bolted from the outside, leaving them alone in the darkness.

"What—" Jom began but NDX held up a hand to silence him. Jom waited. After a moment, a shadow moved in the far corner of the room.

"Hello," a voice whispered to them and Jom's heart leapt into his throat.

"Greetings," NDX said quietly. "Your heartbeat is weak and your core temperature is dangerously low for your species. Do you require assistance?"

A low laugh erupted, quickly turning into a fit of coughing. Jom had heard that type of coughing before. It was the cough the old ones of the village made before dying.

"Can you teleport me someplace warm?" the man said once the coughing died down. "I don't remember the last time I was warm."

"Not presently, no. However, I believe I can help raise your temperature, if you will permit me."

Another fit of coughing. "By all means."

NDX raised a hand and it began to glow on the palm. A soft light lit up the small room, instantly warming them all. Jom looked at the man. He was thin and ragged, with long black hair matted against his face and chest. His clothes were little more than scraps hanging off his gaunt body and his feet were bare. His face was long and had a haunted look to it that invoked both fear and pity in Jom. Jom guessed him to be just a few cycles older than he was. The man leaned forward towards NDX's glowing hand, letting the warmth soak into his body. He remained that way for several minutes before finally pulling back with a small, contented smile on his scruffy face.

"Thank you," he said simply. NDX nodded in response and let the glow die down. The darkness of the cell closed in on them. NDX kept the light on, dimmed down to almost nothing but enough to keep the shadows at bay. They huddled around it so they could see each other.

"Who are you?" Jom finally asked. "How did you get here? I don't even know where here is."

A single laugh floated to Jom through the darkness. "That's a bit of a story. But I guess we have the time, don't we?"

I come from a world called Okorafor," he started, his voice low and sad, barely above a whisper. "Long ago, wishing to expand our knowledge and opportunities, my people took to the skies to live, building great floating cities that ringed the planet's surface. We harnessed anti-gravity and bent the laws of physics to our will. Higher and higher we built into the sky, eventually leaving the atmosphere altogether and lived among the stars in massive citadels that looked down upon our homeworld. The planet, our planet, became nothing more than a basin for resources. Millions upon millions of my people were put to work, gathering raw minerals and food from the surface, then transporting it all to the massive floating cities high above.

I grew up knowing of the cities that hung in the skies above us only through the stories we told and the shadows they cast. The older cities that remained in the atmosphere were, by my time, ghettos where the poor lived, over-shadowed, literally, by cities higher up. My family was among the poorest of the poor. We worked the mines on the surface, spending long days deep underground—a thought inconceivable to those orbiting the planet. When I was old enough to carry a bucket of rocks, I was put to work and haven't stopped since. I hauled the ore from the mine entrance to the transport pad. Over and over again, day after day. Mine to ship, mine to ship.

Every day, long after the sun had disappeared and the cold winds began to blow, my father and mother and two brothers would emerge from the darkness of the mine and we would trudge to our small shack. Mother would sing us songs to help soothe our aching muscles. Songs about the gods and how they created our people long ago. Songs about my people's heroes and how we used to live in peace and freedom. We would fall asleep listening to her sing and, at least for those few hours, we could rest. But then the sun would rise and we would go back to the mine.

One afternoon, I was pushing a cart of rocks to the loading area. It was the latest in an endless line of carts in the middle of an endless afternoon of sweat and heat and the whip of the boss. There was a rumble, then a muffled crash and a dust cloud spewed out from the mine entrance I dropped the cart and ran to the shaft, my only thoughts were of my family; my father and mother and two brothers were all in the mine at the time. I ignored the sting of the whip on my back and sprinted to the entrance.

He paused for a long moment before continuing.

Grey dust choked my eyes and burned my lungs. There was a terrible silence in the aftermath of the cave-in. No cries for help. No screams of agony. Nothing but silence. Even as I ran up to the entrance, I knew what that meant. I slowed. There was no need to hurry. The tears spilled from my eyes, clearing away some of the dust.

Then I felt it. I felt the whip bite into my shoulder. And again into my back. I whirled around. The boss stood there, a grin on his face and he let the whip fly at me again. I moved my head just in time to save my eye from getting plucked out by the leather. Then I saw grey no more. Only red. I sprang at him. I clawed at him. I bit and scratched and punched. There were shouts from the other workers and bosses. Hands grabbed at me. I shook them off. Then, something heavy hit me in the back of the head and I fell back, half-stunned. Only then did my vision clear and I saw the boss. He was lying at my feet, his life blood pumping uselessly into the dirt from the ragged wound I had torn in his throat.

Through all the shouting, I heard someone yell 'Run!' so I did. I ran until my muscles screamed in agony. But I couldn't outrun the bounty hunter ships. This group found me four suns later, half-starved and holed up in a dirty ditch, more animal than man. I've been in this room since. They don't seem in too much of a hurry to turn me in. Or they've forgotten I'm here. Either way, it doesn't matter. I have no one. I'm ready to die.

Jom didn't know what to say. He stared at the man, as much with pity as with compassion. Even NDX, an automaton that could not feel, did not break the silence for several minutes. Finally, Jom forced himself to speak.

"You're not alone anymore."

NDX turned and tilted its head, its motors whirling behind its eyes. Jom held his head up, resolute.

"You're not alone," he repeated. "We're getting out of here and we're taking you with us."

The man smiled a thin smile. "How?" he asked. Neither his eyes nor his voice held any hope.

"I don't know," Jom admitted.

"Have you any idea where the bandits are going?" NDX asked.

The man shook his head. "I hear talk, but it changes from person to person. I get the feeling they are looking for something."

"Looking for what?"

The man shrugged his thin shoulders. "I've heard them talk about a 'Mind Harp.' But I don't know what that is."

"Interesting." NDX turned to look at Jom. "We must continue our journey," it said in a low voice although the man could easily hear them in such a small space.

"We can't leave him here," Jom protested.

"There are greater forces moving into play. We have limited time."

"He can help us."

"Doubtful. He will slow us down. Also, our...mode of transportation...cannot accommodate a third individual."

"I won't leave him," Jom said and crossed his arms, hoping he looked impressive.

"This is not optimal."

"I don't care."

"You owe me nothing," the man said. "If you can leave, you should. I will probably die in this cell. You should not waste your energies on me."

"I can't accept that," Jom told him firmly. "I was not raised to leave someone in need."

"I—I appreciate it." The man shuffled forward. "Then I suppose I should know your names."

"I'm Jom and this is NDX."

The man coughed and smiled his thin smile again. "I'm Macar."

: Dream of the Shadow Saint :

M ACAR? YOUR NAME IS Macar?" Jom asked, feeling his world begin to tilt.

"Yes."

"But—but you—"

"Have had a hard past few cycles," NDX interrupted. "Perhaps we should all get some rest before we plan our next move."

After regarding the automaton for a moment, Macar nodded his assent and moved back into the corner. Jom sat still, unable to move. NDX gently took his arm and they moved to the far wall.

"NDX? How is it possible--?"

"I will attempt to explain," the clock-work boy replied. "However, this is a conversation best left for when we are alone."

"Why?"

"You will have to trust my judgment for the moment. Suffice to say, it is imperative you do not discuss your dream with him."

"Alright."

"I must insist. Can you do that?"

"I—I think so."

"Excellent. Now, you should rest. It has been a troubling sun cycle and we have much to do."

"I don't think I can sleep. My mind is racing."

Just then, Jom felt a small prick in his arm. He looked down but could not see anything in the gloom of the cell other than NDX moving his hand away from him.

"You need sleep," NDX said. "Rest now."

Despite his anxiety, Jom felt himself drifting off and lay his head down on his arms. Soon, he was asleep.

Jom floated above a small dark planet. A dim blue star cast its feeble light on crude stone huts. Jom fell towards the surface, slowing as he approached the ground until he hovered above a decrepit pile of rocks piled into a shelter. From the darkness within emerged a woman carrying a bundle. She had light blue skin pulled tight over hard, angular features. She stood and gazed upward. Her face was an emotionless mask, pupil-less eyes looked to the heavens but no prayer escaped her thin lips. The bundle in her arms squirmed and Jom realized it was a baby. From above, a dark shadow blocked out the dim sun. Jom twisted around to see a large ship landing. The woman waited for the ship, all grey metal and odd angles, to land. A ramp lowered to the ground from the belly of the ship. Two cloaked figures walked down the ramp, their gait halting and strange, as if they were unused to traveling on foot. The bodies underneath the cloaks shifted as they moved and Jom got the impression that they had many appendages hidden within the folds of their cloaks.

The woman extended her arms, holding the baby out to the two figures. They clicked in a strange language and moved forward. They seemed eager to take the child and moved quickly towards the woman. At the last minute, the woman snatched the child back.

"My payment," she scowled.

They clicked to themselves, then one of them reached into its cloak and produced a small bag that clinked as it was passed over. Jom could see yellow skin emerge briefly from the sleeve before the woman grabbed the bag and handed the baby over.

Without so much as a glance at her child, the woman turned and walked back to her hut, counting the coins in the purse. The creature not holding the baby drew a weapon from beneath its cloak and fired. A large, smoking hole appeared in the woman's back and she fell to the ground, dead before she hit. The creature scuttled over, retrieved the bag, and joined its companion. They returned to the ship and left the small world forever.

Jom was pulled along through time and space with the ship. He visited countless worlds across the galaxy in the blink of an eye as the two creatures gathered babies, younglings and children from innumerable planets. Time spun again and Jom found himself on a cold, harsh world looking down into an immense coliseum. The children, grown now to adolescence, were fighting for their lives against one another. Those that could not fight were quickly dispatched by their peers. Limbs and organs flew in every direction as the children fought. The coliseum was filled with all manner of creatures who watched the slaughter in silence, only occasionally making low comments to a companion. The child from the blue star world, now a lithe young man with light blue skin and pupil-less eyes, bested all who came against him, slashing and hacking his way to bloody victory. He could have been more than ten or eleven solar cycles old, younger than Jom. Yet he sliced off limbs and impaled heads with no emotion or regret. His face was blank; betraying no feelings at all as he systematically slaughtered the other children. Blood ran down his thin arms and splashed across his face like a scar. His feet were discolored from wading through the offal that surrounded him. When the tournament was over, he stood alone on the bodies of his fellow orphans.

The boy was taken in chains from the coliseum. Barefooted and nearly naked, he was marched across the unforgiving landscape until he reached the foot of a large mountain. Jom strained to hear the words spoken to the boy but could not. He watched as the boy's captors pointed to the mountain peak and shoved him forward with the points of their swords. The boy climbed. Jom soared around the mountain, watching the boy struggle against the wind and rain, dodge rock falls and bake in the heat of the suns. He grew so thin that his arms and legs dwindled to sticks. Yet he pressed on, finally coming to a great temple built into the side of the mountain peak. A group of monks, clad in robes as black as night, took the half-dead boy into the temple.

Time sped up. Jom watched as the young man was trained in ways that were already ancient when the universe was young. He was taught how to use his mind as a weapon. He learned how to manipulate the emotions of those around him, shaping their desires and fears and using them against his opponents. He learned how to hunt the stars for his prey and how to manifest solid objects from their fear. Jom watched in horror as the man took a hundred victims into an arena and methodically slaughtered them one by one. The terror, sweet and dark and delicious, was harnessed by the power of the man and fashioned into a black sword that dripped shadows. He named the sword Talonn and vowed then and there on the corpses of his victims to use the blade to bring righteousness to the worlds. At a ceremony where a thousand infants were sacrificed, the thin man was granted the title of Shadow Saint by the dark monks. Jom saw him smile then for the first time in his life, for he finally had a name. And with the name came a purpose. He was the destroyer and the seeker. He was the assassin and the savior.

Jom's world spun around. He was whipped about, touching on different times and places. He watched the Shadow Saint roam the planes, using his black blade to carve a bloody path through any and all who stood against him. He started wars, ended wars, assassinated leaders, captured fugitives and impaled emperors. Jom felt his stomach turn at the carnage the Shadow Saint left in his wake. He journeyed from one end of the universe to the other, bringing justice to the highest bidder in the name of his dark gods. And then Jom was spun around again until he found himself in a quiet space on a darkened bridge of a starship.

From beneath his thin cloak, the Shadow Saint stared out at the stars. The bridge of his ship, the Cornelius Grinnell, was empty save for himself and one navigation robot. The rest of his crew had been sent to quarters. The Shadow Saint needed to smell the aether. He was on a hunt.

He stood on the bridge, looking out at the cosmos. He let his gaze sweep back and forth, taking in every one of the trillions of stars visible to him, yet seeing none of them. His mind thought of only one thing: his quarry. His eyes flicked back and forth, scanning nebulas and galaxies, touching each one until a slight flicker caught his attention. He did not let his gaze linger, rather, he continued to peer into the heavens. He brought his eyes back on another sweep. The same star flickered just right. Then he knew he had found the trail. He issued a quick command to the robot behind him and the engines of the Cornelius Grinnell roared to life. The bridge centered on the star and the Shadow Saint permitted a small smile to cross his face.

"Got you."

Jom woke with a start. NDX was staring at him, the soft glow of its eyes more intense than usual. Macar was peering at him from over the automaton's shoulder.

"Are you in need of assistance?" NDX asked. "You were thrashing in your sleep."

"I—no, I'm fine." Jom rubbed his eyes and rose to his elbow. "I was dreaming of a man."

"Please, tell me what you remember."

"There—there was a man. An evil, evil man. He was standing on the bridge of a ship, looking at the stars. He was just looking and looking, then picked one of the stars and started heading towards it."

"Does that distress you?"

"Yes."

"Why?"

"Because," Jom shivered, "I think he's looking for us."

A Desperate Plan

"U S?" MACAR ASKED, TAKING a step back. "You, you mean."

"But why us?" Jom asked, his voice creeping up an octave.

"Unknown at this time," NDX replied. "However, it is obvious we need to get out of this cell quickly."

"And then what?"

"I am processing alternative plans. Let us focus on one problem at a time."

"The door is solid, trust me," Macar said. "I've tried it."

"I do not doubt you, but perhaps we have other avenues." NDX reached down and the small compartment in its side slid open. It removed the vial that housed Dianat and held it up. Its eyes narrowed and it focused on the vial of black liquid. The Water

Banshee stirred in the vial. Jom thought he saw her face float into sight before retreating into the murky liquid of her body. The automaton stood still for a moment, apparently listening to Dianat. Then it nodded and lowered the vial.

"Dianat believes she can create a small passage from this room to the next without attracting the attention of the slicers. Such a quick localized incursion should go unnoticed. She will in effect create a wormhole from this side of the wall to the hallway on the other side. As long as we stay within the tunnel she creates, we will be safe."

"Who? What?" Macar asked, confused. Jom bit back a grin. For once, he wasn't the confused one of the group.

"Is she strong enough?" he asked the automaton, genuinely concerned for the Water Banshee.

NDX nodded. "She believes she has enough energy for a quick portal, yes."

"Who are you talking about?" Macar asked.

"Our companion. She is a Water Banshee."

"A Water—" Macar clapped his hands over his mouth and took several steps back. "A Water Banshee?" he whispered harshly.

"Yes. She is friendly." Macar did not appear mollified by the statement, Jom noticed. He sympathized with the man. Not long ago, he had the same reaction.

"Alright then." Jom moved to the door and placed his ear against the cold metal. "I can't hear anyone on the other side. Can you?"

NDX stepped over and pulled its ear from its housing. It placed the ear on the metal for a moment before returning it to its head.

"Negative. There does not appear to be anyone outside at the moment."

"So we get out of this cell. Then what?"

"We can't take out all of them," Macar pointed out.

"Possibly not," NDX replied. "However, we may not have to if we can reach a life-pod or other means of leaving the vehicle safely. If this is a standard hover train, there will be a number of escape hatches built into the hull. Assuming we are not travelling at too great of speed, we may be able to utilize one to escape."

"Well, what are we waiting for then?" Jom asked. He fingered the dagger in his pocket nervously. He tried to remember the last time he felt safe but it was just a vague memory, something from long ago. The thought of curling up in the corner of his family's hut amid the snoring and heavy breathing of his kin did not make him feel safe anymore. He had already seen too much of the universe to ever think that was safety. He sighed, not because he missed being there, but because he missed feeling that way.

NDX held out its hand and pulled the stopper off the vial. Black liquid poured out of the vial and drifted through the air towards the wall like a sentient storm cloud. Macar suppressed a yelp and took a step away from the Water Banshee as she hit the wall of the cell. Dianat splashed against the metal of the wall, expanding out into a large oval and then began to spin. Faster and faster, she whirled around, turning her body into a vertical whirlpool. The black of her body grew deeper and deeper until Jom could see nothing but inky darkness.

"Go now!" Dianat screamed. Jom and Macar covered their ears at her voice and Jom looked around fearfully, expecting men to burst through the door. NDX ushered them close.

"Simply step through the vortex. You will materialize on the other side. I suggest you keep your eyes closed, however. Unless you are experienced with crossing dimensions, the sight can be unnerving. Hurry. She will not be able to maintain the wormhole for long."

And then it stepped into the spinning vortex. The clock-work boy disappeared into the shadows. Macar looked at Jom with fear in his eyes. Jom shrugged, took a deep breath, squeezed his eyes shut and stepped into the portal.

In one simple step, Jom fell between planes. A hot wind stung his face and his arms and legs turned to ice. He heard his name called out to him and then hideous laughter erupted around him. He wanted to open his eyes and peek at his surroundings. He raised his hands to cover his eyes and felt them restrained by something with claws. Fire erupted around him. He cried out in terror. Then his foot touched a surface and everything went quiet.

"You are safe," he heard NDX's electronic voice say next to him.

He cautiously opened one eye. He was standing in the hallway just outside the door to their cell. Dianat was spinning against the wall and, as he watched, Macar stumbled through, his skin pale with fear.

"It's all right," Jom said, grabbing at the man to steady him. "We're safe."

Macar took his shaking hands from his head and looked around wildly. Only after several heartbeats did he begin to relax. NDX took out the vial and Dianat slowly pulled away from the wall, spinning through the air like a horizontal tornado. She spiraled into the crystal vial. Once she was safely inside, NDX replaced the stopper and returned the vial to its compartment. The door slid shut with a satisfied hum.

"I suggest we find someplace to hide," NDX said and the others nodded. Jom tried not to breathe as they hurried to the end of the hallway. Macar, still pale from the experience of traveling through planes, let himself get led by Jom without complaint. NDX gave directions, relying on his scanners to keep them away from the outlaws roaming the hover train. They found a small space among some random cargo near the back of the vehicle and hunkered down.

"This is ridiculous," Macar said in a harsh whisper, coming to his senses. "They'll find us easy enough here."

"There's nowhere else to go," Jom pointed out.

"A hover train this size should have three emergency pods," NDX said. "I detect two pods still operational on the third deck.

The other pod is missing."

"The third deck? That's where they eat and sleep," Macar protested.

"That is correct. Crew cabins and the mess hall are also located on that deck."

"How are we going to get past everyone?" Jom asked desperately.

"Perhaps Dianat can transport us one at a time to a safer location," NDX suggested.

Jom looked over as Macar shivered. He knew how the man felt. "But what if she gets attacked again," Jom pointed out. "We'd be separated and stranded."

"Affirmative," NDX conceded.

Macar began to cough. He covered his mouth but the coughs racked his body. Jom put his hands over Macar's to help limit the noise until the attack had passed. They looked around nervously. Thankfully there was no one in sight. Jom wiped sweat from his brow.

"Whatever we decide, we should do it quickly."

Static erupted above them from a speaker on the wall. Then, the mechanical voice of the lead bandit came on.

"Congratulations on escaping your cell," he began. "The sensors in the room just went off indicating two men...excuse me, one man and a boy, left the cell along with a wind-up toy. I am curious on how you accomplished it. I look forward to you telling me when you come back. Surely you know there is no place to hide on my ship. I already have men stationed at every escape hatch and life-pod. Come out. Don't make me look for you and I promise you will not be harmed."

They looked at each other. Jom sincerely doubted the man could be trusted and shook his head once. Macar reluctantly nodded in agreement.

"Of course, if we have to search for you, I cannot guarantee you will be treated kindly," the man continued. "I will give you to the count of five hundred to return to your cell. Oh, one more thing. I took the liberty of implanting a small explosive in the man you found in your cell. I hold the detonator in my hand. If you have not returned in time, I will set it off. I would prefer not to have an explosion on my ship. But don't test me."

The speaker shut off. Macar's face had turned ashen.

"There's—there's a bomb in me?" he asked in a small voice.

NDX stared at him for a moment. "My scans do not detect any conventional explosives. However, since I do not know what techno-magic capabilities he has, I cannot guarantee he is bluffing."

Macar stood.

"What are you doing?" Jom asked, pulling him back down and looking around fearfully.

"I don't want to blow up," he said, staring at them. "I'm turning myself in. I've spent so long in that cell; it's beginning to feel like home anyways."

"No! We're getting out of here. NDX, have Dianat take him away first. Maybe there's a limited range on the detonator or something."

"Possible. But it is unlikely that distance would affect it if he is utilizing magic or transplanal frequencies."

"One hundred," the speaker announced.

"What can we do?" Jom pleaded.

"I can turn myself in," Macar replied.

"No!"

"It's not your life you're risking!" Macar raised his voice. "It's mine!"

"Incorrect. He stipulated we all surrender," NDX pointed out. "Therefore we have a stake in this decision as well."

Macar stared at the clock-work boy. "It's not your life," he repeated.

"Two hundred."

Jom thought furiously. There had to be some way to escape! Something they could do!

Then an idea hit him.

"NDX! Does your scan pick up anything unusual in his body?"

NDX turned to Macar and its eyes brightened for a moment. "I detect a number of foreign objects. It appears you have trace amounts of sixteen different metals in your body."

"From the mines, most likely."

"There is a broken blade the size of a small twig embedded in your left thigh."

"Fight. I won."

"There is also a small circular object located near the base of your neck. It is a synthetic alloy of some type. I am unfamiliar with its molecular structure."

"That's it!" Jom said, then quickly clamped his hands over his mouth. "That's it," he repeated quieter.

"That is my guess as well."

"Can Dianat...I don't know, reach in and grab it?"

Macar's face turned another shade of grey. "What? Are you insane? You want a Water Banshee to go into my brain?"

"Three hundred."

"It can work!" Jom turned to NDX. "Right? Can it work?"

NDX was still for a moment as it ran calculations. "It is possible, theoretically. It has never been attempted before so it is difficult to calculate the odds."

"Just do it!"

"No!"

"We're running out of time! Macar, do you really want to be a captive of these people forever? Don't you want to be free?"

"I want to live!"

"Do you want to live, or just exist?" Jom demanded. Macar's face was tight. He was trembling with fright and tears formed at the corners of his eyes. Jom watched anxiously as the man weighed his options.

"Four hundred."

Macar nodded once. Jom turned to NDX. The automaton was already removing Dianat's vial from its compartment in its side.

"The device is exactly three microunits in diameter, located slightly to the left of center at the base of his brain stem," NDX told Dianat. Jom could see her face amid the swirling blackness. He motioned for the vial and held it up to his eyes so he could see Dianat clearly.

"I know you can do this," he told the Water Banshee. "Grab the bomb and take it as far away as you can quickly. Don't get caught with it when time is up."

Dianat nodded. Jom pulled the stopper off. Macar closed his eyes. Dianat spiraled out of the vial and through the air like a tiny whirlpool. She spun right at Macar, coming to a fine point at a spot on his forehead. Jom watched in fascination as she phased right into his body, leaving no trace of her passing. Macar stiffened as she entered him; his eyes sprang open as wide as they could go. He opened his mouth but no sound came out. Then he stiffened and collapsed into Jom's arms.

"Macar!"

"Five hundred." There was an audible sigh. "You disappoint me. Goodbye."

Jom squeezed his eyes shut. He waited an eternity. But there was no explosion. Slowly, he opened his eyes. Macar was still shaking in his arms and his eyes were wide with terror. Tears streamed down his cheeks.

"I'm—I'm still here," he said, his voice trembling.

"We all are," NDX added.

"She did it!"

But then the voice came on the speaker again. "It seems you are much more resourceful than I expected. I will not make that mistake again." The speaker clicked off. They knew the outlaws were already fanning out to find them.

"I do not wish to point out the obvious, we still have our original dilemma of needing to find a way off the ship," NDX said. "And now we no longer have Dianat as an option."

"But we're alive," Jom countered. "And that means everything."

Confrontation

L ET'S GO," JOM SAID, yanking Macar to his feet. Macar visibly pulled himself together with supreme effort and nodded. They hurried down a long hallway, listening intently for the inevitable footfalls of pursuit.

"There are two people approaching from the right," NDX said as they ran. They turned down the first left-handed passageway that presented itself.

"A group of three people are standing at the intersection to our left." They kept going straight, ducking quickly past the hallway when the outlaws weren't looking.

A thousand quick heartbeats went by as they ducked and ran down corridor after corridor, evading the seemingly endless number of outlaws that roamed the ship. Jom knew it was just a matter of time before they ran into a dead-end or NDX's scanners failed them. It wasn't that huge of a ship, he thought. They'll find us any moment. He unconsciously pulled his dagger out and gripped it tightly in his hand. He had a bad feeling it would taste blood soon. As he ran, the blade seemed to pull him forward, like it was seeking death. He tried to push the idea out of his mind and concentrate on avoiding the hunting bandits.

They made it all the way to the second deck before they were found. NDX stopped suddenly, extending its arms to either side to catch Macar and Jom from stumbling forward.

"We are surrounded," it announced, whirling its head around as it scanned the area. Jom looked past the automaton and saw three bandits step into view at the end of the hallway. He spun around as four more outlaws blocked their escape behind them, weapons drawn.

"What are we going to do?" he asked desperately.

"Surrender," Macar replied grimly and held up his hands. Jom scowled at the man but followed his lead. They were outnumbered, outgunned and surrounded. He slipped his dagger back into his pocket quickly and forced himself to stay calm even though every nerve screamed at him to run.

Laughing, the outlaws, all black cloth, drawn weapons and crooked grins, prodded them forward. Macar stumbled once and started coughing. The bandits laughed and shoved him to the floor as his body spasmed from coughing. Jom knelt beside him, gently patting Macar's back to alleviate the coughing as best he could. He was racked with convulsions for several heartbeats. Finally, the attack passed and they were jerked to their feet and hurried along.

They were hustled onto the bridge of the hover train. Waiting for them was the leader of the outlaws, silhouetted by the windows of the bridge. Bright sunlight poured in and Jom realized they had yet to leave the atmosphere of the planet. Either that or they were on another planet entirely. As before, the man was dressed in ragged black cloth that covered most of his body, including the lower half of his face. He stood tall and proud, hands clasped behind his back as the three companions were pushed forward. Jom noticed a number of bandits lurking around the outskirts of the bridge, ready at a moment's notice to jump at their leader's whim.

"I must congratulate you," he said, his metallic voice echoing off the walls. "Few have eluded me quite like you three have, even if it was temporary."

"It was their idea!" Macar blurted out, falling to his knees. "I had no choice! They made me go with them!"

"Silence." He spoke the word quietly, yet it carried across the gap between them easily. Macar shut his mouth and whimpered. Despite himself, Jom scowled at Macar's cowardice. He was scared too. So scared his bowels threatened to loosen. But he would not grovel. His Grandmother had taught him never to grovel. The thought of her sent a sharp pang of longing through the fear. He took a deep breath to steady himself.

"Now," the man continued, "I want to know what you were doing on the surface of this planet. Tell me."

"As I stated previously—" NDX began. The man drew a blaster from beneath his cloak and fired. A flash of light blinded Jom. A loud explosion deafened him. Dazed, he shook his head and saw NDX fall backward. Its left shoulder was smoking. Jom looked at the automaton in horror as his brain processed what he saw. NDX's arm was laying on the ground several paces from its body. The blast had taken its arm completely off. The light in its eyes dimmed to almost nothing.

"No!" Jom screamed and dropped to the clock-work boy. "NDX! NDX!" But the automaton did not respond.

"My patience is at an end."

Jom stood up and whirled around, anger and grief clouding his vision. His hand went to the dagger in his pocket. The barrel of the bandit's weapon, however, was pointing directly at Jom's forehead.

"I wouldn't," the man said, his finger on the trigger.

"We're—" Jom took a deep breath and let go of the dagger hilt. His fingers brushed up against something else in his pocket. "We're searching—"

"Yes?"

Jom's fingers slid across a small cylindrical object and he let his breath out slowly.

"We're searching for the Dowa," he finished as his fingers curled around the miniature flute.

The man stared at him for a heartbeat. "The Dowa do not exist," he finally stated, lowering his weapon slightly.

"We believe they do."

"Why do you want to find them?"

Jom's mind raced as he thought. He looked down at the inert clock-work boy at his feet. "Because...because NDX here needs them to repair him. He's falling apart. On the inside."

The man lowered his weapon the rest of the way and cocked his head, studying both Jom and NDX thoughtfully. Then he let out a loud laugh. Jom and Macar were startled and stepped back a step. The laughter, electronic and cold, echoed off the walls of the bridge.

"So, you're telling me you're just a boy hunting for bedtime story creatures to fix your broken toy?" He laughed harder.

Jom felt the blood rush to his cheeks. "I'm not a boy!" he burst out, feeling his face turn hot. He hated how his voice cracked and that made him angrier still. Macar placed a hand on his shoulder but Jom brushed it away.

"I'm not a boy," he repeated, desperately trying to keep his voice under control, "and NDX is not a toy. The Dowa exist and we're going to find them!" He was so angry and scared he believed his own story. And why not? He had a Dowa flute in his pocket, didn't he? They existed! At least, they did once. And maybe they still did. But his outburst made the man, and the other bandits, laugh even harder.

The man turned and holstered his weapon. "Perhaps we can get a ransom for them," he muttered to his nearest lieutenant.

"Ha! Good luck with that!" Jom blurted out. "My whole village together couldn't afford even a single credit."

"Then maybe I'll just kill you and dump your body at the nearest waypoint!" the man snarled back.

Without thinking, Jom's hand went back to the hilt. He pulled the dagger from his pocket and launched himself at the laughing outlaw with a scream. He made it no further than a pace or two before one of the bandits standing nearby reached out and plucked him out of the air and away from the leader. Still yelling, Jom struggled against the bandit's firm hands. He brought the dagger down wildly, brushing it against the outlaw's arm. Although the dull blade did not pierce the black clothing, a bright red line immediately formed on the man's arm. Jom looked down in surprise as the line burst into flames. The outlaw yelped and dropped Jom. By the time Jom rolled to his feet, half of the man's arm was on fire and he was screaming in pain.

Other bandits rushed forward, beating at the fire with rags and cloaks. But the flames, eager for blood, jumped from person to person, traveling along any surface it came in contact with. Jom felt the heat of the flames and backed away. Macar yelled to him. Jom turned, seeing Macar struggling to pick NDX off the floor. Shaking his head, Jom rushed over to help, the yells of burning people and the stench of burning flesh assaulting his senses. Together, they got NDX up and into Macar's arms. Although he gritted his teeth, Macar stood up straight and nodded quickly to Jom. Jom dashed to the side and grabbed NDX's arm, tucking it quickly between the automaton and Macar's chest. They ran to the door. Jom spared a glance over his shoulder at the conflagration that had now spread to every corner of the bridge. A dark shadow stood in the middle of the fire. Jom stared as the leader of the bandits stepped forward, flames dancing around him. The fire had burned away most of his clothing and Jom gasped as he saw gleaming metal glowing red hot. It encased his arms and legs and most of his face. Cyborg! The leader was a cyborg. Even as he stared, the man laughed and took another step forward.

"Run!" Jom screamed to Macar and they dashed into the corridor.

"The escape pod should be this way!" Macar said, turning down a hallway to his left. Jom was a half-step behind. He felt heat on his leg and looked down. His legging was smoking. He patted at the smoke as he ran. The dagger in his pocket was still warm. He could feel it resist, wanting to go back and taste more blood, wanting to burn more flesh.

"The man—" Jom said between breaths. "That man was a cyborg!"

"I know!" Macar replied, breathing heavily as well. "That's—that's Kala Azar!"

They had no more breath to use and concentrated on running as fast as they could. They found the escape pod around the next corner and hurried in. Jom looked around wildly, seeing banks upon banks of buttons and switches. He put his hands on his knees, trying to catch his breath and make sense of the controls. Macar set NDX down against the bulkhead and hit a switch. The door of the pod slid shut soundlessly, closing out the chaos of the alarms and yelling. Macar pushed past Jom and sat at the pilot's seat.

"Do you know how to use this thing?" Jom asked, trying to will his heart to stop beating so fast.

Macar grunted and hit a few buttons. Jom looked out as large cargo doors opened just outside their cockpit, letting in the light of the outside. Jom saw the landscape speed by incredibly fast. Macar looked around at the various displays, then jabbed at a blinking button. The pod shot forward, knocking them both back. Jom tumbled backwards and desperately grabbed the leg of Macar's chair. The pod careened to the right, then left. Jom saw flashes of colors and lights through the windows. NDX's body slid across the floor of the pod, crashing heavily into the back. Jom tried to regain his feet but suddenly they hit something and his world was thrown into chaos. He fell forward, then back. The roof rushed up, knocking the wind out of him, then he dropped back to the floor. NDX was tossed about with him, colliding with him and the walls. Macar somehow managed to stay in the chair for a moment but the force of the collision was too great and he went flying as well.

Stars exploded behind Jom's eyes and the world stopped moving. Silence. Darkness. He was vaguely aware of something wet dripping into his eyes but couldn't move his hand. Then he felt nothing.

: Dream of the Hypothetical Beast :

THE LAST OF THE three suns dipped below the horizon and a chill wind blew across the plains. Jom shivered and wrapped his cloak tighter around his body. He stood on a high plateau, looking down at the huge marshland below. The delta spread out before him, reaching almost to the horizon. Islands of marsh grass sprinkled the dark waterways. Pockets of fog hung over the stiller parts of the water, keeping both predator and prey hidden. Thin rivers flowed into the marshland from all sides, bringing a steady stream of fresh food to the creatures that lurked beneath the low trees. Jom listened to the calls of the night predators as they woke and roused themselves for the nightly hunt. It was a cloudy night, the moon well hidden behind thick clouds that silently invaded the sky. Yet Jom saw clearly, his dream-sight clear and focused. His gaze centered on a small animal stepping cautiously through the middle of the marsh.

The animal had thick black fur that easily repelled the water. It was small, only a few hands long, and struggled to avoid the deeper parts of the marsh where it would surely drown. A short snout sniffed the air as it carefully picked its way towards solid ground on four short legs. Its small ears were alert and twitching, placing every grunt and snort of the creatures surrounding it. Jom smiled as he watched the creature. It was cute and inquisitive and so very tired of being wet. The day of foraging had been long and it now wanted to reach its nest and sleep. Somehow, Jom knew it was called a Womf and was a rare and timid animal on this world.

A new sound drifted across on the winds and the animal froze. The creature listened as a high-pitched whine grew louder and louder. Jom looked around from his vantage point, trying to place the source of the unnatural noise. There were no settlements or towns within sight of the marsh, only open plains and the occasional copse of scraggly trees.

Suddenly, a bright light pierced the clouds and the night was broken. Jom shielded his eyes as he watched a ship lower itself into the sky just above the marshland. Creatures large and small ran, flew and slithered away from the light that shined down on them. Jom looked to the Womf. Fright kept it frozen to its spot. Jom saw it shivering uncontrollably from fear yet it couldn't move. The light grew brighter, the whine grew louder. Jom had to look away and cover his ears. Then there was a roar of engines and the ship was gone, taking the light and sound with it. The marshland was quiet once more. Jom searched for the creature but it was gone.

Jom blinked. He was in a large room. The cries of a thousand creatures assaulted his ears. Cages towered over him on every side. Animals from countless worlds screeched and chirped and grunted at him, all desperately pleading for release from their prisons. He covered his ears, trying to shut out the horrible din. He looked ahead and saw the Womf from the marshes. The animal was strapped to a large chair. It was a simple metal chair. But it felt...wrong. Jom shuddered just looking at it. The Womf's eyes rolled around wildly as it struggled uselessly to escape the thick chains that held it tight. It cried out in terror as it struggled, tugging at Jom's heart. A low mist rolled around the feet of the chair, dark yellow and noxious. Jom involuntarily took a step back from the mist, knowing that it was evil. Small sparks of green burst randomly from the chair, singeing the Womf's fur. It yelped in pain once, twice, three times before settling into an on-going whimper, exhausted by its futile struggles.

Jom moved towards the chair, wanting, needing to free the poor creature. At the edge of his vision, he glimpsed a figure. He turned to look, but it was too quick and ducked behind the cages. Jom set his jaw and took another step forward. Then he saw the shadowy figure behind the chair. A shrill laugh erupted and there was a click. Energy flooded through the chair. The yellow mist rose up, surrounding the Womf. It cried out in pain and Jom staggered backwards as bolts of sickly green energy lashed out at him. He stumbled and fell.

Jom shook his head. He was in a different room. The Womf, exhausted and hungry, lay curled up on a cold metal floor in the center of the featureless room. Jom looked around and saw two figures standing to the side. Their features were hidden in shadows but he knew one of them was a Technomage by the arrogant way he stood and the fine fabric that covered him from head to toe.

"This? This is a weapon? Why do you waste my time?" a voice snarled.

"Watch, my Lord," a second voice hissed.

A door slid open to Jom's right. A large brute of a person walked into the room. He stood at least five heads taller than Jom and was made of solid muscle that flexed as he walked. His grey skin was studded with small quills that dripped a thick blue liquid. Jom took a step back, trying to make himself small against the wall. The man looked like he could tear Jom apart as easily as a leaf and laugh while doing it. He strode into the center of the room and looked down at the Womf, a disgusted look on his face.

"Is to eat?" the man laughed.

The Womf looked up at the man, shaking with fear. But instead of attacking, the man gasped and stumbled back. He cursed in a tongue Jom had never heard. The Womf took a tentative step forward and the man began to cry. He dropped to his knees, tears streaming down his face. Then, with a final cry of anguish, the man fell face-first to the floor, dead before he hit.

The Womf jumped back in panic. When the man didn't move, it curled back into a ball and shivered, cold and alone.

The door slid open again. This time, five reptilian creatures slithered in. They had four short legs on opposite sides of long, thin bodies. Dark red scales covered them and sharp teeth glinted from long snouts.

The creatures ran into the room, sniffing the air for prey. The one nearest the dead giant ripped into the grey flesh, tearing off a huge hunk. The other creatures chirped and scurried over. Grunts and hisses erupted as they fought over the meal. The Womf squeaked and backed away from the carnage. One of the reptiles saw the Womf move and leapt towards it. The Womf let out a small whine. The reptile skidded to a halt in front of the Womf and cocked its head. Then, without warning, it let out a loud cry of anguish and dropped to the ground dead. The other reptiles looked up from their feast. Seeing their dead companion, they snarled and ran towards the Womf. Again, one look from the Womf and they fell dead to the floor.

"What happened?" the first voice, the voice of the Technomage, demanded.

"The eyes," the other voice hissed. "The eyes are the windows to the soul, my Lord. This creature has so much pain and suffering in its soul that it spills out through the eyes. All that look into its eyes feel the overwhelming crush of sadness and pain. They instantly fall dead from so much suffering. It is my greatest achievement. It will be your greatest weapon. None can stand before it and live."

Jom looked to the shadows. He saw the taller figure extend his gloved hand. A brilliant bolt of purple energy shot from his palm and lanced across the room to the creature. The Womf cried out as the energy burned its eyes out. Jom's heart was shattered as he watched the poor creature writhe in pain on the floor.

"Fool," the Technomage said. "Now what power does it possess?" He turned and left the room.

"My apologies, Lord Ku'baba. I will work harder." And the other shadow left, leaving the wounded Womf whimpering in pain.

Jom raced forward to the Womf but space twisted around him and he woke.

A Fair Trade

JOM BLINKED HIS EYES several times. Something wet and cold was dripping into his eyes and he wiped away blood. His head was pounding. His body ached. He looked around, trying to make sense of his environment. He was in a twisted heap on the floor of the escape pod. NDX was partially on top of him and he gently pushed the clock-work boy off. He patted his arms and legs, making sure nothing was broken.

"NDX? Can you hear me? NDX?" The automaton made no response. Its eyes were dull. Its gears were quiet beneath its battered shell. He looked around the tumbled equipment that was scattered about the cabin. "Macar?" That elicited a groan from near the front of the vehicle. Getting painfully to his feet, Jom shuffled over to the cockpit area. Macar was sprawled across the chair, hand on his bleeding side where a small piece of metal was protruding.

"Are you all right?" Jom asked, looking for something to help stop the bleeding.

"I—I think so. Nothing seems broken, at least." Macar righted himself with a groan and pulled the metal out, gasping as he did so. Jom quickly handed over a strip of cloth torn from his shirt to help stop the bleeding.

"Can you stand up?"

Macar nodded and, with Jom's help, got to his feet. He swayed for a moment and needed to steady himself with a hand on the back of the chair but waved away more assistance.

"I'll be fine. Just—just need to catch my breath." Another round of coughing hit and he had to sit down in the chair, holding his side and wincing in pain as the attack ran its course. Finally, the coughing died and he nodded to Jom.

Jom nodded back and looked out the windows of the cockpit.

"Where are we?"

"Not far from the hovertrain," Macar replied. "We didn't travel far before crashing."

"I thought you knew how to fly this thing," Jom said accusingly.

"Considering you don't fly an escape pod like this so much as steer it, I do," Macar answered. "These things aren't made for much, just to get you safely to ground."

Jom grunted but bit back his response. He looked around the cabin. "So now what?"

"We need to get some distance between us and the pod. They'll track the pod soon enough. These come equipped with homing beacons. To locate survivors. We shouldn't be anywhere near here when that happens."

"Agreed. We'll have to carry NDX, though."

"That will not be necessary," a mechanical voice replied. They looked back to see the automaton sit up and whirl its head around to look at them. The light in its eyes brightened as it surveyed the wreckage. "I will be able to travel on my own."

"NDX!" Jom stumbled forward, his feet still unsteady, and gave the clock-work boy a hug. "I was so worried you were done for!"

"The blast, though unexpected, did minimal internal damage. I automatically went into preservation mode until the danger had passed."

"I could have used your help," Macar said quietly. "You're heavy," he added.

"My apologies. It is an encrypted program. I will attempt to rewrite it to avoid such difficulties in the future. For now, however, I agree with your assessment. We should vacate this vehicle immediately."

As quickly as their bruised and battered bodies were able, they scavenged the cabin for supplies, finding emergency food paks and all-weather cloaks. Jom used some loose cables to tie NDX's arm to the back of its torso. Macar even found a small blaster pistol and stuffed it into his waistband. Within the span of a few heartbeats, they were ready. Macar hit a button on the wall and a door slid open, letting in bright sunlight. They jumped down onto loose brown gravel amid small dried-out bushes.

"So," Jom said, shielding his eyes from the sun, "where to?"

"We need to get as far away from this pod as possible," Macar replied.

"Yes. But which direction?"

NDX swiveled its head around, scanning the area. "I suggest we go perpendicular to our original course. Our pursuers will most likely assume we continued along the same path."

Macar nodded. "Fine. Let's go."

Jom looked around. "There are mountains in that direction."

He pointed to their right

"It is agreed then. We will make for the mountain range."

Macar was ten steps ahead of them before Jom even had a chance to shoulder his pack. He looked at NDX but the automaton did not seem perturbed by the man's behavior. Together they hurried to catch up with him.

They spend the remainder of the day trudging across a restless landscape. Winds whipped dust and dirt around them. Scrub bushes bent and swayed, beaten down by the heat of the sun and swiping at their legs as they passed. Small creatures darted between shadows, hissing at them as they walked by. Jom's headache gradually subsided in favor of tired legs and sore feet. The mountain range in front of them gradually, slowly grew larger, eventually blocking out the sun. The cool shadows were a welcome relief from the sun until the sweat on their skin turned cold. Soon, Macar and Jom were pulling out their cloaks to keep warm.

The sky deepened in color and they looked around for a place to shelter for the night. The winds died off as they picked their way over and around a field of large rocks that formed the foot of the mountain. The rocks provided shelter from the wind, at least. The deep shadows between boulders suggested safety.

"We can stop here for the night," Jom said but Macar shook his head.

"There's no sight line. We'd be sitting ducks for anyone who came this way."

Jom grunted but didn't say anything. Better than a damp cave, he thought. Still, NDX did not disagree so Jom put his head down and they continued up the side of the mountain, picking out footing among the loose gravel. Walls of rock rose around them, funneling them down a narrow path that snaked up the mountain. Maybe an old river bed, Jom thought. He looked at the stone that rose higher and higher as they climbed, scanning every nook and cranny for bandits. They were almost a third of the way up the side when they looked ahead to see a woman standing in front of them about thirty paces off, blocking their path.

The figure was striking to see. Her tall body was completely wrapped in a deep red fabric. It encased her long legs and arms, broad shoulders, every part of her tall body. Long strips of the fabric hung from every part of her as well. These strips seemed to have a life of their own and floated about in the wind, encasing her in a cloud of red that shimmered in the half-light of dusk. No patch of skin was left uncovered. Her hair was wrapped in fabric as well, cascading from the top of her head in long, thick braids. Even her fingers were individually wrapped in red. She held a long pike in her hands. Although it was not pointed at them, it was obvious from the way she held it that she could bring it to bear in an instant. Piercing green eyes gazed at them from between strips that wrapped around her head. The fabric was expertly wrapped around her face to allow her to speak and eat without exposing any skin.

"You do not belong here," she stated, her voice as hard as the desert. The strips of fabric undulated in the breeze, giving Jom the impression of snakes growing out from all over her body.

"Here we go again," Jom mumbled just loud enough for Macar to hear.

"Our apologies," NDX stepped forward. "We are lost."

"Yes, you are," the woman agreed. "And in great danger."

Jom looked around nervously. He saw movement in the shadows as four other figures stepped forward. They were all dressed like the first woman except the colors of their attire differed from person to person. One was in blue, another in black and two were wrapped in light grey. They all carried long spears of dark metal. They all had the odd strips hanging off their bodies as well that moved on their own accord in the shadowy light.

"We mean no offense," NDX continued. "We are hoping to find shelter for the night."

"We have shelter."

"May we impose on your hospitality then?"

The woman cocked her head to the side. "Why would we take in strangers? It is nothing to us if you die out here tonight."

"Let the Murtocs feast on their bones," one of the others said. Jom thought it was the one in black.

The red woman raised her hand to still the other. "What do you offer in exchange?"

"We carry no currency, unfortunately," NDX replied.

"We have nothing," Macar spat.

"We have stories!" Jom blurted out.

Everyone stopped and the woman in red stared intently at him. He felt his ears turn hot from the scrutiny. She absently played with one of the thick braids that hung from her head as she thought.

"Indeed?"

"Ye—yes." Jom looked her in the eyes, trying not to let his legs tremble too much. "We'll trade. A night of safety for a night of wonder."

Her eyes sparkled at the statement and Jom thought he could see a hint of a smile underneath the fabric covering her mouth.

"Very well. That would make a fair trade."

Macar nudged him in the ribs. "I hope you know some good ones," he whispered.

"I learned from the best," Jom replied, sparing a quick thanks to his Grandmother.

She turned and the others closed ranks around them, spears held loosely but kept ready. They walked a short way to a slim opening in the rocks. They would have walked right past the opening without ever seeing it, it was so well hidden among the shadows of the stone. The woman in red ducked inside with a quick movement. With a glance at Macar, Jom took a breath and stepped into the darkness of a cave. He found himself on a path that led into the interior of the mountain. Torches blazed in hollows chiseled into the rock at regular intervals and Jom could clearly see the red woman waiting for him a few paces ahead. Without a word, she turned and walked down the path. Jom hurried to keep up, occasionally glancing over his shoulder to make sure Macar and NDX were following.

The woman led them deep into the mountain. Every so often, she would turn down a side passage. After several such turns, Jom lost his sense of direction. Side passages branched off on either side and the woman would take them, seemingly at random, first in one direction, then another. There were numerous times Jom thought they walked past the same intersection or rock formation and he got the uneasy feeling they were being led on a winding way through the tunnels to stop them from finding their way out easily. Jom wondered if they knew NDX would not be so easily fooled. At least he hoped so. The automaton's scanners hopefully were still functional.

Finally, they were led through a small opening and Jom stopped. Spread out before them was a sight of unparalleled beauty. A number of huts were spread among large leafy trees along the floor of an immense area. Campfires blazed here and there throughout the village. The light of day struck the far wall, illuminating green leaf and blue water. Jom saw a merry stream snake its way across the area from a waterfall to their left. The spray of the water caught the fading light and a rainbow arched across the village. Jom looked up, saw the sky high above and realized the mountain was hollow, like an empty volcano. The walls of rock that surrounded the village were covered with alcoves and caves filled with people and animals. Bright winged creatures with long necks and large beaks cawed as they flitted about while villagers busied themselves with weaving, cooking, skinning, drumming and singing. There was laughter in the air and dancing among the fires. Everyone was garbed like their escort. Long strips of colored fabric flowed around bodies as they walked and ran and danced, creating a whirlwind of color that dazzled Jom's eyes. He smiled, letting a delighted laugh escape his lips, then realized the woman in red was watching him. She nodded in approval and led them down the path and into the village.

The strangers were greeted with a mixture of curious stares and open laughter. They whispered among themselves as Jom and the others passed but not in a fearful way. They seemed more intrigued by the visitors than anything. The children were fearless, scampering up to the party and yelling in delight. Even Macar could not resist the happy children that ran between his legs, trailing colors as they weaved in and out among the party. Jom laughed at his bemused grimace. NDX was especially intriguing to the villagers. They crowded around it, touching its dented metal skin in wonder and murmuring to themselves until the red woman shooed them gently away. Jom noticed that the vast majority of villagers were female. He saw only a handful of males; all dressed in green and keeping to the outskirts of the crowd.

They were led to the center of the village to a large open circular area. A great fire blazed in the center of the clearing. People were gathered together in groups, cooking and eating, dancing and singing. Jom tried not to stare at one group eating. He saw the vegetables in a woman's hands, then the wind picked up, the strips of blue that covered her body fluttered about, and the food was gone. He blinked, trying to watch closer, but they moved on and he lost sight of her.

Jom and the others were brought to a series of sitting stones near the center and Jom sank down gratefully, his legs sore from the long trek. The red woman disappeared into the crowd. The guards remained, Jom noticed, but kept back and stood unobtrusively near the edge of the sitting area, keeping to the shadows and not disrupting the festive mood that welcomed Jom and the others.

Food and drink was brought to them. Platters of a variety of odd-looking fruits and vegetables with small pieces of meat scattered among them were placed in front of them. Jom and Macar eagerly dug in, mumbling thanks between bites. Jom couldn't remember the last time he had eaten a proper meal and continuously thanked their hosts. There were murmurs when

NDX politely declined to eat. A woman wrapped in white stepped forward, looking concerned. She knelt beside NDX.

"Are you in much pain?" she asked gently.

"I feel no pain," NDX told her. She touched its damaged shoulder, then the arm strapped to its back.

"How is it possible?"

"I am not a biological being," NDX explained. "I am a clock-work boy, made from gears and springs."

She looked at him, a thousand questions on her face. "You are a golem?"

NDX tilted its head slightly. "In a sense, yes. I am."

"Is this, then, the first wonder of the night?" a voice asked. They turned to see the woman in red step into view. The other villagers bowed and stepped back.

"I am Ravola. We welcome you to Cloudburst Tribe." She extended her hands, palms up, and bowed her head.

Jom and the others stood and returned the gesture.

"I am Macar, a mine worker." Macar attempted to keep the haunted look from taking over his face, no doubt feeling the sting of loss. As if to emphasize his words, a round of coughing hit. The others waited politely while the woman in white gave him a bowl of liquid to drink. The coughing subsided almost immediately. Ravola nodded to her, then to Macar.

"I am ND-7-2349-X, servant of Abla'than'abla." Ravola nodded.

"I am Jom of...of the unnamed village." At this, Ravola tilted her head, studying him yet again, then nodded.

"We welcome you all. Know you are safe while in our village. Now, please, finish eating. Then we would hear your stories."

The night progressed pleasantly. After they had had their fill, the bowls were removed. Settling in by the warmth of the fire, Jom told them many of the stories he had heard from Grandmother; tales of giants and stories of spirits. He told them of the Dowa and the Revitalizers. He talked about the Sun Boy and the Lurkers that lived under the black waters. He then told them of his own adventures, from the moment he was pulled under the waters by a Water Banshee to escaping the cyborg pirate that very morning. He left out details about finding the Phobetor Chair after NDX gave him a slight nudge, nor did he mention his dream about Macar. Macar took over at the point of them finding him in the cell, telling of his loss and subsequent capture. When they finally finished, the night was deep, the great fire was low and the moons were high in the night sky. With gentle words, Ravola sent the villagers to their beds.

She stood and gestured to a small hut behind them. "You may sleep there tonight. It has already been prepared for you. At dawn, I will escort you to the other side of the mountain. Your pursuers will not think to look for you there and you may safely continue on your way."

"We thank you," NDX said. "Your kindness is greatly appreciated."

She nodded. "As I said, a fair trade." She turned and walked off into the shadows, leaving them to rest.

Kala Azar

DESPITE HIS EXHAUSTION, JOM could not sleep. So much had happened in such a short time. His mind whirled with questions that had no answers.

"NDX," he whispered. "NDX, are you awake?"

The clock-work boy stirred. Jom heard gears moving under its metal skin. It turned its head towards him, the light in its eyes growing a bit brighter.

"I sense no danger," it said. "Are you unwell?"

"No...I mean, not really." Jom sighed. "I just need to talk."

"Proceed."

Jom tried to put his thoughts in order. "Can we trust these people?" he finally said, deciding he may as well begin with their immediate situation.

NDX did not answer immediately. Its gears spun within. Then it nodded. "There does not appear to be sufficient cause for alarm at the moment. They appear to be sincere. They have provided us with sustenance and shelter and have asked little in return."

"What do you know of them?"

"Nothing you do not. There is no record of a Cloudburst Tribe within my databases."

"Doesn't that concern you?"

NDX tilted its head. "Not at all. It is impossible for my system to carry information about everything. I do not have sufficient on-board memory for that. The Master would assuredly know, but I am unable to contact him at the present time."

Jom sighed again.

"Is there more you wish to discuss?"

"Do you think the bandits will come after us?"

"Unknown. That depends entirely on which is more important to them: us or the object they appear to be searching for."

"Macar mentioned a 'Mind Harp'."

NDX nodded. "That is correct. He overheard some of the pirates discussing it."

"What is it?"

"I do not know. There is no record of that either."

"When we were escaping the ship, Macar said the man's name was Kala Azar. I saw him. He's a cyborg."

Again, NDX was silent for a moment while it analyzed the information. "Interesting. I do have a record of a man named

Kala Azar."

"Tell me what you know."

The red sun shone brightly, bathing the city in rose-tinted light. Thin towers spiraled up into the clear, pink sky, their stone walls twisted by the Master Shapers to resemble the coiled scales of the World Serpent. Hundreds of towers, each shaped like a serpent, dotted the landscape. The surface of the towers glinted brightly in the soft light, giving the impression of something both slimy and rough. At the top of each tower, the serpent's head opened to reveal a large room open to the sky. Some of these platforms served as council chambers, some as laboratories and, in the case of the tallest tower, the throne room of Para Sann.

Para Sann, sovereign king of the Vacc, son of Para Lurr, sat on his serpent throne and smiled. Before him, two priests from the Egg sect knelt before him, an infant in their hands. His son. The babe's skin was smooth, with just a hint of scales under the thin surface. Para Sann smiled wider. The bloodline was pure. The mother had not lied about her lineage. He gestured and the priests hurried off, taking the infant with them to feed him the mother, whom had been killed just after childbirth, while the meat was still fresh. Para Sann stroked the head of the great serpent at his side and let the red sun warm his cold blood.

Years passed and the babe, Sihh, not yet Para, lived a hard life. He was instructed in combat by the Fang sect, taking beatings every day until he could best his teachers. He was taught the rituals by the Venom sect, learning how to appease the World Serpent with sacrifice and blood. Then, in his sixteenth sun, came the day when Sihh stood before his father, sword and spear in hand, and challenged him for the throne. Tradition dictated that the son must win the throne from his father with steel and blood. With a snarl and hiss, Para Sann leapt from the throne. Metal clashed with metal as father and son fought while members from all the sects stood to the side as witnesses. All afternoon they dueled. Blood flowed from both their bodies and the priests smiled, knowing the World Serpent was pleased with the sacrifices being made that day.

But the red sun, avatar of the World Serpent, suddenly moved behind dark clouds and the Venom sect murmured words to ward off the bad omen. As the fight continued, a rumbling was heard across the city and the Fang sect tightened grips on halberds and swords. Sihh knocked Para Sann down and raised his sword to plunge into his father's heart. At that moment, Coilrock, the mountain to the east, home of the World Serpent, exploded with fire and ash. Burning clouds rolled down into the city. The ground shook buildings apart like shed skin. Sihh was knocked to the ground by the quake. A piece of masonry fell from above, crushing Para Sann as lava flowed into the city. Thousands were burnt as the river of fire entered dwelling holes. Whole generations of eggs cooked in their shells. Chunks of flaming rock fell from the sky. One crashed into the throne room, spewing lava into the air with a great explosion. Burning rocks fell on Sihh, melting his face and body.

When the ground had stopped moving and the dust settled, Para Sann was dead and Sihh rose to his feet, stumbling over to his father, half-dead himself. He raised his sword to the fiery skies in triumph, claiming the throne. But those still alive from the sects turned their backs on him amid the rubble. He did not make the kill. He did not spill the lifeblood. He could not claim the throne. Furious, Sihh leapt at the priests and warriors, killing several before being forced by his injuries to abandon his claim, his throne and his name. The warriors of the Fang rose up against him and drove him from the throne room.

He fled.

He stumbled through the broken palace, hounded by the Fang until he reached his personal shuttle and left the city to burn, leaving only curses and vows to one day return and take what was rightfully his.

Mad with pain, half-dead from his injuries, Sihh let the autopilot take him where the World Serpent willed. For twelve cycles, his ship wandered the stars as he floated in and out of consciousness, kept alive by the on-board life support of his ship. He barely felt the pull of the tractor beam that finally locked onto his ship, nor did he hear the hiss of the door opening. Shadows loomed over his broken body. The Weaponmongers of Jogaoh were astounded to find the prince of the Vacc lying on the floor of the shuttle. They argued back and forth, waving their arachnid limbs wildly as they decided what to do with him. In the end they took him and healed him, in their own way. His melted flesh was replaced with gleaming metal. His shriveled organs were removed and processing chips added. He was made into a living weapon and they looked upon him with pride. The Weaponmongers had created their ultimate weapon.

When he finally woke, he saw he was no longer Sihh, prince of the Vacc. That man had died many cycles ago. He looked at his metal body. He heard his mechanical voice. His left eye, his Vacc eye, cried a single tear for his loss. His mechanical eye shed no tear. He took the name Kala Azar, "Pestilence" in the Weaponmongers' tongue. He went out among the stars, cutting a bloody path through the planes, always looking for some way to exact his revenge and claim the throne.

Jom was silent. He couldn't believe they had escaped such a madman.

"I wonder why he didn't just kill us," he finally said.

"The only reasonable response would be because he believes we have something he wants," NDX replied.

"But what?"

"Because I know where the Mind Harp is." They turned and looked at an awake Macar in astonishment.

"You? How?"

"I may have....changed the details of my past a bit."

Revelations

JOM STARED AT HIM in stunned silence for several heartbeats. Eventually he found his voice, although it was higher and more desperate than he would have liked.

"What? You...you lied to us?"

Macar shrugged. "Yeah. I needed to get out of that cell. You were my only option."

"You lied to us?"

NDX placed a hand gently on Jom's arm. "It would be best for you to explain yourself," it offered.

"You lied to us!" The shock had worn off. Now, anger flared up within Jom's breast. He jumped up, bringing the others to their feet as well. "You lied to us!" he repeated, louder than intended.

"Please," NDX said, "lower your voice. Let us not bring anyone else into our quarrel."

Macar looked away for a moment, then met Jom's accusing eyes. "What do you want me to say?" he demanded. "I needed you to help me." He paused for a second. "You would have done the same."

"No," Jom shook his head. "No, I wouldn't."

"Well," Macar looked away again, "then I guess you're a fool."

NDX stepped between them. "Perhaps you should explain exactly how you know the location of the Mind Harp."

Macar sighed heavily. "It's not like I completely lied to you," he began. "I did lose my family in the mines. That much is true. And I was captured by these bandits. That wasn't recent, though. And I wasn't exactly captured. I joined them. I had been on the run for so long. I needed somewhere safe. Somewhere where I didn't have to sleep with one eye open, constantly looking over my shoulder, expecting to see the bounty hunters. I've spent the last five cycles with them. After I proved myself, of course."

"What does that mean?"

Macar gave Jom a hard look. "I killed an innocent. For no reason. And I've done it since. Many times over. Everyone on the crew is expected to pull their own during a raid. If someone gets in our way...we are expected to take care of the problem quickly and cleanly."

Jom felt a chill go down his spine.

"I'm not a good person. Get that through your head. I used you to get out of that cell and I don't regret it."

"Please, continue with your account," NDX said.

Macar nodded at the automaton. "A little less than a cycle ago, while we were looting a transport ship we had disabled, I found an old Latuip."

128

"A what?"

Macar coughed, looking at Jom the whole time. When the attack had passed, he straightened a bit and continued. "You really don't know anything, do you? Latuips are one of the older races on this plane. They're small things, barely past my waist. Look like pets, lots of hair, big ears. But they're smart. They know things."

"That is correct," NDX interrupted. "Latuips are small, human-oid creatures. They are a communal species, prized throughout the planes for their knowledge. They value information above all else and spend the first part of their long lives learning everything they are able from their community. Their capacity for information is unmatched among sentient species and even surpasses many artificial entities. However, once they tell a fact, it is forever erased from their memories. It is theorized that they actually give the information to another, taking it from their brains and passing it on, leaving nothing where the information once was. For this reason, they are not only valued but, if captured, are kept under strict conditions by their captors. If someone had once asked it a question the owner wished to know, they would be unable to respond because they simply do not know anymore. In addition, they communicate telepathically. So if you would ask one a question, you and only you would hear the answer in your head. They are considered the ultimate dispensers of knowledge in the universe and have been long captured and sold as commodities. That is why they live in hiding, rarely seen by outsiders."

Macar nodded. "This Latuip was old, even for their kind. Fairly useless, actually. Most of its knowledge had been told. Still, I knew Kala Azar would reward me for taking it to him."

"And let me guess, you asked the Latuip where the Mind Harp was." Jom crossed his arms over his chest. Macar nodded again.

"I didn't mean to. I had brought it onboard to him. Kala Azar asked it what could help him reclaim his throne. For a moment, the Latuip and Kala Azar stared at each other. After a moment, Kala Azar spoke. 'Mind Harp? I've never heard of such an incredible thing. Finally I will have my throne!' I blurted out in excitement 'Where is it?' before I knew what I was saying. I was asking Kala Azar but the Latuip answered instead. Suddenly, I heard the location being spoken to me. In my mind. The words just appeared in my head. I looked at Kala Azar. I've never seen him so angry. I thought he was going to kill me right then and there. But he didn't."

"Because he needs you to tell him where it is," Jom finished.

"Yes. He threw me in that cell until he could figure out a way to wring the information from me. But I know him. As long as I keep it to myself, I live. The moment he finds it, he will kill me. Slowly."

"Does he still have the Latuip?" Jom asked after thinking for a moment.

Macar gave him an amused look. "You think to steal it, boy? Good luck with that."

Jom turned to NDX. "It could help us."

"While the knowledge would potentially make our journey considerably easier, the risk involved is too great."

Jom thought for a moment. "What if we trade him? The Mind Harp for the Latuip?"

"And why would I show you where it is?" Macar demanded.

"You owe us your life, for one," Jom countered, letting his anger rise to his voice. "We saved your life. Without us, you'd still be in that cell, probably getting tortured and half dead."

Macar laughed. His laughter turned into coughing. "So you want me to throw that freedom away? Like I said, boy, if Kala Azar gets the Mind Harp, my life is forfeit."

"He won't need you anymore."

"He'll hunt me down regardless for making him work so hard to acquire it. I know him. He won't let me live out of spite."

"In addition," NDX said, "giving a weapon to such a person is morally questionable at best."

"So we give him a fake!" An idea quickly formed in Jom's brain. "We get the real one, create a fake and give him that in exchange for the Latuip. By the time he figures it out, we'll be long gone."

They were silent as they considered the plan. Macar shook his head.

"You're insane. He would never take such an insult lying down. He would go to the edge of the galaxy just to find you. And when he did, and he would, he'd kill you so slowly you wouldn't know anything but pain for cycles."

"I agree that this is a very risky plan," NDX added. "We would make a very dangerous enemy."

"We seem to be doing that already," Jom noted wryly. "And, we'd end up with both the Mind Harp, whatever that is, and the Latuip. Surely we would have the advantage."

"We must also consider the possibility that the Latuip cannot give us the information we seek," NDX pointed out. "As Macar said, it is very old."

Jom twisted his mouth. "I haven't thought of that," he admitted. "Still, isn't it worth it to try?"

"No!" Macar stated. "It's not. He's insane, I tell you. You're insane. You do not want to cross him."

"Listen, all you have to do is take us to the Mind Harp. After that, go run away," Jom spat.

"Running away has saved my life more than once," he replied.

Jom grunted in response.

"Perhaps we should sleep on it," NDX said. "We have much to think about. We will discuss this further in the morning."

"Agreed." Macar lay back down, turning so his back was to them. With a sigh, Jom lay down as well. He heard NDX shut down, its motors slowing to almost nothing. Despite his whirling

thoughts, he soon fell into a dreamless sleep.

Jom opened his eyes slowly. He heard birds calling outside and blinked as his sight adjusted to the dawn. He turned over and looked about the empty hut. It took his sleepy brain a heartbeat to realize he was alone in the hut. As the thought penetrated, he sat bolt upright, looking around wildly. Neither Macar nor NDX were in the hut. He scrambled to his feet and yanked the curtain aside that covered the doorway. Bright light blinded him. He shielded his eyes and scanned the area.

Brightly-colored villagers were everywhere going about their business. They laughed and hummed and sang. The younger children ran after one another while the older ones carried firewood or water buckets back and forth. Jom spotted NDX to his right, sitting with Ravola. She was dressed in the same red fabric as the day before, the streamers flowing off her body seemingly of their own volition. Jom studied the crowd but saw no sign of Macar. He hurried over to the clock-work boy.

"Bright sunrise," Ravola greeted him, bowing her head slightly at his approach. Jom pulled up short, forcing his legs to move slower.

"Um, good morning." He bowed. "Thank you for your hospitality."

"It was our pleasure." Jom thought he could make out a small smile behind the fabric.

Jom turned to NDX. "Where is Macar?" He hoped his voice didn't sound too worried.

"He left the hut just before sunrise," the automaton replied.

"What? Where did he go?"

"I am currently tracking him moving away from us towards the rim of the valley in that direction." It pointed to Jom's left.

"What? Why did you let him leave? We need him!"

Ravola suppressed a laugh. "He is an excitable one, isn't he?" she asked the clock-work boy.

NDX gestured for Jom to sit down next to him. "There is no need for concern. Ravola has assured me he cannot leave the valley without the aid of the tribe. He is engaged in a futile exercise."

"But what if he finds a way out? Or contacts the bandits?"

"In the unlikely event he succeeds in the first, he would most likely lead us to the location of the Mind Harp. After all, that is the only thing he has to trade for his life, whether with us or Kala Azar. In the event of the second, then our part of their story would most likely end. Kala Azar would have no further need for us and would continue his pursuit of the Mind Harp with Macar."

Jom puffed several breaths out through his cheeks. He knew NDX was right. It was always right. Still, he didn't trust Macar.

"Perhaps," Ravola said gently, "you feel so strongly about his behavior because he is not like the man you met in your dream?"

Jom's jaw dropped and he stared at the woman.

"How—how do you know about my dream?"

"I have informed Ravola of our quest and your part in it," NDX said. Jom turned to the automaton.

"Why?"

"It is in our best interest that she is well-informed of our intentions if she is to accompany us," it explained.

Jom stared dumbly at them both until his brain gave up and he sat down in confusion. Ravola stifled another laugh.

"You need my help," she explained. "You will not survive the wilds of this world without guidance. And you need protection. I can provide both."

He slowly nodded his head. "What about your tribe?" he asked.

Ravola looked around at the villagers. "They can fend for themselves just fine. We are well protected here, even from one such as Kala Azar."

"I suggest then, if we are all in agreement, that we should gather supplies and retrieve our wayward companion."

With that, they split up. NDX and Jom were led to a young blue-clad girl named Lowsh who helped pack supplies for their journey while Ravola left to make final arrangements with her council for her absence. Lowsh glanced shyly at Jom as she gathered dried fruit and leaves for them. He watched in rapt fascination as her blue fabric swirled around her lithe body. Each strip moved on its own. He looked up to see her staring at him. He felt his face grow warm and turned away, followed by soft giggles. He quickly stuffed his supplies into his pack, hoping she didn't see him blush.

They reunited in the main square just as the sun was peeking over the rim of the mountain wall behind them. Ravola carried a small pack slung over her shoulder and her spear. A short sword hung from a belt around her waist. She handed Jom an identical sword and belt. Jom buckled the belt on and instantly felt safer, although the weight of the sword threw his balance off a little. He patted his pocket to make sure his dagger was still there as well, mentally reminding himself to talk to NDX about the effect the dagger had on the bandits when he had a chance.

Macar was found easily enough. He was climbing the rock wall of the mountain at the edge of the valley. He had only made it about a quarter of the way up by the time they reached him. After several calls went ignored, Jom became frustrated.

"How are we going to get him down?" he demanded. NDX and Ravola looked at each other.

"I will fetch him," she said, handing the clock-work boy her spear and pack.

Jom looked on in confusion as Ravola walked over to the rock wall. She spread her arms and the streamers of fabric that dangled off her arms and back came to life, stretching out towards the rocks. Jom realized then that the streamers were not just part of her garment, but were in fact part of her body. They were tentacles that were wrapped in fabric. He watched as she grabbed hold of rocks in seven or eight different spots and quickly crawled up the wall. She barely even had to use her legs and arms, relying instead on the twenty or so tentacles that branched off her limbs to scurry up the rock. He watched dumbfounded as she scrambled up the rock wall as quickly as a spider.

Macar, seeing her approach, pulled out his blaster but managed to fire off only one shot that Ravola easily avoided before she was on him. The weapon was seized by one tentacle while ten others picked him off the rocks and down they came. Within heartbeats, Macar was standing before them, red-faced and defeated.

"Just leave me be!" he pleaded.

"No," Jom shook his head, trying to concentrate on the man before him and not on the woman to his side. "We need you now. You're going to take us to the Mind Harp and that's all there is to it."

Macar looked around at the group in resignation.

"This is suicide," he said.

"We all die," Ravola replied. "What matters is how, not when."

Macar shook his head but did not argue. He seemed resigned to his fate. He hung his head.

"We need to head towards the dawn," he said, his voice weary.

Murtocs and Swints

WITH RAVOLA LEADING, THEY quickly navigated the tunnels that snaked through the walls of the mountain. The sun was not yet halfway across the sky when they emerged from the darkness. She kept them going, leading them into the foothills surrounding the mountain until late in the day. By the time they made camp for the night, the mountain was in the distance, almost hidden behind large leafy trees and rolling hills. She led them to a sheltered area deep among the trees. There was a simple hut nestled between towering bushes. Jom would have missed the shelter completely if Ravola had not called a halt and pulled branches aside, exposing the small structure.

"We will be safe here for the night. There are few large predators in this area that could bother us," she said. Jom was only a little reassured by her phrasing, imagining all the small predators that could chew off a toe or finger while he slept.

While Jom gathered twigs and branches for a small fire and

NDX scanned the area and kept watch, Ravola cleared out the shelter. Her tentacles whirled around her as she moved around the campsite, tying rope, weaving leaves and breaking branches simultaneously. By the time Jom returned, the shelter was clean and all were sitting comfortably on mats of leaves around a fire. Jom looked around in astonishment and Ravola let out a light laugh.

"There are advantages to having a Gex with you in the wilderness," she said.

Jom laughed too. "I see that." He dropped the wood near the fire and sat. NDX passed him a small handful of tangy berries.

"I—I didn't know you were called Gex," he admitted.

Ravola shrugged. "Our species is not well-known. We mostly stay near our villages."

They enjoyed a light meal and casual talk. Ravola told them a little of her village and Jom told her a couple of Grandmother's stories. Even Macar seemed to lighten a little, occasionally joining in the conversation. As the night deepened, they turned in, trusting in Ravola's knowledge of the area and NDX's sensors to keep them safe. Jom noticed that the clock on its chest was almost half of the way wound down but thought better than to mention it in front of Macar.

From his bedroll, Jom stared up at the stars through the slits in the roof of the shelter. They were not his stars. He tried to find the gods he knew but could not. No Dragon-King. No Water Wheel. No Harvest Goddess. He felt small. He always felt small when he looked at the stars. But this was different. As tiny as he felt looking up at his stars back in his village, seeing these strange lights made him realize that everything he knew was less than a drop of water in a lake. The universe was so much more than he ever thought. Here he was, so far away from his home that he couldn't even see his stars. And who knew how much further he would go yet. He wrapped his arms around his chest and turned over. But sleep eluded him now, pushed away by his thoughts. With a sigh, he got up and walked quietly to the edge of camp.

He walked to a small rise where he could see the surrounding landscape through the trees, waving away the thrips that buzzed around his ears. Scattered copses of tall, double-trunked trees dotted the landscape, towering over banks of bushes that swayed in the light night breeze. A small river, its waters dark with night, meandered between the hills. Jom thought about going down to the river but decided against it. Lurkers were bad enough. There could be worse in this strange land.

"Can't sleep?" a soft voice said. He turned to see Ravola walking up to him. He hadn't heard a single footfall as she approached.

"No," he admitted. He sat on a fallen tree trunk and she joined him.

"The calls of the night have always soothed me," she said. "I love to lay awake through the night, listening to the echoes of the Murtocs as they hunt. It's soothing, in a way."

"Murtocs?"

"They were a species that lived on this world long ago. You can still hear them, even after all these cycles, if you know how to listen."

"Tell me about them."

She shifted slightly. Most of her tentacles were wrapped around her body, providing extra layer of warmth from the cool night wind. Jom tried not to shiver in the cool night breeze.

"I'll tell you the story as I first heard as a child," she said with a smile.

There was once, many thousands of cycles ago, a race of creatures called Swints. They had two legs and walked upright like we do. Smooth green skin covered thin bodies. Long light hair cascaded down their backs. But there was more to them that that. They were six-dimensional beings. They existed on a plane higher than ours, casting only their four-dimensional shadows into our world. If you hold a ball to a light, it casts a shadow. That shadow is only two dimensions—a circle, even though the ball is three-dimensional. So it was with the Swints. They appeared here as living creatures moving through time—four-dimensional—yet they were so much more than that.

As their shadows moved through this plane, they attracted the attention of the Murtocs. Large, grey-skinned predators, the Murtocs were all teeth and claws and evil. So it comes as no surprise that, one day, they sniffed the air and smelled a new odor. Running swiftly across the land, they crashed through the forest and beheld a group of Swints in the valley below. With poisonous drool dripping from their fangs, they leapt at the Swints. But, just as you cannot harm a shadow, the Murtoc's attack was fruitless. They swiped at the Swints, yet no flesh was torn from body. They snapped their jaws at Swint heads, yet no bones crushed between their teeth.

Nevertheless, the Swints were startled by this attack and fled. The Murtocs pursued. For several suns, the chase continued, the Murtocs literally chasing shadows. Finally, the leader of the exhausted Murtoc pack called a halt. Grumbling, they watched the Swints speed away, helpless to capture their prey for the first time in their existence as a species. The howls of the Murtocs filled the valleys that night as they vented their frustration.

Many cycles passed and the Murtocs evolved, gradually gaining speech, fire, technology and society. The predators of old slowly grew into murderous, vicious creatures that could think. And think they did. The driving force, the single purpose they had, was to kill the Swints. What started off as a chase across the plains had grown into an obsession that shaped the Murtoc culture. Their religion cast the Swints as evil, as the antithesis of everything that a Murtoc represented. It became the duty of every Murtoc to find and destroy the Swints. And so they continued to hunt the Swints, using ever more complex weapons. First sticks, then fire and traps. The Murtocs discovered over time that they could control the fires they built and fashioned weapons to hurl destruction from a distance. Still, all was for naught. After all, they were still chasing shadows.

Their brains evolved, growing ever more complex. So too did their weapons. Then came the day that the Murtocs tried a new weapon. A group of Swints were moving along a river. The Murtocs fired their new weapon and the sky was set on fire. The Swints cried out in pain. The energy from the Murtoc weapon had penetrated into the Swint's home dimension, burning them. The Murtocs roared in triumph as the Swints fled. The Murtocs pursued, firing their weapon again and again. Each time, the fabric of the planes was pierced and the Swints cried. Of the five Swints that were attacked, only one escaped with its life. The others perished. The Murtocs stood over the bodies of the Swints and laughed. Finally, they would eradicate their world of the Swint vermin. Their holy war was at a turning point.

The Murtocs quickly built more of their terrible new weapon. Hunting parties were sent out in every direction. It was soon a common sight to see the sky light up as the Murtoc found and killed any Swint they could find. As the Swints were murdered nearby, the Murtocs took to moving further and further across the land, spreading death as they went, lighting up the skies with their murderous fire.

Eventually, the sun rose on a day when there were no more Swints to kill. The Murtocs hunted far and wide. But none were left. They had all been killed. They looked around in wonder at their Swint-free world. But their elation soon turned sour and dread fell upon the Murtocs. Their very reason for existing had always been to hunt

Swints. Now there were no Swints left to hunt. They had no purpose anymore. In desperation, they took to hunting the other creatures of the world. But nothing proved to be a challenge and they were easily slaughtered. They were no Swints. Then, inevitably, they turned on themselves. Only fellow Murtocs could provide the challenge of the hunt and they murdered each other with toothy smiles. The sky once more lit up with fire as the Murtocs warred among themselves. For a time, they gleefully hunted each other across the land, killing their own kin with the same relish as they once killed the Swints.

Before long, only two Murtocs were left. They aimed their weapons at one another, knowing their race was at an end but unable to stop their drive to kill. Even at that moment, they couldn't stop themselves. One fired, killing his opponent. As the charred corpse fell, the lone remaining Murtoc gave out one final roar of victory, turned its weapon on itself, and blasted the Murtocs into history.

The Warrior Queen

S O NOW, THOUSANDS OF cycles later, you can still hear the echoes of the hunt at night, reminding us to not repeat the mistakes of the past."

They listened to the cries of Murtoc ghosts for a few heartbeats. "You know a lot about this place, don't you?" Jom asked her, staring out at the landscape before them.

Ravola nodded. "I've lived among these hills and trees my whole life," she replied. "They are my friends. My family."

"Home is important," he said quietly. "You don't really realize that until you're away."

Ravola wrapped her arm around his shoulder and gave him a light squeeze. "Home is always with you," she replied. "It's in your heart, in your thoughts. It's a part of you that can never be taken away."

She was quiet for a moment, then began to speak softly, letting the light night wind take her words across the valley.

Although I grew up here, I haven't always been here. I was born under the Blood Moon—the last moon of winter when the hunters of the forest are hungry and desperate. They move closer to the villages and are bold in their attacks. It is a dangerous time for the newly born. The young are vulnerable and the predators fierce. Only the strongest born during the Blood Moon survive. My mother died fighting off the animals who would feast on my flesh. Instead, they carried her away into the night and I was left without a family.

But I survived. As new shoots emerge from the ground in the warming time, so too did I grow. The warriors of the village, impressed that a newborn survived such a dangerous time, took me and taught me their ways. By the time of the next Blood Moon, although I was still small and young, I killed on my first hunt. I was welcomed back from the hunt, riding on the shoulders of the other warriors and there was a feast in my honor.

With the next turning of the seasons, I was sent away on the Great Hunt. Only the strongest warriors who come back with a trophy are given the honor of wearing the Blood," she stroked the red fabric that covered every bit of her skin, "and it was time for me to prove I should wear it. I left my village, my home, and traveled across this world. I was on a hunt for the Gowal, a terrible beast that lives among the swamps and lowlands many cycles away.

My people grow up with legends of the terrible Gowal. They stand as tall as two of us, with thick white hide that oozes poison. A thick shield of bone covers the back of its head, protecting its neck. The shield tapers to a razor-thin edge that can fell a tree in one swoop of its head. Their feet end in claws larger than your head that can rip a body to shreds in an instant. As a child, I heard of the many Great Hunts the warriors had been on, how the Gowals would crash through the trees, trampling anything that got in their way. I listened as they told of how they trapped these great beasts with pits and snares, only to have the Gowals leap out of the pit or tear the snare from the ground with its powerful muscles.

And now it was my turn to hunt this creature and bring back proof of conquering it. Only then would I be allowed into the warriors and wear the red cloth that signifies the Blood. I journeyed across the land in search of the Gowal. I hunted for food. I foraged. For three turns of the seasons, I survived in the wilderness, hunting the elusive beast.

Many nights, as I lay on nothing more than a bed of leaves, I stared up at the stars and thought about my tribe, safe behind the walls of our mountain. I listened to the cries of the night hunters. At first, I was wary and cautious. But, as time went on, I came to love those cries. As I grew in strength and wisdom, I also grew in boldness. I challenged the predators of the forest. I defied the storms that threatened to drown me and tore down trees around me. I wore my scars with pride.

Finally, I came across tracks that could only belong to the Gowal. Immense prints that you could sleep in. Excited, I hurried on, following the great tracks until the ground grew soft and turned to mud. Without realizing it, I stumbled into the swamps. Mud sucked at my feet and drained my energy. It was then I looked up to see a Gowal standing over me. Its eyes were black as night, its tusks sharp, its claws scratching at the mud. It huffed once and nearly knocked me over with the force of its breath.

Looking around desperately, I spied a thick vine hanging above my head. I swung my pike, cutting it in two. Grabbing the nearest half, I pulled. It held and I pulled harder. The mud pulled back, sucking me deeper. Then I felt something push me up. I looked over my shoulder to see the Gowal helping me escape the sucking mud with its massive trunk.

I was in shock. I froze. But it pushed me again, using its strength to help me. I pulled myself out of the mud and swung over to solid ground. Seeing I was safe, the Gowal turned and lumbered off through the brush. I lay on the ground, gaining control of my breathing, clutching my pike, waiting for the Gowal to charge through the swamp and impale me with its great tusks or trample me with its tree-trunk feet. But it never came. I stood, trembling with anger.

"Anger? Why?" Jom asked.

"I had faced the great beast. I had looked it in its eyes. And it had turned its back on me. Worse, it had helped me. I was like a gnat to it. My blood boiled. I would prove I was no gnat! I would bring the beast to its knees and, when it was lying at my feet, I would look it in the eyes again and it would know which of us was the victor before I ended its life.

I went after it, this time keeping my eyes on the ground as well as my surroundings. The Gowal led me deep into the swamp. Thin, moss-covered trees towered over me, dripping with moisture. Strange animals called to each other among the still waters of the swamp. I felt a hundred eyes on me as I tracked the Gowal. For three dawns I followed the great beast, eating things that slithered in the water, sleeping among the branches. Finally, I spotted it ahead of me, slowly making its way through the brush.

I let out a cry for blood and plunged ahead. The Gowal spooked and took off. The soft ground trembled as it ran. I followed as quickly as I could but it was too fast and disappeared from sight. But I didn't slow. I ran on, following its path through the green. Suddenly, a loud scream rent the still air. I skidded to a stop and listened. Another scream echoed across the swamp. I moved forward cautiously now, keeping my senses alert. I stepped into a clearing and saw the Gowal in front of me. It was lying on the ground. It screamed again, a scream of agony and pain. Walking forward, I saw that the Gowal had stepped into a sinkhole and twisted its leg. It lay there in incredible pain. I approached it, seeing its injury.

I looked into its eyes. It looked into mine...

Ravola paused. Jom, breathless from the story, waited until she had taken a few deep breaths, before speaking.

"Did you kill it?"

Ravola stared ahead for a moment, and then spoke quietly.

"I couldn't. I couldn't. For the first time in my life, I couldn't kill. All my life up until that point had been nothing but training and battle and hunting. I didn't know any other way. But, as I stood over the Gowal, I couldn't bring myself to slay the beast, even knowing that my future with my tribe depended on it." She stared down at her hands, wrapping her tentacles tighter around her body.

"What did you do?"

"I repaid my debt." She raised her head proudly as she spoke. "I helped immobilize the break. I built a fire to keep the Gowal warm and, with both fire and steel, kept the predators at bay while it mended. I helped it recover its strength, its power, its dignity.

We formed a bond during those long suns and moons. We came to understand each other in a way I had never thought possible. We became...friends. I named her Yapar, a name that means 'Proud' in my language. When Yapar was healthy enough to walk again, I no longer trailed behind; I walked beside her as a companion. We emerged from the swamp and she led me to where others of her kind gather. I found myself surrounded by scores of Gowal, all crowding around me, curious and wary. But my friend trumpeted my worthiness and they allowed me to stay.

When it came time for me to return, Yapar blocked my way. At first I thought she would not let me leave. Even then, even after all that had happened, I was still foolish. But Yapar kneeled down, wanting me to ride atop her. The other Gowals trumpeted and jostled me forward. Amazed, I climbed up her shoulder and sat astride her broad back. She stood and trumpeted, announcing our friendship to the world.

We left the Gowals, traveling back through the swamp and onward back to my village, me directing Yapar with gentle pressure from one knee or another. Together we crossed the land, protecting each other from the other hunters, finding food to share.

Eventually, we reached my village. Five Blood Moons had come and gone since I had left. My people had given me up for dead. None had ever been away for so long and come back. But not only had I survived, I returned from the Great Hunt carrying no trophy, but instead riding one of the great Gowals as a friend. My people were astounded. They didn't know how to react at first. Many ran in terror. Others threatened Yapar. But none crossed me. I had done something no one had ever done before, had never even thought of doing.

For, you see, it wasn't that I had conquered the Gowal. I had done something infinitely more difficult. I had made a friend. I had stayed my hand out of compassion. And I had become stronger because of it.

I was declared a warrior queen. I donned the Blood. I rose through the ranks of the Blood and became first among the warriors. Yapar stayed with me for a cycle. When the next Blood Moon appeared in the sky, I went with her back to her tribe. She needed to be with her people, just as I needed to be with mine.

When the Elder Queen went to her last hunt five cycles ago, I was honored with the mantle of leader of my tribe. And one day I will pass on my responsibilities to another. The Blood Moon tells us it must be so.

She turned to Jom. "But all that time I was alone, I carried my tribe, my home, in my heart. I never forgot them. I never abandoned them. You must do the same now. Hold them close. Never let them go. And one day, you will return to your Grandmother."

"I will."

Jom smiled and hugged her. Together, they listened to the cries of the Murtocs float across the valley.

The Screaming Moor

A T DAWN, THEY RESUMED their journey. The emerald sky was clear and a light wind blew through the gigantic fronds of the trees. Macar insisted they continue towards the dawn sun. Ravola shook her head, insisting that there was nothing in that direction other than rock and wind. In the end, she relented only because NDX detected signs that Macar was lying--no elevated heartbeat or increased body temperature. Jom had his doubts as well, but stayed quiet. His hand was never far from his short sword though, nor his eyes too far from Macar.

The walk was easy. The hill country gradually flattened out. The tall trees grew shorter and thicker and the grass coarser. After stumbling for half of the morning trying to keep his sword from slicing his leg, Ravola dropped back to walk side-by-side with him.

"Strap it on your back. It will be much easier for you," she said.

"You don't wear yours that way. And I'm almost as tall as you."

"Yes. But I have worn a sword most of my life. You have not."

Jom sighed. She helped him loosen the belt and strap it over his shoulder, under his pack. Jom grunted, acknowledging the better fit. He practiced grabbing the hilt and pulling the sword free a few times, making sure he wouldn't slice his shoulder off in the process.

"Do not try to grow up too quickly, Jom. That will come soon enough."

"You're right. I know. I'm sorry."

"There is nothing to apologize for," she assured him.

"I want to contribute, but it seems I always mess things up," he complained.

"How so?"

"Take Macar, for example," he said, lowering his voice. "I met him. In my dream, I mean. But he's nothing like that man I dreamed. I was wrong. Maybe I'm wrong about looking for this Mind Harp too. Maybe I shouldn't have insisted on saving him in the first place."

She gave a light laugh. "Sometimes dreams are powerful messages from the gods. They should be listened to very carefully for the gods do not like to state their intentions simply. They couch their words in strange symbols and images."

"I guess."

"And sometimes, a dream is just a dream," she said with a smile and walked ahead, leaving him to his thoughts.

"That helps," he grumbled to himself.

A little while later, they came to the crest of a large hill and stopped. Spread out in front of them was an immense barren plain. There was literally nothing in front of them as far as they could see; only pebbles and small rocks that danced in the wind that roamed freely across a landscape of featurelss, flat land.

"As I said, nothing but rocks and wind."

"How far does it go?" Jom asked, peering into the distance. The plain extended to the horizon.

Ravola shrugged. "None of my people have ever seen the other side. There are no way stations, no water, nothing to hunt, nothing at all. The sun can rise and set many times before you cross it. In your language, its name translates loosely as 'The Screaming Moor'."

"Screaming?" NDX inquired.

"The wind has nothing to stop it. It comes here to play, to be free. You can hear it coming long before it reaches you. It screams in delight as it speeds across the moor."

"And you want us to go there?" Jom demanded.

"I don't want to go anywhere," Macar spat. "But if you want the Mind Harp, we go that way." He pointed directly into the moor.

"What exactly did the Latuip tell you?" NDX turned to Macar.

He gave a short laugh. "Why would I tell you that?"

"Perhaps you misinterpreted what the Latuip told you."

"And perhaps once I tell you, you'll kill me."

"Oh please!" Jom exclaimed. "You should know by now we're not going to kill you."

"I might," Ravola muttered under her breath.

"Listen, if you tell us what the Latuip said, you can go! How's that for a bargain?" Jom spread his arms wide. "We won't need you anymore anyway. You can go. Hide in a cave somewhere. Run until you collapse. Get yourself killed. I don't care!"

"Jom has a point," NDX said. "If you tell us exactly what you know, word for word, we would no longer require your services and you would be free to leave."

"How would we know he speaks true?" Ravola demanded. "He could say anything just to get away."

Jom nodded. "He could. But we have to trust him to be the man we think he is." He stared at Macar until the man looked away.

Macar sighed and took a deep breath, weighing his options. Then he looked at them, his eyes clear.

"'Towards the dawn, where the air never sleeps, stands the Obelisk of Seven Keys. Walk the path that disappears until you reach the eye that never closes. There the Obelisk stands guard over the Harp of the Mind.'"

They were all silent as they processed the words. Finally, Jom threw his hands in the air.

"What does all that mean?"

"Uncertain," NDX said. "We have traveled towards the dawn and are now on the edge of a place where the 'air never sleeps', so I would posit we are on the correct path."

"My people have heard tales from other tribes of a tall black finger that thrusts out of the rock in the middle of the moor," Ravola added. "It is said to be the hand of a god and is guarded by the spirits of the dead. Whether these stories are true or not, though, I cannot say."

"Great," Jom said, sitting down in a huff. "Hand of a god. Dead spirits. And we don't have seven keys either."

"Can I leave then?" Macar asked.

Jom waved his hand at the man. "I don't care." He was dejected and felt defeated.

"We no longer need your assistance," NDX told Macar. "We will not prevent you from leaving."

"Good." And with that, Macar turned his back on them and quickly disappeared back into the surrounding bush.

Jom didn't even look up as the man sprinted down the opposite side of the hill. Ravola stood over Jom, looking down on him, her fingers softly drumming the shaft of her spear.

"Well?"

He looked up at her, his face screwing into a scowl. "Well what?"

"We should get moving. We should make use of the daylight we have left."

"What's the use?"

NDX tilted its head. "Are you not willing to continue?"

"I don't know." He sighed into his chest. "I just don't know anymore."

Ravola hunched down and placed a hand on his shoulder. "Our journey will not be easy. But turning back accomplishes nothing."

"What if we fail?"

She shrugged her shoulders. "Then we will most likely die."

He stared at her. "That doesn't make me feel any better."

"It should." She stood. "Live for something or die for nothing. The choice is yours." She turned on her heel and joined NDX.

After a moment, Jom got to his feet and walked over to them. Ravola smiled through her red fabric and placed a hand on his shoulder in encouragement.

"I detect no life forms within range," NDX said. "If there are any dangers ahead, I cannot sense them."

"There are dangers," Ravola confirmed. "But your sensors will not be able to help us, I think."

"Do we have enough supplies?" Jom asked.

Ravola took a quick inventory of their packs. "We have enough to last us two suns, maybe more."

"That's not much. You said this moor goes on much further than that."

"I doubt we could carry enough supplies to cross it completely," she replied. "But let us spend a moment foraging here before we enter the moor. We'll gather what we can."

They nodded and spread out, picking tiny yellow berries and digging up tubers in the hard ground. Jom found a small rill that snaked through the tall grass and filled their waterskins. Shortly, they regrouped and took their first steps onto the moor.

Within a short time, they could barely remember anything but the moor. There was nothing to look at. The hill country quickly disappeared behind them. There were no trees, no rivers, no life at all in any direction, only the wind and the rocks. They barely talked. The wind took their words as soon as they spoke and carried them off into the distance. NDX led, using its scanners as best it could to keep them heading in a straight line. Jom followed the automaton, staring at its footprints as they disappeared in the ever-changing, wind-blown gravel under their feet. Ravola brought up the rear, keeping a keen eye to the horizon on all sides, her body tense and alert. Near dusk, she whistled sharply and the others stopped.

"We are being followed," she said when they huddled together.

"Where?"

"Behind us. Whoever it is has been following us for most of the afternoon."

"Why didn't you say something sooner?" Jom asked, looking back the way they had come. He barely saw something moving near the horizon. He squinted but couldn't make out any features.

Ravola shrugged. "There is no place for us to hide. And I was curious to see how long they would continue the pursuit."

"We should stop here for the night," NDX said. "We will make camp and wait for whoever it is."

"I don't like this idea," Jom said. "Every time we wait for someone to catch up with us, it goes bad."

"What do you suggest?"

"We set a trap. Let's be on the offensive for once."

Ravola nodded. "The boy has a point." She looked back, judging the distance. "It will be some time before they reach us. Plenty of time to set a snare."

"Let's do it then."

NDX and Jom erected their shelters and dug a small fire pit while Ravola made the trap. Jom tried to watch her but couldn't see what she was doing; he heard her chanting but the wind stole her words. A short time later though, she joined them around the shelter and nodded. They ate a few berries, trying to conserve their supplies best as they could. The sun dropped below the horizon and the wind picked up, howling in their ears incessantly. The darkness of night spread over them like wings from an immense bird. The tiny fire struggled to keep alive, barely able to survive in its pit, fighting with the wind every second. Their shadows leapt around in response and Jom lost his thoughts in watching them dance across the barren land.

There was a yelp from just outside their circle. Ravola was instantly on her feet and rushed into the darkness. NDX and Jom heard a short struggle, then a figure stumbled into the light of the fire with Ravola right behind.

"You!"

"Yes," Macar said, looking away. "Me."

"Why are you following us?" Jom demanded.

He stared at his feet and didn't speak. Ravola nudged him with the butt of her spear and he gulped.

"I—I realized you all are my best chance for surviving. I...I need you."

The words didn't make Jom feel nearly as satisfied as he had hoped. But he couldn't help a tiny smile from creeping onto his face at Macar's reversal.

"No more problems?" he asked. "No more fighting every step of the way? If you're with us then you're with us."

Macar nodded his head. "I'll help any way I can. Just promise me you'll do what you can to keep Kala Azar from killing me."

"We obviously will do whatever is within our power to ensure that," NDX said.

Macar nodded. He broke out into a coughing fit. Ravola reached into her pack and took out a small vial of milky liquid. She passed it over to Macar, urging him to drink. After a moment's hesitation, he did. His coughing stopped immediately. He looked at Ravola in wonder.

"It coats your lungs from the metal that has damaged them. It will not last forever but it will ease the attacks."

"Thank you." He looked at them in turn. "Thank you all."

"We should rest," Ravola said. "The wind will not make it easy to sleep, but we must try."

Ravola was right. The constant wind screamed in Jom's ear all night long until it became a part of his thoughts. When he finally passed out from exhaustion, his dreams were nothing more than Water Banshees screaming at him all night. When he woke as the sun was rising, he was just as tired as when he had lain down the night before.

The sun rose and set twice with no change to their surroundings. Jom's feet hurt from walking on stones. His ears ached from being continuously buffeted by the unforgiving wind. His eyes stung from the dirt and dust that rode the wind. To pass the time, he told himself every story he knew. He began with the stories Grandmother had taught him, so long ago. When he had repeated all of those, he told himself the story of his journey so far. Then he told himself about his dreams. Then he started over again.

When they stopped for a rest, Jom could barely make out more than a few paces in front of him. His skin ached from the constant barrage of dirt and pebbles thrown into him by the ever-increasing wind. Particles clogged the air around them, streaming past their eyes and blurring their vision. The roar of the wind drowned out any conversation. Jom looked ahead, seeing nothing but a brown wall. As he blinked his eyes, trying to keep the tears from getting whisked away, he realized that a wall of wind was approaching them. Frantically, he yelled and grabbed the others, pointing to the storm bearing down on them.

Ravola's tentacles shot out, wrapping around them and pulling everyone in close. NDX extended its arms, providing as much support as it could. They huddled together, low to the ground, and braced themselves. The storm came upon them in moments, blasting them with dirt and rock. Their breath was snatched from their mouths and Jom struggled to remain calm. He felt them sliding across the moor as one, pushed by the extreme force of the wind. Jom closed his eyes, holding onto Macar and NDX as tightly as he could. His arms and legs ached from the strain. His back felt raw from the barrage of stones thrown at it. Even Ravola's embrace began to falter as the winds continued.

Then, the hurricane abruptly stopped. One moment they were straining not to get blown away, the next, they were falling backwards, no longer propped up by the force of the wind. The storm raged in front of them. Jom saw the curving wall of the hurricane extend in a great arc to either side. A few paces before them, the wind whipped around at tremendous speed. But where they now knelt, the air was calm. They were in the center of the storm. They were safe. He looked around in wonder. Then his eyes landed on a tall pillar of black stone that rose from the barren ground in the middle of the eye.

"Look!" he pointed. "The Obelisk! We made it."

Journey of the Seven Trials

T HEY APPROACHED THE OBELISK cautiously. The column of black stone jutted high into the air, its surface smooth except for various carvings etched into the hard stone. Jom gazed at the obelisk, amazed that it could rise so high yet be so thin. It did, he had to admit, look like the finger of a god poking out of the moor. Jom looked around, his grip tight on the hilt of his borrowed sword. He expected a horde of evil spirits to rise up out of the rocky ground and attack them. He fervently wished Dianat was still with them. But the Water Banshee was gone, probably on a different plane, hopefully still alive and not blasted into nothing by the bomb she took from Macar's skull.

The air was still. No wind blew. The sudden absence of wind was disconcerting and Jom shook his head, trying to adjust to the silence after so many days of constant noise. Jom looked up and saw clear sky above them, surrounded in a wide circle by the raging storm.

"The eye that never closes," he said. The others looked up.

"Aye," Ravola replied, her voice tight.

"There are symbols etched into the stone of the obelisk," NDX said. The others moved closer, their eyes not nearly as sensitive as the automaton's sensors.

Strange lines looped and crossed each other in bands around the obelisk. Jom counted. Seven bands of writing. And in the middle of each, on varying sides of the pillar, were holes of different sizes and shapes. One per band.

"Seven bands of writing. Seven holes. For seven keys," he muttered.

"I've never seen this language before," Ravola said.

"Nor I," Macar added.

"NDX?"

The clock-work boy approached to within a few paces of the obelisk. After a moment of whirling gears and clicking levers, it shook its head.

"There is nothing comparable in my database," it announced.

"I—I know this," Jom said, his voice barely a whisper.

The others turned to him in amazement.

"You?" Macar asked. "How could you know this language?" Doubt clouded his words.

"I've seen this writing before."

"Where?"

"In a dream."

"Do you know what the bands say?"

"I'm—I'm trying to remember." He studied the hieroglyphics intently. He remembered seeing them and instantly knowing what they meant. But now, in the waking world, it was difficult to remember.

He reached out his hand, wanting to touch the strange symbols. Ravola grasped his hand just before it touched the black stone. Jom looked at her and she shook her head slightly.

"Perhaps it would help if you told us the dream," NDX offered.

Jom nodded and they all stepped back a few paces.

I don't know if I remember all of it. I dreamt it a long time ago, when I was just a little child. I'd forgotten the dream until just now. But I remember some of those symbols...

It started with me standing on mountain. A world was spread out below me. I was higher than I had ever been in real life. I was above the clouds. In the distance, a number of peaks broke through the clouds from the world below. I was standing next to a girl. She was shivering. The air was thin and cold, and she was wearing only a light cloak. Her hair was black and long, pulled back into a single braid that went down her back. To her side stood a man. He was bent with age but his eyes still shined brightly. He gestured with a gnarled hand at the landscape below them.

'Look, Gellfaxi,' he said, pointing to the peaks that rose above the clouds. 'See the Seven Mountains?'

'Yes, Master.'

'You must travel to each of them. They are the homes of the gods. Take only your vila-stick.'

'Yes, Master.'

'You will be tested.'

'Yes, Master.'

'Go.'

She began the long climb down the mountain, stumbling sometimes, tripping and catching herself or, more often, not and sliding painfully back down the slope. By the time she reached the base of the mountain, she was beaten and bruised. Her vila-stick—a long metal pole with a sharpened point on one end and a nasty hook on the other—helped her clear the brush aside as she struggled forward. For many moons she traveled, living off of brown moss and green river water, fighting off the vicious creatures that dropped on her from the branches above her like shadows falling from the sky. Finally, she stumbled through the last of the wilderness and found herself at the foot of another mountain. She looked up in despair. The top of the peak was covered by clouds.

Steeling herself, she began the long climb up, trying to ignore the cold wind that bit her and threatened to knock her from the rocks. She rested in cracks and hollows in the cold stone and ate what little moss she could find. She put bits of snow in her mouth for water. Finally, after what felt like an eternity, she reached the top, barely able to stand. Before her was an orb of blue light that pulsed in the thin air. It was a god manifesting on her plane of existence. She knelt before the god and the light moved through the air towards her. It touched her skin, burning a symbol into her right hand, then disappeared, leaving her alone on the peak.

Jom pointed to the bottom band of writing. "That's the symbol," he said, indicating a large, circular glyph in the middle of the band.

"What does it mean?" Macar asked.

"It's the name of the god. Sotark. The god of Strength."

"Please, continue."

The god had given her renewed vigour. Or, perhaps, had shown her she had the fortitude within her all along. She stood, looked around until she spotted the next closest peak, and then began her descent. The way was still difficult, but now she felt less tired, less defeated as before. When she reached the bottom, she found herself on the shore of a great lake. The next peak lay on the opposite side, barely visible through the haze that drifted over the deep water.

She had never been a strong swimmer. She gazed across the water and despaired. Then, pushing aside her doubts, she looked around the area. Spying a small copse of thin trees, she took her vila-stick and went to work. Within a short time, she had lashed together a crude raft. Without hesitation, she pushed herself out onto the lake, using her vila-stick to slowly row out from shore. She had barely left the shore before the first attack came. A long, sinuous creature erupted from the dark water, its mouth filled with jagged teeth. Without hesitation, Gellfaxi swung her vila-stick, hooking the creature in the side of its head. It let out a squeal as the hook bit deep into its brain. It shuddered once, then died, almost upending the raft when it collapsed. She hauled it up as best she could, letting most of its length trail behind in the water. She sliced into the meat of the monster and feasted. Her stomach knotted up briefly but quickly relaxed. It was the only food she'd had in moons and she was not going to let it go to waste.

After she had her fill, she let the corpse sink into the water and rowed on. There was a disturbance as the corpse was fought over by other creatures just under the surface. Thrice more she was attacked as she rowed across the great lake. Three times she fought off the monsters from the deep and fed on their corpses. By the time she reached the far shore, she was weary yet hopeful. She scaled the mountain, feeling the wind once more but ignoring it as best she could. At the top, a red ball of light was waiting—another god. The god burned a symbol onto her left hand and disappeared. She looked down and nodded. It was the name of the Aeartsa. The goddess of Justice.

Her journey continued. She braved ice and fire, desert and jungle. On each mountain top, she received the blessing of a god. They seared their names into her flesh: Soele, the god of Mercy, Sutriv, the god of Bravery, Isalut, the goddess of Loyalty, Adzam Aruha, the god of Wisdom and Hcolom, the goddess of Sacrifice. Finally, she stood on top of the last mountain, her flesh covered with the six blessings of the gods. One more god, one more symbol and she will be complete. As the last god burned her, she felt her body die, unable to hold all the gifts the gods had bestowed on her. Yet, in that very moment, she was reborn, becoming more than just a corporeal being. She was one with the godhead. She rose into the sky; her light shone down, burning away the clouds that obscured her world. She smiled and the suns broke through the clouds. Now, she would turn her planet into a paradise. She rose into the clearing sky to begin her greatest work.

"And then I woke up," Jom finished.

"That is a beautiful story," Ravola said.

Jom shrugged. "Like I said, it's just a dream I had."

Macar laughed. "Even I know by now that your dreams are never just dreams." Jom shot him an unreadable look, carefully keeping his face neutral.

"Anyway, that's what the symbols mean. They're the names of the gods," he said, keeping them on track. They walked over to the obelisk and Jom pointed to the various glyphs, beginning with the lowest.

"Strength. Justice. Mercy. Bravery. Loyalty. Wisdom. Sacrifice."

"So now we need to find seven keys that have those symbols?" Macar asked.

"I—I don't think so," Jom said, staring at the glyphs. "Now that I'm looking at them, that doesn't seem quite right to me."

"What do we do, then?"

They studied the obelisk thoughtfully. Then, Jom pulled the Dowa flute from deep in his pocket. He cradled the small instrument for a moment, thinking of a simpler time from not so long ago. Through all his journeys, he had so few reminders of his village, his Grandmother.

"This is supposed to be a Dowa flute," he said, showing the others. "The Dowa were known for their loyalty to their masters. Even to the point of ruin, they did not abandon the people who created and cared for them. And once their masters were gone, they couldn't continue either. They lived only to serve."

Jom stepped up the obelisk and walked around until he was staring at the fifth hole.

"Loyalty. This is for the key of loyalty. This is to honor Isalut." He slid the flute into the hole. There was a click. A low humming began from inside the obelisk.

"What did you do?" Macar demanded.

"I think he figured out the riddle," Ravola answered.

"Quick! We need something to represent the other keys!" Jom said.

"Perhaps this will help," NDX said. It opened the compartment on the side of its torso and withdrew the container that had housed Dianat. The clock-work boy walked up to the seventh key. "Sacrifice. For Hcolom." It slid the vial in. Another click. The humming grew louder.

"And this for Justice," Jom said, pushing his dagger into another hole. "A heart for a heart, according to the story. Aeartsa would like that, I hope." A third click. Now they could clearly hear something moving within the pillar.

"That leaves Strength, Mercy, Wisdom and Bravery," NDX said.

"NDX, place your hand in the Wisdom keyhole. You have the most knowledge of anyone here."

"Knowledge and wisdom is not the same thing," it pointed out.

"But you are wise as well," Ravola assured the automaton.

NDX paused for a moment, then nodded. It untied its severed arm from its back and slid the hand into the hole. "In honor of Adzam Aruha." Another click.

"Ravola, you have Strength," Jom said. She shrugged and placed a tentacle into the hole. "For Sotark," she murmured. After a moment, she nodded. "It does not hurt."

"Mercy and Bravery are left."

"Jom should take Mercy," Ravola said. "You are the kindest of us."

"Are you sure?" Jom eyed the hole nervously, then laughed, answering his own question. He gently placed his hand in the keyhole. "Please, Soele, accept my gift." There was yet another click. He felt something lightly grab his hand. He felt he could remove his hand if need be and was assured.

"Macar, you're last."

Macar looked at the hole for Bravery. "I don't think this will work. I'm not a brave man. You've said it yourself."

"I believe you are," Jom told him. "It doesn't matter what you were in the past. It only matters what you are now. And right now, you will be brave."

He took a deep breath and nodded. Hesitantly, he put his hand in the keyhole. "For Sutriv then."

And then hell broke loose.

Battle for the Mind Harp

SEVERAL EVENTS HAPPENED SIMULTANEOUSLY. First, the obelisk fell into itself. The obsidian surface of the pillar folded inward, like some god took the thin sheaf of reality and creased it over and over again, bending it into smaller and smaller pieces. The hard stone of the pillar turned flexible and began to dismantle itself. Jom and Macar's hands were caught for an instant as the obelisk collapsed and Jom panicked. He yanked his hand out even as Ravola cried out a warning. Jom stumbled backwards onto the hard rock. Ravola and NDX leapt clear from the folding stone, the automaton just barely able to get its severed arm out of the shifting reality.

A loud roar shattered the air. It took Jom a heartbeat to realize the roar was not coming from the pillar. He looked up to see a large object break through the storm that raged around them. Black metal glinted in the murky light as a ship crashed into the ground just inside the storm wall. Jom gasped in recognition. Kala Azar's hover train dug up a huge swatch of ground as it skidded to a halt.

The pillar continued to collapse and through the chaos, Jom noticed a light growing from the middle of the folding stone. He turned back towards the obelisk. As the pillar folded into nothing, a bright light erupted from the center of where the obelisk had stood. Jom shielded his eyes against the light, trying to peer into it. Ravola gave another shout. Suddenly, the back half of the hovertrain exploded in a brilliant ball of fire. The ground shuddered from the force of the explosion, throwing Jom to his knees. Then another shape emerged from the storm. A shape Jom recognized instantly from his dreams.

The Cornelius Grinnell burst through the storm. It was a huge, ugly ship, all odd angles and barrels of weapons sticking out of the hull in every direction. Jom's heart almost stopped at the sight of it. Memories of his terrible dream flooded back into his brain. Weapon fire erupted from the massive ship, slamming into the side of the hover train. Another explosion rocked the area, throwing them all to the ground. A hand clamped down on Jom's shoulder. He looked up into NDX's face.

"Get the Mind Harp!" it told him. It yanked him towards the light, turned and joined Ravola. Together, they moved forward, blocking Jom from the figures emerging from the burning hover train. Even from that distance, Jom could make out the silhouette of Kala Azar as he strode from the wreckage. He was surrounded by a dozen of his men. But for the moment, their attention was not on Jom. They hefted large blasters and began to fire at the ship hovering above them. Brilliant blasts of energy slammed into the Cornelius Grinnell and the ship listed to the side. It moved away, then lowered towards the ground. The bandits continued to fire on the ship, blasting chunks of metal from the skin of the ship.

A beam of pure white light shot down from the underside of the ship to the ground. When it faded, a tall, thin cloaked figure was standing on the moor. In one hand, he held his ebony blade that dripped darkness. The shadows flowed around him, concealing him. The Shadow Saint raised a hand and bright red energy shot from his hand into the bandits. Kala Azar leapt to the side just as the energy hit his men. They screamed for an instant before disintegrating. The cyborg rolled to his feet, two blasters appearing in his hands. He fired at the Saint. The Saint ducked the energy beams, his movements too fast to watch, too hidden by the darkness that swirled around him. Another blast of energy erupted from his palm, lancing the ground around Kala Azar.

"Go!" Macar yelled at him. Jom shook his head to clear it. The sounds and explosions were making it almost impossible to concentrate. Macar joined NDX and Ravola in front of him, protecting him from the fighting. Jom turned towards the light. In the middle of the brightness, he could just barely make out an object. He took a deep breath and, pushing his fears aside, reached into the light. He felt his hands touch something warm. The light pushed against him and pulsed around him. He steeled his nerve and pushed back, feeling the resistance as something both physical and mental. He felt the light in his head as much as around his hands. Unbidden and unwanted, doubt crept around the edges of his mind and he felt the light grow stronger. He let his mind focus on the doubt and it grew. It formed a wall, keeping him out. He hesitated. The light blocked him out, forming a barrier he could not break. Then, he remembered the keys.

Strength and Justice. Tempering what he could do with what was right. Mercy and Loyalty. Bending the law but staying true to it at the same time. Bravery and Wisdom. Standing up in the face of adversity and knowing when it was necessary. And finally, Sacrifice. Knowing there were bigger stakes than just him. He smiled. The doubt faded. He gave himself to the light, letting it wash over him. The sounds of battle dropped away as the light engulfed him. He closed his eyes and banished the doubts, the worries from inside and felt his fingers touch the Harp. He pulled, bringing it out of the light and to him. The light died as the Harp was removed from the remains of the obelisk.

As the light faded, he looked down at the object in his hands. It was a solid cylindrical piece of blue crystal. Deep grooves were carved into the sides, seven groves repeated seven times. The symbols of the seven trials were also carved into the crystal. Jom brushed his fingers across a set of grooves and felt a surge of confidence wash over him. He saw that the symbol above the grooves he had touched was for Bravery. An idea formed in his head. He turned the Harp around until he saw the symbol for Wisdom and lightly skimmed his fingers across the grooves.

He stumbled as his mind expanded. He knew instantly how to use the Harp. By balancing the seven virtues, he could manipulate the planes. By playing the seven notes, he could control minds and bodies, time and space. No wonder the Latuip directed Kala Azar to this! With the Harp, anyone could destroy or rebuild the universe at will! He shuddered at the power he held in his hands. Kala Azar could use Justice as reason enough for destroying his homeworld. Anyone, for that matter, could manipulate the seven aspects to suit their own designs. He looked down and saw his fingers still touching the Wisdom grooves. Jom smiled and nodded. He knew he needed to hide the Harp. It was too powerful. It needed to disappear. He was a fool to look for it but now that it was in his hands, he needed to hide it somewhere no one would ever find it again.

But first, he needed to save his friends. He looked up at the battle raging. NDX, Ravola and Macar were fighting with a group of Kala Azar's bandits. Ravola was a whirlwind of slashing metal and stinging blows as she whipped her tentacles around three bandits, attacking them from all sides at once. They desperately attempted to get her in a crossfire but could not pin her down. She leapt about wildly, her tentacles always striking from behind or the side as she whirled around. Macar was engaged with a bandit near her, fighting desperately over a blaster that lay on the moor a few paces from them. NDX was under fire from several more bandits, its personal forceshield glowing a bright yellow as blaster fire pinged off it. Behind them all, Kala Azar and the Shadow Saint continued to trade blasts, each dodging the other's fire. The hover train was smoking from several fires. A handful of bandits were desperately trying to extinguish the flames before the ship exploded while several more continued to blast the Cornelius Grinnell, hoping to bring the massive ship to the ground.

Despite the danger that surrounded him, Jom sat down, crossed his legs and placed the Harp in his lap. Concentrating hard, he carefully placed fingers on the grooves for Strength, Loyalty, Justice and Wisdom. Then, he closed his eyes and gently played the Harp.

The immediate response was silence. Jom cautiously opened one eye to see everyone stopped. Time itself, in fact, was suspended. Blaster fire burned the air in lines of energy that stretched across the ground. Ravola hung in mid-air like a puppet. Everyone was frozen. Jom played Loyalty and his friends were released from their stasis.

"Jom! What happened?" Macar shouted, grabbing the blaster from the ground and pointing it at the frozen bandit. NDX surveyed the situation and lowered its forceshield, despite three energy blasts a hands-width from its face. Ravola tumbled to the ground, springing instantly to her feet.

"It's all right!" Jom yelled before either Macar or Ravola could kill their opponents. "They can't hurt you now!"

"I see that," Ravola said, stopping her sword just short of cutting off a bandit's head. She stepped back and studied her foe. "How did you do this?"

"I—I played the Harp," Jom explained. They all walked over to him, staring at the Harp in his lap.

"You know how to use it?" NDX inquired.

"Somewhat. Not really. It's actually a good teacher," Jom explained sheepishly.

"Then let's leave before they regain movement," Macar said, eyeing the bandits warily.

"They can't move until I release them," Jom said, getting to his feet but being careful not to play any of the grooves. "At least, I don't think they can."

"Interesting," NDX said, studying the Harp.

Ravola gave a short snort. "Too bad. It was a good fight."

"Can your new toy get us out of here?" Macar asked.

"Yes. I think. But first, I need to know something."

Leaving the others behind, Jom walked across the battlefield to the Shadow Saint, cautiously ducking under frozen blaster fire and around immobile bodies. The Shadow Saint was frozen in mid-jump. The shadows that concealed him were static and still. A burning line of blaster fire sizzled in the air, lancing across the distance from one of Kala Azar's pistols. Jom carefully ducked under the energy and approached the tall figure. Sitting down again, he placed fingers on Strength, Mercy and Wisdom and gently played.

The Shadow Saint moved slightly. Although still frozen in mid-air, he turned his head to look at Jom. Ravola held her sword at the ready behind Jom and Macar fingered his blaster.

"Can you hear me?" Jom asked.

The Shadow Saint smiled beneath his cloak. "Yes, Jom, I can hear you."

Jom's heart beat faster. "How—how do you know my name?"

"I know many things. I know you better than you know yourself."

"Why are you hunting us?"

"Silly boy. I was paid, of course."

"By who?"

"By someone who wishes to remain anonymous at this time. I'm sure you understand."

"I don't understand. Tell me."

The Shadow Saint turned his head to look at his hand. Jom's gaze followed the Saint's. The fingers of his hand were twitching, flexing against the force that held them. The Saint turned back to Jom and smiled again.

"Your time is running out."

"You can't move until I let you." Even as the words came out of his mouth, Jom knew them to be untrue. He strummed the Harp again, willing the man before him to stop moving. But the Saint continued to flex his fingers. Then his wrist began to move, as well as one of his feet.

"You have no idea what you're doing, boy."

"Jom, I think we should leave," NDX said from behind him. The others agreed. Reluctantly, Jom got to his feet.

"I'll find you, you know," the Saint said. "It doesn't matter where you go. I'll find you." He flexed his arms, almost free.

"Jom..." Macar said urgently.

Jom looked down at the Harp and placed his fingers. With a final look at the Shadow Saint, he played the Harp and a brilliant light exploded around them.

The Last Quadrant

WHEN HIS VISION CLEARED, Jom found himself on an island of black rock floating among a sea of stars. A shimmering dome of white energy arced above them, enclosing him and the others in a half-circle of breathable air. Jom looked around, seeing NDX, Macar, Ravola and...someone else. A small, hairy man was standing among them. He had deep maroon skin and long scraggly black hair that hung in his face, obscuring most of his features. A nose as pointed as his ears twitched as he looked around at them with beady eyes. He was wearing dark leggings and a loose top, secured by a simple leather belt, all of which looked ancient and worn.

"Um...hello," Jom said.

The man looked up at Jom and nodded but did not speak.

"The Latuip!" Macar said, stepping forward. "It's the Latuip I--we captured."

The Latuip turned to look at Macar, his face unreadable behind the mat of hair. Jom tried to figure out if the creature was bitter at his capture or merely perturbed. Maybe he didn't even understand what was happening. He didn't seem nearly as confused as the rest of them. He stood passively, as if he was waiting for someone to take charge.

"How did we get here?" Ravola asked. "Did you simply wish it?"

Jom searched for the correct words. "Not exactly. I wanted to be safe. For us all to be safe. And.."

"And?" Macar prompted.

Jom sighed. "And for us to complete our journey." He sat down on the cold rock, cradling the Mind Harp in his lap. "I'm tired. And scared. I just…I just want to finish this stupid quest and go home."

"Interesting," NDX said. "The Mind Harp must have interpreted your unspoken desires. It brought the Latuip along with us as the most efficient means of completing our quest. It searched your mind."

"But where are we?" Macar asked, looking up at the multitude of stars that surrounded them.

"My internal star chart suggests we are somewhere in the Last Quadrant."

"The Last Quadrant?" Macar exclaimed. "But that's…"

"On the edge of forever," Ravola finished for him.

"I don't understand. What's the Last Quadrant?" As he asked the question, Jom's eyes fell on the Latuip. Jom saw the small creature's eyes twinkle and then his mind exploded into colors, shapes and sounds.

In the center of the universe there is a silver star. It glows with a light that is both holy and unnatural. It is the beginning and, some say, the end. It is the oldest star and will be the last one to burn out when the universe finally ends. It was the first light and will be the final one as well. Surrounding the star are five planets, each one more lush and beautiful than the last. They spin in perfect orbits around the silver star and each one is a birthworld for one of the five First Races.

The First Races were the beginning of all the intelligent life that came to inhabit the countless worlds of the universe. They were the immortal Mother Races, the original denizens of the universe. From them sprang every sentient creature. One planet was nothing but water and from it sprang all the sea-dwelling and finned races. This planet was called Iad. Another was composed entirely of air and gas. From it came the winged ones, the feathered creatures, and was known as Sfo. The planet of rock and dirt was Ord. The planet of fire was Ewr. And finally, there was a planet of light. No shadow marred the surface of the planet. No night ever fell on it. Its jeweled composition reflected the silver star's light back and forth across the surface, bathing the planet in continuous day. It was called Iah.

Time passed and the races evolved. They built societies and cities of fire and cloud, rock and water. They spread across their worlds, conquering their own planets, then they reached out past the limits of their atmospheres to the next planet. Water met fire. Rock found air. At first, there was war as they struggled to understand themselves and each other. These first wars unleashed death upon the universe. Before that, there was no dying, no destruction, only everlasting life. But the wars changed that. Now, the Races could die. More importantly, they could kill. This new-found power scared them even as they embraced it. The race of light, the Iahians, urged the others to lay down their arms. They realized they were on a precipice. Either continue to kill each other and doom them all to oblivion, or turn away from the destruction. The others almost annihilated each other before they saw reason. They finally put aside their weapons just as they were on the verge of destroying their worlds and worked together. Devoting their energy to the common good, they repaired the damage their wars had caused, making their planets better than before. Then they turned back to the stars and were soon exploring the universe, first in great ships, then with nothing but thought. They transcended their physical limitations and became immortal once more.

They spread out across the universe, seeding planet after planet with life as they explored the cosmos. Like a great wave, they traveled outward from the center, expanding in every direction. For untold billions of cycles, they journeyed to the far reaches of the galaxies. They did not stop until they reached the edge of the universe. There, they were brought to a halt. Something stopped them from progressing. Something blocked their way. They realized they had come to The Wall of Forever. The end to everything. Beyond this point, there was nothing, literally nothing. They were at the limit of the universe. They could go no further. But, as they gazed into the Abyss beyond reality, they could not accept that this was the end. After so long, they had become explorers. All they knew now was looking to the next horizon. They sought the hidden, the unknown. Beyond the Wall, they knew, was ultimate knowledge. They had conquered the universe. Now, they would travel beyond every known realm and explore the Unknowable. And so they gathered in this Last Quadrant, this edge of the universe. Every member of the Five Races came, called together to bend their wills to this final push into true immortality. This was their destiny—to transcend this universe and enter the next. Working together, they bent time and space, intent of piercing the Wall. Whatever was beyond the Wall was rightfully theirs. They were the first. They would be the last.

Jom shook his head, clearing the images that lingered behind his eyes. He looked at the Latuip in amazement.

"What happened?" Ravola asked, quickly reaching his side. "You went blank."

"I—he told me about the Last Quadrant," Jom mumbled, pointing at the small creature.

"The Last Quadrant is unknown territory," NDX said. "No explorer on record has penetrated very deeply into this sector of the universe."

"Can't get much safer than that," Macar muttered, kicking at pebbles.

"Very true," NDX agreed. "This must be an old outpost or waypoint used by one of those previous explorers."

"Did they succeed?" Jom asked.

"Did who succeed at what?"

"Did the First Races pierce the Wall of Forever?"

NDX shrugged. "There are no records that I know of that say one way or the other. Perhaps the Master knows."

"Does it matter?" Macar asked.

Jom thought for a heartbeat. "Maybe. I don't know. I feel like it does, but I'm not sure how."

"Perhaps we should focus on our quest?" NDX suggested.

Jom nodded. They needed to find the Phobetor Chair and bring it back to Abla. Jom turned to the Latuip.

"Where is the Phobetor Chair?"

Jom was greeted with silence. No thoughts, no images exploded in his mind. After a moment, he shook his head. "Nothing."

"Which means he's been asked that question before," Ravola pointed out.

"Which means we are running out of time," NDX added. "There may be others looking for the Chair as we speak."

"Try a different question," Ravola suggested. "Your dreams give you insight."

Jom took a deep breath and thought. The Latuip watched him with interest.

"What's your name?" he finally asked.

The Latuip tilted his head and Jom thought he could see a small sad smile cross its half-hidden face.

SEBUIT NEBT UAA KHESFET SEBAU EM PERT F

The voice was strong and old, the kind that rumbled in the chest before leaving the body. Jom took a step back, steadied by Ravola's strong hand. The words vibrated through his body. Jom steadied his nerves, trying to adjust to this odd way of communicating.

"Um. Can we just call you Nebt?"

The Latuip nodded once.

"Everyone, this is Nebt." They all greeted the Latuip. The small creature seemed pleased by the attention.

"It is amazing that no one has ever asked him that in all his years," Ravola said in wonder.

"It's sad, isn't it?" Jom agreed. "But you're worth a name to me." He smiled warmly and Nebt gave a quick bow.

"Now, Nebt, do you know where the Phobetor Chair is?"

Nebt did not respond.

"Can you take us to the Phobetor Chair?"

Nothing. Jom puffed out a couple breaths. "Anyone have any ideas?"

They asked the question a thousand different ways. They tried countless permutations. Through it all, Nebt stood there, silent and unmoving, his eyes glinting. There was no sun to gauge the time, no deepening of the day or rising of a moon to track how long they sat there. But their stomachs told them. Their heavy eyes told them. Jom assumed NDX had an internal chronometer but didn't ask how long they've been on this desolate rock. He didn't want to know. The clock on NDX's chest told him they had been there too long. They needed to figure out their next move quickly. Eventually, though, he ran out of ideas, as did the others. He lay down on the hard black rock in frustration. It wasn't comfortable. It didn't matter. Soon, he was fast asleep.

: Dream of the Swarm :

TECHNOMAGE GRAAA SAT ON his throne and frowned. Before him, a thousand monitors showed him his empire, beaming him images from every corner of his domain. Creatures of every size and shape passed before his eyes, stepping in and out of view of his omnipresent surveillance. Countless worlds flew his flag above their capitols. His shocktroopers marched across a thousand battlefields and occupied millions of cities at the slightest hint of uprising. They crushed revolt with a heavy hand, setting an example to the other worlds. Millions upon millions of creatures called him 'Master.' He was in complete control of his empire. He took a small amount of satisfaction from that fact. After being exiled here from his own plane by the other Technomages, jealous stupid cretins that they were, he fought hard to conquer this plane of existence and take it for his own.

And yet, Graaa was unhappy. He was the undisputed ruler of more worlds than he could track. A single word from his thin lips sent billions to their deaths. His fist held the galaxy in a steel grip. But as Graaa looked at the monitors, he saw resentment in the eyes of his subjects. The disrespectful way that one held his head. The subtle look of protest this one had as a shocktrooper moved her along. He saw the spark of independence behind their obedience. He saw rebellion hidden in their hearts. Even with the greatest army this plane had ever seen, Graaa feared it was only a matter of time before his grip would loosen.

This would not do.

His empire would last forever. His will would guide the universe to glory. His hand would never let go. But how could he ensure that? How could he stop rebellious hearts? How could he squelch their pathetic attempts at freedom? How could he make them understand they were better off with him in control? How could he get them to see the universe as he saw it, to think like him?

A toothy smile grew across Graaa's oily face then. The answer was obvious. Ridiculously obvious. He leapt off his throne, hurrying to his inner sanctum to begin work. For many cycles, he shut himself away in his laboratory, harnessing dark forces and bending them to his will. His generals pounded on the solid door of his sanctum demanding an audience, but received no answer. His advisors wrung their hands and whispered among themselves, unsure if they should continue to plot against their lord or if his seclusion was some elaborate trick to catch and execute them. Inside the sanctum, Graaa worked nonstop. He didn't have much time. He knew his subjects were lifting their heads as rumors spread across his empire. Rumors that he had died, that he had been assassinated. That he had gone mad. They began to tentatively raise their faces to the sky. Thoughts of rebellion formed in their minds. Images of freedom clouded their vision. As he harnessed the dark science and forbidden energies, Graaa grinned. How utterly sweet it was to give them one last bit of hope before taking it away forever!

Finally, the door to the sanctum opened and Graaa emerged from the shadows. In his hand he held a small weapon. The only thing remotely remarkable about it was its dull grey color, a grey that sucked in the surrounding light, giving only the barest color in return. The guards on either side of the door snapped to attention at his appearance, startled to see him after so long. The Technomage pointed the weapon at one of them and fired. An oily beam of grey energy slithered out of the barrel, roiling across the air to the guard. When it touched the guard's uniform, it spread quickly across his body, covering him from head to toe in its sickly grey energy. Graaa watched in delight as the greyness seeped into the guard, draining all the color away. He smiled his toothy smile as the light in the eyes of the guard was replaced by grey and the skin turned grey and then the mind turned grey.

Graaa spoke, his voice coming from two mouths at once.

"Excellent."

They turned and fired on the other guard, watching in delight as the grey took over. Satisfied his/their work had not been in vain, he/they went back into the lab and began replicating the weapon. Three sets of hands worked in unison. Where once there had been three minds, now there was only one: Graaa.

He could never achieve perfect unity, ultimate peace across his empire as long as there were differing points of views. He could never make every last one of his subjects agree with him. Too much independent thinking. So he needed to take away that independence. He created a weapon that didn't simply override the victim's thoughts or suppress their desires. That could be reversed. That control could be broken. No, his weapon took away thoughts, leaving nothing but a grey mass that was filled with an extension of his own mind. It replaced independent thought with unity. Once converted, he saw through their grey eyes and felt with their grey hands and thought with their grey minds.

You can't rebel against yourself.

His grey vision expanded exponentially as he converted more and more of his subjects. He stalked his palace in three directions. Three more were quickly added to his mind. As he walked the hallways, he began work on more weapons while continuing to convert his subjects. In little time, he was a hundred strong. As more weapons were produced, he spread out across the surface of the planet. He walked with a hundred feet. Then a thousand. Soon, as he continued to swarm over the planet, he took to the stars as well, looking to the next planet with a million eyes.

Planet after planet, filled with billions of lifeforms, turned grey and uniform. Graaa pushed further and further, becoming a swarm of grey that left nothing untouched. He continued to grow exponentially as he went. He spread out like a blanket across the universe, reaching the limits of his empire, turning it all grey. He saw his subjects flee as he advanced but simply laughed. Sooner or later, all would fall to him. All would become him.

Worlds banded together to resist him, of course. They tried energy weapons and magic, science and prayer. But he was a wave that washed over everything. Those that resisted were forced to fall back before him or become grey. Many fought valiantly. There were many heroes in the war against the grey. It did not matter. All fell to him in the end. Nothing could stop the swarm that was Graaa.

The physical creature that once was Graaa was no more. Now, trillions of beings spread across the universe were

Graaa. They were the same, even if their corporeal bodies differed. His consciousness encompassed everything now. There was no more dissent. There was no thought of rebellion. There was only the grey.

Occasionally, a traveler from another plane would appear among the grey. An explorer would pierce the aether and enter his universe. Graaa always tried to learn how they transversed the dimensions but they never gave up their knowledge and would eventually be assimilated into the grey.

But he waited patiently. Sooner or later, he would learn how to cross the planes. Then, the grey would grow again. And he would exact his revenge on those that exiled him so very long ago.

Jom woke with a start and looked around wildly. Nothing but the black of space and the white of stars. His heart seized up. Was he in the grey? But then his eyes fell on the red of Ravola's outfit and the gold of NDX's body and he relaxed.

"Are you unwell?" NDX asked, coming to his side.

"I—it was just a dream."

Macar snorted from where he was sitting near Jom. "Your dreams are never 'just' dreams, boy."

"He speaks the truth," Ravola agreed. "Tell us about it."

Jom told them about what he had seen. How the swarm of the Technomage Graaa moved across a universe, engulfing everything until there was nothing but grey. As he spoke, he shuddered at the memories of what he had seen.

"That sounds horrible," Ravola said softly.

"It was."

"And it is true," NDX added. "At least as far as we know."

"What do you mean?"

"There have been a couple messages, sent transdimensionally, from explorers over the cycles. The messages were always short and clipped off before they could talk at length. But they spoke of a plane that was of one mind. Every sentient being was part of a hive-mind. We do not know much else, only that the dimension is strictly forbidden. The threat of the swarm entering our plane is too great a risk. Even the most intrepid explorers do not dare chancing an encounter with this swarm."

"So he never was stopped?" Jom asked.

NDX shook his head. "Again, we have very limited information. But it appears as if this Technomage did, in fact, succeed at conquering his entire universe."

Jom shuddered again. "Let's not go there."

"I couldn't agree more," Macar said.

Jom looked around. His stomach growled loudly. "We need to get going." He glanced furtively at the clock on NDX's chest. "We're running out of time."

"Do you have any ideas?" Macar asked.

Jom thought for a moment, staring at Nebt who was standing silently a bit apart from them. "Maybe," he finally said.

: Music of the Harp :

WHAT'S YOUR PLAN?" MACAR asked. Instead of answering, Jom got to his feet and walked over to the Latuip. He hunkered down next to Nebt. The small man watched him intently.

"The Water Banshees weren't the first experiments with the Phobetor Chair, were they?"

Nebt's eyes sparkled and he shook his head.

"There was a creature called a Womf. It was tortured by the Shield of Ku'baba at a Citadel. Do you know where the Womf is buried?"

Nebt continued to stare at him.

Jom swore under his breath. "I was positive that would work," he mumbled. "I doubt many know about the Womf."

"Womf?" Ravola asked.

Jom shook his head. "I'll explain later. I thought he would know where a creature had died..." A sudden thought sprang into his brain. He stared at the Latuip.

"Nebt, is the Womf still alive?"

Nebt smiled and nodded. Jom's heart skipped a beat and he looked at the others with a grin. "I think we lucked out." He took a deep breath and thought about his next move.

"Nebt, where is the Womf?"

Jom closed his eyes and braced himself for the flood of images that was going to explode in his brain. After a moment of nothing though, he let out a long sigh. Frustrated and disappointed, he opened one eye only to see Nebt calmly staring at him. Opening his other eye, Jom realized that the Latuip was pointing. Jom followed Nebt's finger to an outcropping of black rock in the distance. It was half-hidden in shadows and nondescript, easily passed over.

With a look at the others, Jom got to his feet and they hurried to the outcropping. A small hole had been carved into the rock, hidden by the natural formations of the rock. A single door could be seen in the shadows and they looked at it in wonder.

"Can it be?"

"This is a sparsely populated part of the universe," NDX said. "It would make sense to have a base of operations here if you did not want to be found."

"So the Mind Harp didn't bring us to just a random outpost." Jom looked at the Latuip in wonder. "But how could it have known this is where we needed to be?"

"The Mind Harp must have read your desires and gathered the information from Nebt, then teleported us," NDX suggested. "Together, they brought us here."

"You think the Harp...asked Nebt where to go?"

NDX shrugged. "I do not pretend to understand the forces at work here. I can only speculate. But I believe that is too simplistic of an explanation. After all, if Nebt was asked the question, he would no longer have the answer for us."

"Great," Macar said. "So let's find this Womf thing and get the chair and get out of here!"

"That won't be as easy as we'd like," Ravola said. She was studying the door intently. "The passageway is shielded. I doubt any of our weapons will be able to penetrate it."

Looking closely, Jom could make out a faint shimmer of energy around the door. NDX stepped over and swept its sensors across the shield.

"Latent gravistar pulses. Ravola is correct. None of our weapons can pierce this type of energy."

"There must be another way in," Macar suggested.

"Possible. But how can we explore the rest of this planetoid outside of the atmosphere dome?"

"So we have to go in this way," Jom said. "There's got to be a way in."

"I see no input pad or code device," Ravola offered, searching the surrounding rock.

"Nebt, how do we get past the shield?" Jom asked.

Nebt stared at him calmly.

"Really? You've been asked that before?" Macar exclaimed. "I thought this was a secret entrance!" Jom shot him a look and Macar turned away, pretending to study the door with Ravola. She suppressed a laugh beneath her fabric but did not say anything.

"NDX, how does the shield work?"

"Gravistar energy comes from a large number of gravitons that have been condensed to such a degree that they...."

Jom held up his hand. "Let me rephrase the question. Is there a way we can disrupt the energy to the shield?"

"Theoretically, if we hit the shield with a counter-pulse of equal but opposing wavelength, it should negate the energy wave and disable the shield."

"How do we do that?"

"We would need a Type IV ion displacer."

"We don't have one of those."

"No, we do not."

"But we have one of those," Macar said, pointing to the Mind Harp in Jom's pack.

Jom was silent for a moment. "I—I don't really know how to use it," he protested.

"I can't think of a better time to learn," Macar responded. "We're stuck on a barren rock in the middle of the Last Quadrant. There are at least two psychopaths hunting us. We're down to the last of our food and water. I wouldn't bet on you being able to learn at your leisure at some future point."

Ravola placed a gentle hand on his shoulder. "He has a point. Now's the time."

Jom took a deep breath and nodded. He sat down and pulled the Mind Harp out of his pack. Carefully, he placed it in his lap and thought. He knew nothing about wavelengths and gravistar energy. All he knew was that they needed to get through that door. He placed his fingers on the keys and closed his eyes. Strength. Strength to do what he needed to do. Wisdom to know how. And Bravery to face the unknown. He trailed his fingers across the Harp.

In his mind, he saw bands of energy in front of him, like waves on a lake. The energy pulsated in regular intervals across his field of vision. Concentrating, he strummed the Harp again, imagining the energy from the Harp flowing out towards the waves. Pushing with all his will, he saw the music as a new energy in his mind's eye. Slowly, it emerged from the Harp, forced out and directed by his thoughts. Jom gritted his teeth as he pushed. Then, he realized he was going about it in the wrong way. He took a deep breath and simply let the music emerge instead of forcing it. The music responded instantly, flowing out of the Harp like a gentle wave. Jom directed the music towards the shield. The energies collided and Jom could feel the gravitstar pulses repelling the harp-energy.

"Do not attempt to fight it," he heard NDX say at his side. "Let the two forces join."

Jom concentrated harder and moved his fingers across the Harp. The energies struck again. This time, Jom willed the music of the Harp to mingle with the shield. He saw the two forces combine and heard a low buzz.

"The shield is getting stronger!" Macar said.

The energies reinforced each other, making the whole stronger. The tips of the waves, buoyed by the music, rose higher, pushing everyone away. Jom could feel the shield expanding outward.

"Now Jom, move them out of sync with each other."

Jom shifted his thoughts, moving the music sideways from the pulses instead of with them. Sweat rolled down his brow. He squeezed his eyes tighter, focusing all his concentration on moving the music of the Harp. His fingers absently strummed the keys as he struggled. In his mind's eye, he saw the two energies moving together as one. Then slowly, ever so slowly, the music moved out of sync with the shield energy. There was a cacophony as the energies moved apart. Jom resisted covering his ears with his hands and tried to stay focused. He moved the music further away. The sounds assaulted his mind and tears ran down from the corners of his eyes. Then, with a final push, the music moved far enough so the peaks of the gravistar met with the valleys of the music and vice versa. Suddenly, there was silence.

"You did it!" Macar yelled from somewhere to his left. "The shield's down!"

"Hold the music, Jom. Give me a moment," NDX said. Jom heard shuffling and the gears of the clock-work boy grinding. He kept his focus on maintaining the music, gritting his teeth from the effort.

Finally, NDX said he could relax and Jom felt Ravola's hand on his shoulder. Relieved, he broke off his concentration, letting the music fade. He opened his eyes, blinking away the tears. NDX and Macar stood by the open door. Ravola looked at him with a mixture of concern and pride and helped him to his feet.

"Well done," she said.

"Thanks," he mumbled, stumbling and weak from the effort. Ravola easily supported him as they walked towards the opening.

They stopped at the door, peering inside. Darkness lay in front of them. Taking a deep breath, Jom turned to the others.

"Ready?" They all nodded. NDX removed its severed arm from the straps and held it up. It touched a few loose wires and a finger began to glow brightly. With the clock-work boy leading the way, they entered the shadows.

: The Labyrinth of Night :

A LONG NARROW HALLWAY descended at a gentle angle. They were forced to walk in single file down the passageway; NDX leading the way holding the light high, then Macar, Nebt, Jom and Ravola bringing up the rear. There were no doorways or side passages. The corridor was, in fact, completely devoid of any features. It was simply a long metal hallway. And yet, Jom felt a growing sense of oppression as they descended further into the complex. He could almost feel the weight of the rocks above pushing down on them. Everyone had their weapons in hand, as if they all sensed the same foreboding presence.

They eventually reached an intersection. Corridors went off into the darkness in three directions. Waving the light down each passageway, they could see no difference between them.

"Well? Now what?" Macar asked.

"Uncertain. My scanners have a very limited range and this

appears to be a large complex. This metal appears to be restricting the effectiveness of my sensors as well."

Jom looked down the various hallways. "I guess we pick one?"

They chose the left-hand passage. Ravola took out her dagger to carve a marking into the metal in case they had to backtrack but the metal would not yield to her blade.

"Unusually hard material," she commented, trying again to scratch the surface.

"I will be able to keep track of our route," NDX said.

"That won't help if we get separated," Macar pointed out, peering into the darkness with trepidation.

"True."

After a moment's thought, Ravola ran the dagger across one of her tentacles. She barely grimaced as the weapon cut. Jom looked on with concern but she shrugged it off. She used the blood to mark the wall and nodded to the others.

The next hallway was shorter and curved gently to the left. Then it straightened out. Before long, they were at another intersection and again had to choose. Ravola marked the metal wall and they continued. Three, five, ten intersections went by. It did not take them long before they realized they were in a maze of featureless corridors.

"I don't like this," Macar muttered as they turned down yet another hallway.

"What choice do we have?" Jom asked then stopped short. "Did you hear that?"

They all halted and strained their ears. A low grating sound echoed down the passageway to them, like metal scraping on metal.

"What's that?" Macar whispered loudly.

"I don't want to find out," Jom replied and they hurried down the corridor, pausing only to mark yet another intersection.

As they moved down the corridor, they saw something ahead. Up until then, all the corridors had been featureless with smooth, unadorned walls. As they walked though, they saw alcoves on both sides of the corridor. Cautious, they approached the first one. Lying within the alcove was a body. Ravola and Macar quickly brought their weapons up but the body didn't move.

"Wait!" Jom said, looking intently at the body. He stepped forward. The body was thin and tall. Its limbs, two legs, two arms, were unnaturally long, ending in thin fingers and toes. But Jom's gaze was drawn to its face. There were no features on the head at all; no eyes, no ears, no mouth, nothing. Just a lump of flesh attached to the shoulders.

"What is it?" he asked.

NDX studied the body for a moment, analyzing and processing. "I believe it is a synthetic creature," it said. "I have heard of such things. They are called Syntries. They are designed to protect."

"Protect?" Macar asked, stepping back slightly and looking down the hall at the other alcoves. "How do they protect?"

NDX shrugged his shoulders. "I assume they have defensive capabilities built into their bodies."

"Let's move," Ravola said, also eyeing the way ahead. "But not that way."

"Logic suggests that the way that is guarded is the way we must go," NDX pointed out.

"Even so, I'd rather see if there's a way around these things."

They started back the way they had come. But, when they turned down the previous corridor, they saw that alcoves had appeared along that path as well, interspaced along both walls.

"That sound must have been parts of the walls opening for these things," Macar said. "We've been walking past them all along. We just didn't know they were there."

"Which means," Jom said, "that they're everywhere. This place is filled with them."

NDX nodded. "It appears we will have to pass by them regardless."

On alert, they moved forward. As they approached each alcove, they slowed and, weapons ready, filed past. But the Syntries remained still. Another intersection, another decision, another quick cut to mark the way. As they turned the corner though, they heard something and froze. It was a subtle sound, easily missed if not for it echoing down the silent corridors of the maze.

"It sounds like someone is moving," Macar whispered. The others nodded. Moving slowly, they approached the first alcove. The Syntry was laying in its alcove as the others before except one leg was hanging down. Ravola stepped forward and leveled her sword at the creature but it did not move. They hurried past only to find the next Syntry in the same position. And the next.

"It's like they all move at the same time," Jom whispered as they hurried along.

Turning down the next corridor, they again heard the sound of movement. Ravola motioned for them to wait as she investigated. After a moment, she called them forward. The Syntry was again lying fully prone in its alcove.

"They went back the way they were," Macar said, looking into the next alcove a little way forward.

"Which suggests we are going the wrong way," NDX said.

Ravola nodded grimly. "It appears I do not have to mark our trail any longer. The closer we get to the center, the more these creatures will awaken."

"Meaning we'll have to fight an army of them to make it through," Macar said sourly.

"Do we have any other options?" Jom asked.

"It appears not," NDX replied. They went back to the intersection and chose a different path. Again, the Syntries responded so they moved forward. After another few turns, they again heard movement. The Syntries were now sitting in their alcoves. Ravola fingered her sword, tense from this threat of violence.

"We should kill them as we go," she said, eyeing the sitting creature. "Thin their numbers."

NDX shook its head. "Attacking them may set them all off immediately. I would prefer we not fight until absolutely necessary."

But they were all nervous, walking past these strange, silent creatures. Just as they got used to seeing the Syntries sitting as they walked past, they turned a corner and could see the creatures standing. Again, Ravola went first, approaching the creature with sword at the ready. But it did not attack. It simply stood in front of its alcove, staring at the opposite wall. Now they hurried past as a group, looking over their shoulders to make sure the Syntry didn't move. Jom could feel them watching him, even without eyes. His hands were clammy and he clutched his short sword tightly. He looked over his shoulder again and gasped.

"They moved!" he said, bringing them to a halt. They turned to see the Syntries standing now looking at them.

"And in front!" Macar said. They all swiveled around to see the creatures in the next corridor standing towards them as well.

"We must be getting close," NDX said.

As they approached, the creatures still remained motionless. They did not attempt to block passage. Once Jom and the others moved past though, they turned, as if they were watching the group. Steeling their nerves, they moved forward. After a few corridors, Jom noticed the creatures were not standing in front of their alcoves anymore and called a halt.

"Look! They're a few steps away from their alcoves," he pointed out.

"They are beginning to close in on us," Ravola said. She looked behind them at the Syntries they had just passed. "Look, even the ones behind us have moved towards us."

"We'll never get past them all," Macar said.

"We have to."

As they took a few steps forward though, the Syntries in front of them moved towards them. For each step the group took, the creatures took one as well, closing ranks. Finally, they were within striking distance of the first one and Ravola, eager for combat, swung her sword, taking off the head of the nearest Syntry with one clean swipe. A black, thick liquid poured from the body as it collapsed to the floor. As the head bounced across the corridor, the other Syntries tilted their heads back and a scream erupted around them. Looking around wildly, Jom saw the creatures behind them in the same position. But still they did not attack.

"Why aren't they coming for us?" Macar asked, pointing his blaster at the nearest one.

Ravola shrugged. "This one is dead, at least."

"Look!" Jom pointed to the body at their feet. Where the black liquid poured from the body, smoke curled around the metal of the floor. "The blood. It's eating away at the metal!"

"Acid. And a powerful acid at that if it can eat through such strong metal," NDX said, taking a step away from the pooling liquid.

"We need to go," Macar said.

Step for step, the Syntries approached them as they moved ahead. Ravola, dispatched each as they came within reach, careful to not let the black acid spill on her. Each time she killed one, the others screamed, as if they all felt the pain of the blade. As they went, the creatures continued their slow march forward. By the end of the corridor, the Syntries were already coming from the next passage. Smoke drifted around them and they heard the sizzling of the acid on the metal. NDX cautioned everyone to not breathe the vapors and they wrapped cloth around their mouths to protect themselves from the searing smoke.

"We have to move faster!" Jom yelled. "We'll get trapped by the acid!"

Nodding, Ravola ran ahead. The Syntries matched her stride for stride. But, instead of impaling them, Ravola leapt and slammed into the creatures, knocking them down and into one another. Jom and the others ran ahead, avoiding the long fingers that now reached out for them. Jom saw black acid dripping from the fingers of the Syntries and yelled a warning to the others. Macar joined Ravola in knocking the Syntries back so the others could run by. But the army of creatures grew in number. With horror, Jom looked back to see Syntries from other corridors advancing on them from behind as well. Soon, they would be overwhelmed by sheer numbers.

"We can't do this forever!" Macar exclaimed, narrowly avoiding a Syntry hand.

Jom grabbed his head with his hands and thought. Then, out of desperation, he sat down in the middle of the corridor and pulled the Mind Harp from his backpack.

"What are you doing?" Ravola asked, stepping close, sword ready. "It's too dangerous to stop. We need to keep moving."

"We have to try something," he responded. He tried to clear his mind of his fears and concentrate on finding a way out but the screams and yells around them distracted him. He gingerly placed fingers on the grooves for Bravery and Wisdom and closed his eyes. With a gentle strum, he opened his mind to the energies of the Harp.

He saw himself rise above his body. The ceiling of the hallway disappeared and he rose above the labyrinth. Further and further he rose, seeing more and more of the impossible maze they were stuck in. Corridors branched off in every direction with no logic or reason. He saw hundreds of Syntries walking the corridors of the maze, all converging on their location. He looked further out across the maze, astounded by how large it really was. It extended to the limits of his vision. They were in the middle of nowhere. Fighting down the despair, he willed his body forward, concentrating on finding the center. He saw it, ahead of them and cried out.

"This way!" he yelled. But they could not hear his psychic words. He looked down, memorizing as much as he could of the right passages to take, then dropped back into his body. His eyes flew open.

"I know the way! At least some of it."

"Lead on," Ravola said, helping him to his feet. Jom directed them as they pushed, shoved and stabbed their way through the screaming synthetic army. When Jom was unsure of the way, he halted the group and dove back into the Harp's world, getting a new perspective on the maze. As he used the Harp, it became easier for him to call up the power he needed to find their way. As he came back to his body, he held on to the vision, letting it overlay his normal sight. Soon, he was able to point the way using the Harp's power to guide him from his body. They made quick progress now through the labyrinth, slowed only by exhaustion and battles. Eventually, though, they reached a large circular room. They turned a corner and suddenly they found themselves in an immense room.

Jom immediately recognized it from his dreams. Hundreds of cages of different sizes and shapes were stacked all around the room. They were piled on top of each other and covered every available surface. Each held a different species but there were no noises coming from any of the cages. Jom looked into the nearest cage. A strange ten-legged feathered creature stared at him blankly. It took him a moment to realize that the creature was in some sort of stasis. He looked at the next cage. This one held something that was all long claws and mouths. But again, it did not move, frozen in a stasis field.

"Quick!" Jom said. "Look for a small furry animal. Its fur is black. Four legs. Short snout. And—and it's been blinded."

The others looked at him questioningly for a moment, then moved off in different directions, searching the various stasis cages for the creature. Jom heard movement coming from the labyrinth and gulped. They would be trapped in this room if they didn't get out quickly.

"Jom! Over here! I think I found it!" Jom ran over to Macar who was peering into a cage. "Is this it?"

Jom looked in and his heart leapt. Inside, perfectly suspended, was the Womf. It was thinner than he remembered from his dream and the fur around its snout had grey streaks now. Where its eyes once had been, there was only scar tissue. But it was alive. After so many cycles, it was alive. Jom looked around the cage.

"How do we open it?" he asked.

NDX was there in a moment, softly pushing him to the side. "Let me take a look," it said, its electronic voice gentle. It studied the stasis cage for a moment. "It appears to be a simple amber field. Disabling it should only take a moment."

"We may not have that long," Ravola said. The others looked at her. She pointed towards the entrance of the room. The entrance to the room was blocked with hundreds of Syntries. They crowded into the room, arms outstretched, fingers dripping black acid that sizzled as it ate away at the metal. Slowly they approached, cutting off any hope for escape.

"Now what?" Macar asked, gripping his sword tightly.

"I—I don't know," Jom admitted.

: Reunion :

RAVOLA AND MACAR STEPPED in front of Jom, weapons ready as the synthetic army slowly advanced. NDX quickly touched buttons on a small control pad on the side of the stasis cage. Nebt stood near Jom, looking intently at the Womf suspended in the cage. Jom fingered the hilt of his short sword nervously, wishing he still had his rusted sun dagger. But it was lost amid the ruins of the Obelisk, a sacrifice for the Harp that hummed quietly in his mind and his pack. He steeled his nerves and stepped forward, joining Ravola and Macar.

A loud shriek split the air shattering Jom's thoughts. Out of the darkness, a geyser of smoky liquid erupted from the empty space between them and flew through the air at the Syntries. Jom watched as a Water Banshee tore through one of the creatures, its fluid claws gouging out deep valleys of fake flesh as it flew by. The Syntry screamed in pain and dropped to its knees. The Water Banshee disappeared into the flank of the second creature with a splash, emerging a heartbeat later from the other side of its torso. It was dead before it hit the floor—its internal organs taken to another plane in the blink of an eye. The spirit weaved around the Syntries, a primal force of shrieks and death. The creatures screamed as the Banshee circled around, swiping at them with its own long talons. Chunks of flesh flew about and Jom and the others had to protect themselves from airborne bits of acid-ridden synthetic flesh. The screams of the dying monsters were indistinguishable from the screams of the spirit. The Banshee made quick work of the entire army, slicing them to ribbons efficiently and mercilessly. Soon, there was an impassible barrier of remains, keeping the thousands of Syntries still out in the maze at bay.

The Syntries, what little remained of them, collapsed onto the metal floor amid pooling acid and viscera. The Banshee wheeled through the air and turned towards Jom and the others, its face a terrible mask of fury. Ravola lifted her sword, her face grim and determined. But NDX quickly stepped forward, blocking her attack.

"Dianat!" it said loudly, "it is good to see you!"

Confused, Ravola lowered her weapon slightly. Macar kept his sword up though, Jom noticed, surely remembering his last encounter with the spirit.

"Dianat?" Jom looked at the Water Banshee closely. In the gloom of the room, it was impossible for him to say for sure it was their friend.

"The Master knew you would come!" she shrieked, her words echoing loudly off the walls of the room.

"Of course!" NDX said. "After leaving us, you went back to Abla'than'abla, didn't you?"

"Yes!"

Jom's ears hurt from the Water Banshee's shrieks. But there was another sound in the room. Concentrating, he heard a small whimper. He looked down to see the Womf peering out from the now-deactivated stasis cage. It was trembling in fear from the back of its cage as it cautiously sniffed the room. Jom bent down slowly.

"It's all right," he said softly. "You're safe now."

The Womf looked up at the sound of his voice and moved further back into the cage, pressing itself against the far wall. Jom slowly extended a hand out, murmuring reassurances while he did so. The Womf sniffed at his hand, cringing. Jom smiled despite himself.

"You're safe. Nothing is going to hurt you anymore," he whispered, letting the Womf get used to his smell. He reached into his pack and pulled out a hard piece of bread. He extended his hand, offering the bread to the frightened creature. The Womf smelled it, then quickly grabbed it with its small mouth. Two bites and the bread was swallowed. Jom laughed and fed it another piece, then another.

"It must have been ages since it last ate," Ravola said from over his shoulder.

The Womf let out a small squeak at the sound of her voice and scuttled backwards into the cage again. Jom offered more bread, gradually coaxing it closer. He looked up at the others, a smile on his face and tears in his eyes.

"He's going to be all right?"

They nodded in agreement.

"We're all going to be all right," Ravola said, crouching next to him. "But I don't think we should stay here for long. There are still many dangers about."

"Actually," Macar said from across the room. "I think we're safe enough for the moment." He touched a pad near the entrance and a heavy metal door slid into place, slicing through the remains of the Syntries, sealing them within the room. A strong fan in the ceiling sucked the deadly vapor of the acid from the room, leaving nothing but synthetic flesh cooling on the floor. "I think this door will hold for a while, even with the acid eating away at it. But let's not take too long."

NDX nodded. "Then let us rest here for a short while before continuing."

They made themselves comfortable. Ravola dug out a few dried fruits. NDX placed its severed arm in the center of their circle and Jom was pleased when it emitted a comfortable heat. They gathered around and settled in for a rest. Jom thanked Dianat for coming for them and introduced her to Nebt and Ravola.

"I apologize, Dianat," NDX said to the spirit that flitted about the edges of the light. "I had to leave your vial behind."

"Perhaps this will work?" Macar said. Nebt was holding out a small cylindrical container to him. He took it from the Latuip and held it up. Dianat gave a shriek of delight and poured into it. Macar's hands shook as the Water Banshee entered the container but did not drop it. Once Dianat was safely inside, he screwed the top on and gingerly handed it over to NDX.

"Thank you. That will suffice."

Jom closed his eyes, enjoying the warmth and the talk, almost forgetting the danger they were in. He felt something in his lap and looked down. The Womf had crawled into his lap and curled up, fast asleep. Jom laughed quietly and the others looked at him.

"You wouldn't think he'd be tired after sleeping for so long," he said to them.

"He?" Ravola raised an eyebrow.

Jom nodded. "I think so."

"And what are you going to call him?" Macar asked.

Jom thought about it for a moment. "Pula. It means 'Little Dreamer.'"

Ravola smiled through her fabric. "I like that." One of her tentacles reached over and gently stroked the Womf's head. It murmured at the touch and nestled further into his lap.

"What I don't understand," Macar said, "is how that little thing will lead us to the chair we're looking for."

"NDX, can Dianat take us to it?" Jom asked, deflecting the question for a moment while he gathered his thoughts. "She was our original guide, after all."

The clock-work boy was silent for a moment as it communicated with the Water Banshee by means beyond Jom's understanding. Then it looked up at them.

"She tells me that the energy signature of the Chair is no longer where it was. It has been moved since she was last here."

"Great." Macar snorted. "So we have a Latuip who can't tell us anything, a pet that can't see anything, and a Water Banshee who doesn't know anything. Terrific."

Jom shot him a look of irritation but said nothing. Instead, he looked down at Pula, softly stroking his fur. "When I dreamt of the Chair," he began, "I felt that a connection was forged between the Chair and Pula here. He was one of the first to feel the full effects of the chair and it made a link of some sort with him. I think I can use that connection to lead us to where it's hidden."

"He's been in stasis for a very long time," NDX pointed out. "How can you be sure there's still a connection?"

Jom shook his head. "Stasis didn't break the hold. I—I felt him suffering ever since I had the dream. He's been hurting the whole time."

"It is a miracle he is still whole," Ravola murmured.

"He's not. At least, not yet. But that's why I had to save him. I couldn't let him suffer any longer."

"You did the right thing," Macar said, an odd tone in his voice.

"It is settled then. Once we are rested, Jom will attempt to lead us to the Chair. I suggest we all get some sleep."

"Are we safe here?" Jom asked, eyeing the door.

NDX nodded. "I believe so. My sensors will alert us if anything attempts to break into the room."

And with that, they settled in for some much needed rest. Jom carefully lay down on the hard floor, gently moving Pula into his arms. The Womf murmured quietly and snuggled in closer to his chest, breathing a long sigh of contentment.

The Story That Had Never Been Told

JOM TOSSED AND TURNED as, one by one, the others drifted off to sleep. His eyes wandered around the room, seeing the shadows of all the cages scattered about the room. His thoughts turned to the other victims of the horrible experiments that had gone on here. His gaze slid across the shadowed figures of his friends and landed on Nebt. The small man was sitting by himself a little distance from them. His eyes glittered in the darkness and Jom realized the Latuip was awake and staring at him. Propping himself up on an elbow, careful not to wake the sleeping Womf, Jom regarded the strange man.

"Thank you for your help," Jom said quietly. Nebt nodded once, a small smile crossing his face.

"Tell me about yourself. Can you do that?" Nebt tilted his head, considering Jom's words. Finally, with a quick nod, he got to his feet and shuffled closer to Jom. Sitting back down, Nebt held Jom's gaze for a moment, as if considering how much he would reveal to the young boy, then his eyes sparkled and Jom's mind exploded.

Two suns spun around a gas planet, one white and the other blue. The planet had no solid ground, no core; it was just a dense ball of chemicals that gradually dispersed into the nether. Graceful cities shaped like spheres hung in the haze of the planet's atmosphere, held aloft by great engines that used the gas of the planet to push against the weak gravity. Inside the spheres, safe from the toxic gases that surrounded their cities, the Latuips lived. Besides the engines, the only other sounds of the cities were the hum of the machines that scoured the universe for knowledge. Countless arrays, antennas, telescopes, and other instruments poked from the shell of the spheres, looking out into the galaxy. Events were observed, studied and recorded in a massive network that crisscrossed the planet like a web. The Latuips moved quietly through among the machines, analyzing, interpreting and observing. Nothing in the universe escaped their attention.

Jom watched as youngsters, their skin a smooth, light red, spent the endless days of their childhoods studying. Their instruction was constant and pervasive. They swam in a river of data, absorbing everything that was put in front of them as their elders looked on, one eye on their charges and the other on new information as it came in. The sphere cities of the Latuips were the largest repositories of knowledge in the universe. Its citizens did nothing but memorize and learn. Their lives were dedicated to knowledge and facts.

Jom's vision focused on a young Latuip standing before a group of adults. Without needing to be told, Jom knew he was watching Nebt, many, many cycles ago. Although they spoke no words, Jom could hear everything that passed telepathically between them.

"It is time for you to go on a Gathering," they told him.

Nebt nodded his head. He knew this time would come, as it did for many. He tried to keep his face from breaking out into a prideful smile. Only the best students were sent on a Gathering. He was to be sent out among the stars to see that which could not be seen from their home. Even with all their sensors and machines, there were some events, some knowledge that simply had to be gathered in person. To experience and report, to catalogue and record, and then to bring that information back to the homeworld, that was the duty of the brightest and best of the Laptuips. He had been an exceptional student. This was his reward, to see first-hand the wonders of the universe and bring that knowledge back to his home.

"In order to protect our world, we must now do that which is forbidden."

The thought-words chilled him. Nebt steeled himself. Every Latuip dreaded this moment. The Rite of the First Questions.

His entire life had, up until now, been spent learning and absorbing the knowledge of the universe. But, because of their nature, this learning was done without questioning. No Latuip asked another a question, for the knowledge would leave the one and enter the other. Nothing new would be gained, only transferred. This was anathema. Knowledge was to be shared, not hoarded. But now, he would have to suffer through the worst test of their society.

"What is the name of this planet?"

Nebt gasped as the knowledge was torn from his mind and taken by the elder. He felt a hole in his brain. He felt incomplete.

"How do you get to your home planet?"

"What system are you from?"

"Which sector is your planet?"

On and on it went. The elders asked him any question that could lead others back to their planet. If an outsider ever discovered where they lived, their society would be destroyed, their people taken, their precious knowledge forever hoarded and eventually forgotten. Finally, after an endless series of questions, they stopped. Nebt cried as he lay on the cold stone, feeling around in his mind for something that was no longer there. He wept for what was lost to him forever.

Gentle hands picked him up and wiped his tears. A small object was pressed into his palm. Nebt looked down at it. It was a pendant.

"This will bring you back to us, when you are ready. Hold it and say 'home'. Only you can activate it. Keep it safe."

Jom's vision pulled back and he watched Nebt rocket out into the universe. The young Latuip explored the universe, traveling from one end of the stars to the other. He saw planets born and planets die. He witnessed wars and violence but also beauty beyond comprehension. As he traveled, he observed and remembered. Thousands of cycles came and went and still he did not return to his home planet. He was fascinated by the variety and wonder of the cosmos.

Latuips live a very long time. But they are not immortal. Jom watched as his skin deepened in color and wrinkles slowly etched their stories on his skin. Time spun around him and Nebt grew old, as most things must. Finally, fate

212

caught up to him and he was captured.

It happened quickly. One moment, he was observing an asteroid destroy a primitive planet from one of its moons, the next he was grabbed by three Roxxians—large rock-like creatures who are known across the galaxy for both their ferocity and their art—who took him to their planet. Nebt was strapped into a chair and pelleted with questions. The priest sculptors of Roxx took turns asking him questions about every subject they could conceive. Not since the Rite of the First Questions had Nebt been traumatized so horribly. Bit by bit, the majority of his knowledge was ripped from his brain to be scribbled down on the Roxxian slate scrolls.

Many cycles later, after the priest sculptors had exhausted their questions, Nebt was dropped off at a space port, hardly more than an empty shell of his former self. Various creatures came upon him, asking him questions. But he had hardly any answers to give and was pushed to the side, useless and forgotten. Then he was found by Macar and taken to Kala Azar.

Jom blinked as the vision faded from his eyes. He rubbed his eyes as they cleared. Nebt sat across from him, waiting patiently for Jom to recover. Finally, Jom, careful not to wake Pula, reached over and squeezed the small Latuip's hand.

"I'm so sorry. I didn't realize how much pain it causes you to answer questions."

Nebt smiled a small, sad smile.

"I promise I won't ask you anything unless it's really important. Is that all right."

Nebt nodded once, patted Jom's hand, then lay down to sleep.

: Following the Ribbon :

JOM WOKE TO SOMETHING licking his face. He opened his eyes, saw Pula and smiled. The Womf was sitting on him, eagerly licking him awake. He laughed and pushed him off his chest but Pula came back at him.

"Are you hungry?" he asked between giggles. The Womf gave him one last lick, then sniffed about for food. Jom sat up and looked around. The others were scattered about the room. NDX was studying some of the control consoles. Nebt stood quietly off to the side, watching as always, his dark eyes reflecting everything he saw. Macar paced the room, idly looking through the equipment, presumably hunting for useful items to salvage. Ravola sat in the middle of the room with Dianat's container in her lap. She was speaking quietly with the Water Banshee. Curious, Jom cleared his throat and she looked up.

"How can you talk with her?" he asked, absently breaking off a piece of bread for Pula.

"She speaks on a higher frequency than you can hear," Ravola explained. "But my ears are slightly more sensitive."

"How is she?"

Ravola smiled through her fabric. "She is well. And she appreciates your concern. After she took the bomb from Macar's body, she tunneled through the dimensions. She released the bomb before it exploded. But the shockwave knocked her through the aether and she had a long way to travel through the planes. By the time she made her way back to the ship, you had escaped. So she went back to her Master for further instructions and he sent her here."

Jom nodded. "Thank you again, Dianat."

Ravola nodded. "She says you would do the same."

Jom blushed and concentrated on playing with Pula for a short time.

Eventually, everyone slowly moved closer and Jom knew it was time to go. He looked from face to face, seeing their confidence in him.

"I—I don't really know if this is going to work," he began. "But I think we should stay close with each other. Just in case."

"Dianat says that, although she cannot encompass all of us, she can provide a buffer of sorts," Ravola relayed. Jom nodded and Ravola opened the container while he sat down. Dianat erupted from the container like a screaming geyser and swirled around them, herding them closer. Jom placed the Harp on the floor in front of him and picked Pula up, setting him in his lap. Pula gave a short squeak and licked his hand. Macar, NDX and Nebt all came in close. Ravola stood over Jom, reaching her tentacles out to the others. They all grabbed hold and she placed her hands on Jom's shoulders. Dianat extended her body around them, enclosing them within her smoky protection. Jom could see through her—she was stretched thin in an attempt to protect them all. He took a deep breath and concentrated.

He placed his fingers on all the Harp's chords. He didn't know what was going to happen and wanted to be ready for anything. He closed his eyes and concentrated on Pula. Lightly brushing the Harp, Jom's vision opened. He saw the Womf in his lap, looking at him with unseeing eyes. Jom suddenly realized that Pula had sight after all, despite his eyes getting burned out. He saw the world around him in a way Jom never could. Pula, like all Womfs, could see souls. That was why he had been captured in the first place. He had been the perfect candidate for the Shield's experiments. He saw souls and, with the power of the Chair, could burn them as well.

Jom's heart expanded in his chest as he communicated with Pula. Their words were looks and thoughts, enhanced by the power of the Harp. Jom told Pula how he knew of his suffering from his dream and how he had to rescue him, had to free him from the endless torture he was enduring. Pula nudged Jom's arm in appreciation. Then, taking a deep breath, Jom told Pula of what he needed to do.

We need to find the chair that hurt you, he said in his mind. If we don't, others will find it and use it to hurt others like you were hurt. Will you help us?

Pula whimpered and burrowed deeper into his lap. His small body shook from the thought of the Chair. Jom placed a hand on Pula's head, gently stroking his thick fur. Pula whimpered again. Then he looked at Jom and licked his arm. He was afraid. But he trusted Jom.

I know you've been hurt so, so bad. I know you still hurt. I promise I will protect you. No one will ever hurt you like that again.

Pula licked him again. Jom looked up. He strummed the Harp again, letting his vision expand. He thought about Pula and all the horrible things that had happened to him. A tear escaped his eye and ran down his face as he concentrated. He felt the warmth of Pula's small body next to him. He saw the energies of his friends around him. Then, he shuddered. There was something in the air. Some strange energy that made him shiver. Jom touched the Strength and Bravery cords and his vision grew stronger. He could see a small, thin line of green energy snake around them. It was evil. Pure evil. Jom knew immediately that it was the energy of the Phobetor Chair. Pula whimpered in his lap, sensing Jom's recognition of the energy, and placed a small paw on Jom's arm, giving him strength. A thin offshoot of the energy was connected to Pula. Jom focused on the ribbon of sickly green energy. It twisted about the room, like a ribbon in water, before disappearing. Jom looked at the point where the ribbon vanished and strummed the Harp again. The veil between planes parted and he saw the ribbon flow out of this plane into another.

"We're going through the dimensions," he said out loud. "NDX, project your force shield as far out as you can. Dianat, encircle us. Everyone stay as close together as possible."

He heard the others prepare and he concentrated on following the ribbon through the dimensions. He saw Dianat's and NDX's energies wrap around them. Pula climbed up onto his shoulder and he set the Harp in his lap. Everyone crowded in close, grasping each other tightly. He pushed them forward, as one. A part of his brain felt his body lift from the floor but he ignored the physical sensations, focusing entirely on the ribbon of evil energy. He kept strumming Loyalty and Strength as they began to move through the air, held together by their combined efforts. Then, without hesitating, they plunged through the veil into the space between space.

He felt the world shudder around him as they passed through the membrane. He remembered his previous trips through the planes and shivered involuntarily. Pula nuzzled his neck, letting him know he wasn't alone. Jom pushed them on, following the ribbon as it meandered through the dimensions. They passed from one plane to another and another, pursuing the energy of the Chair. Jom kept his eyes closed tightly but could hear wind and screams, rain and laughter as they moved from one plane to the next. He felt creatures dart out of the aether at them. But between NDX's shield and Dianat's claws, they were quickly repelled. He pulled them along as fast as he could, using the sickly green energy as a rope to pull them along. As they moved, he saw the ribbon slowly grow in size, becoming stronger and stronger. He knew they were getting closer. He kept moving as quickly as he could, not wanting to spend any more time in the aether than necessary. Some part of his brain registered Dianat's screams as she fought off Slicers and other denizens of the aether. The tendril continued to grow in strength. Jom pulled them forward.

Pula squeaked and brushed against his neck. Jom tried to calm him while maintaining his hold on the ribbon. But the Womf squeaked again louder. He pawed at Jom's ear, forcing Jom to turn his head.

That's when he saw they were being pursued.

Travelling along the ribbon behind them was a black bird-like shadow. Wide wings flared out on either side, flapping madly in the aether as it pursued them. Although he couldn't see any details in the shadowy figure, Jom instantly knew who it was that was coming for them: The Shadow Saint.

With ice in his heart, he pushed them on, strumming the Harp faster. A surge of adrenaline exploded through him. He felt a shudder as they dropped out of the aether onto a new plane of existence and he willed everyone to hold on. The ribbon continued to grow in size and he pulled them forward as fast as he could. The energy of the ribbon burned him as it grew in intensity. He could feel the evil radiate off it and wanted nothing more than to let go, forgetting he ever knew of it. But he didn't let go. He had to drag them onward. They had to find the Chair before it was too late. He glanced over his shoulder. The Shadow Saint was quickly gaining on them. Steeling his nerves, he grasped at the ribbon and pulled them along as fast as he could, ignoring the searing iciness that burned his soul.

Pula gave out a loud squeak of warning and Jom looked back just in time to see the shadow surge forward. A talon reached out of the darkness. Jom cried out just as the shadowy claw grabbed at them, knocking them off course. They tumbled through the air, jarring to a sudden stop. NDX's shield bent at the impact, just barely protecting them from the force of landing. They hit the ground hard, scattering apart. His concentration broken, the energy of the Harp faded. Jom's eyes flew open and he lost sight of the ribbon even as the darkness descended on them.

: The Dark Wild :

JOM GRABBED PULA AS they hit and tucked him against his chest. They rolled across a hard surface. His shoulder exploded in pain. The Mind Harp flew out of his reach, bouncing off into the darkness. Jom felt his body come to a rest but couldn't move; the landing had knocked the breath out of him. Pula whimpered and squirmed in his arms and Jom relaxed his grip. The Womf fell to the ground next to Jom, wobbling from the impact. Jom's vision swam. Shadows leapt about in front of his eyes. He heard moans and groans from the others but couldn't see anything in the darkness.

Then, a small light flickered into existence. NDX held up its arm, shining a weak light about them. Jom shook his head, clearing his sight. Everyone was accounted for, scattered about like so many rag dolls.

"Is—is everyone all right?" Jom asked between sucking in deep breaths of air.

"Why can't we have a soft landing once in a while?" Macar asked, holding his head and getting unsteadily to his feet.

Jom looked around. They were surrounded by darkness. There was no light other than NDX's, and that was unsteady. Jom looked at the clock-work boy.

"Are you hurt?" he asked. NDX swiveled its head around erratically.

"I still function," it replied. "My internal gyroscope is recalibrating. I will be fine. Although I suggest we leave this place immediately."

"What do you sense?"

"Danger," Ravola answered. She peered into the shadows, sword and dagger in hand. "We are not alone here."

Jom held his breath and then he heard it—scuffles and footfalls in the darkness around them.

"Something is out there!" he whispered sharply.

"Many somethings, if my scanners are accurate," NDX responded.

The darkness that surrounded them was too thick for Jom's eyes to pierce but he trusted his companions. He picked up Pula and put the Womf on his shoulder, then scanned the area for the Mind Harp. He saw it lying on its side at the edge of the weak light's reach. Even as he started towards it, a slithering slimy tentacle snaked out of the darkness and wrapped around the Harp. Jom gave a shout as the Harp was pulled out of the light and into the shadows beyond.

Ravola leapt forward. She hurtled her dagger as she vaulted through the air. The blade flew through the intervening distance, connecting with an audible thunk with whatever lurked in the dark. A high-pitched scream rent the air. Ravola landed near the edge of the light and reached forward, retrieving the Harp, dripping with thick clear ooze, and her dagger, dripping with thin green blood. As she turned to give the Harp to Jom, three more thick tentacles shot out of the dark and wrapped around her body.

Dianat's shriek pierced the darkness and the tentacles holding Ravola shuddered, loosening slightly. It was enough for her to use her own tentacles to pry her sword hand free. With a flash of steel, one of the creature's appendages dropped to the ground, spurting green blood on her red-wrapped legs. Dianat screamed again. Jom thought he saw the Water Banshee as she attacked the monster from the darkness but couldn't be sure. It was one shadow attacking another. Ravola backed into the light, holding her dripping sword at the ready while Dianat dispatched the creature.

Then another yell caught his attention. He turned to see Macar waving his sword menacingly as two crab-like creatures emerged from the shadows behind them. Large sharp pincers snapped the air in front of him, each easily large enough to cleave him in two.

"I need some help here!" Macar yelled, barely dodging a pincer.

Jom drew his short sword and ran towards him. Pula clung to his shoulder tightly, whimpering in his ear. One of the creatures turned its eye stalks towards Jom and shifted to intercept him. Jom skidded to a halt well out of range and flourished his dagger. Pincers snapped the air and the creature scuttled forward on short legs, ready to slice him in half. From the side, a rock struck the carapace of the creature. Jom looked to see Nebt hefting another rock, a peculiar smile on his face. He wound up his small arm and launched the rock, striking the monster in an eye. Jom jumped forward while the creature was stunned and sliced through the eye stalk with one swipe of his dagger. The creature squealed and hurried back into the shadows, pincers snapping furiously.

The light flickered, reducing their area of safety. Jom and Macar stepped back, holding the other crab creature at bay.

"NDX! Can you brighten the light?" Jom yelled over his shoulder. But the light did not grow stronger. He turned to see the clock-work boy on one knee. It was barely able to hold its arm up for the others and the light continued to flicker and dim.

"NDX!" Jom ran over to the automaton.

"My apologies," NDX said, looking at Jom with its gold eyes. "I am afraid I am unable to help you."

Jom looked down in horror at its chest. The clock had wound down. NDX struggled to its feet with Jom's help.

"NDX, why didn't you say something?"

"The trip through the aether affected my...internal chronometer. This...this was unexpected. Only...only the Master knows how to extend time. There...there was nothing....nothing you could do..."

With a last burst of energy, NDX brightened the light, flooding the area with intense white light. Creatures in every direction shrieked and ducked back into the shadows. But then the light faded out and they were left in utter darkness.

"What happened?" Macar screamed.

"It's NDX! His clock has run out!" Jom felt the tears in his eyes but ignored them.

"Dianat!" Ravola yelled. "Where are you?"

"Here!" came the reply and Jom felt something brush past him. The Water Banshee screamed as it circled them, keeping the creatures at bay.

Jom felt something on his arm and jumped, but Ravola's spoke into his ear.

"It is me," she reassured him.

"Macar! Nebt! Come to me!" Jom yelled. "Keep as tight as possible. Dianat is protecting us but we need to stay close!"

"We need light!" Macar's voice said from his right.

Dianat screamed in warning. Ravola's tentacle wrapped tighter around Jom's wrist. Pula whimpered in his ear. Suddenly, Dianat's scream was cut short.

"We need...." Ravola began. Jom heard a sound. It was the same sound he had heard as a child watching the butcher of his village. The sound of steel cutting through meat.

"You need a miracle," a voice said. Ravola's tentacle slid off his wrist. A red light flared to life. Standing over Ravola's body was the Shadow Saint. Dianat was held in some sort of stasis bubble behind him. A dark stain slowly spread out from the middle of Ravola's back. Her blood dripped from the end of the Saint's sword.

"You need a miracle," he repeated.

: Casualties :

THE SHADOW SAINT REACHED down and casually wiped Ravola's blood from Talonn on the fabric that covered her.

"You've been quite a bother, you know," he said to Jom.

Pula let out a low growl from Jom's shoulder.

"How nice. A pet." Even though the darkness hid his features, Jom knew the Saint was smiling underneath his hooded cloak, barely seen among the swirling shadows that bled from his ebony blade. Jom instinctively put a hand on Pula to still him. He fingered his dagger with his other hand. He glanced down at Ravola's body. She wasn't moving and the dark stain of blood grew, spreading over her back. He choked back tears and willed his knees to stay steady.

The Saint lifted his head slightly as Macar and Nebt stepped into the red light. Macar gave a cry of anguish at the sight of

Ravola's body and hefted his weapon. Nebt brushed against Jom's side and Jom glanced down. The Latuip was staring at him intently, an odd sparkle in his eyes. Nebt reached up and Jom passed Pula to him. The Womf gave another low growl but settled in Nebt's arms. Jom turned away but Nebt nudged him again, more insistent. Jom suddenly realized what the small man was attempting to do. He thought quickly.

"I still don't understand why you're hunting us," he said to the Shadow Saint.

"I told you," the assassin replied. "I'm being paid to. Quite handsomely, I might add."

"You won't succeed," Jom said, hoping his voice sounded confident.

The Saint laughed. "I believe I already have."

"No." Jom shook his head. "There's a way to stop you." He looked down quickly at the Latuip, making contact with Nebt's eyes. "Isn't there?"

Nebt shrugged as if to say 'close enough' and Jom's mind exploded. He grit his teeth, keeping both eyes riveted to the Saint as his brain was flooded with images. He felt like his entire head was on fire but he did not take his eyes off the shadowy figure in front of him. In the space of a heartbeat, he knew what he had to do. His heart jumped into his throat and his hands turned clammy. A cold feeling of dread came over him at the thought of what lay before him. But his friends' lives were at stake. He had to save them. He had to protect Pula. He lifted his head and stared at the dark figure in front of him.

"Step away from my friend." Jom glared at the Saint in defiance. The Saint glanced down at the body at his feet. He nudged her with his boot.

"I don't think she cares anymore."

Macar stepped forward. "Don't you touch her you animal!" he yelled. The Saint turned his attention to Macar.

"Are you ready to join her?" he asked in a hiss, raising his black blade, the darkness flowing around him like a living entity. Macar took another step forward. Jom threw his dagger. The Saint easily deflected the small blade. Macar leapt, bringing his weapon down hard. But the Saint was ready and parried Macar's attack. Jom rushed forward. The Saint stepped back, swinging his sword in a wide arc to keep Jom at bay. But Jom didn't pull up in time. He was caught by the tip of Talonn and rolled to the ground. Macar shouted and renewed his attack on the Saint.

Jom looked down to see a deep gash in his arm. Blood flowed from the wound freely and his hand tingled. He got to his feet in a daze. Macar and the Saint were engaged in a fierce battle. Jom knew Macar wouldn't last more than a handful of heartbeats against the assassin. He looked around and spotted Dianat, helpless in the binding spell. Jom cupped his wound with his hand, letting his palm fill with blood. Then he flung the blood at the Water Banshee. Scarlet drops rained down on the binding spell. Dianat let out a liquidy howl as the blood covered the magical field caging her. Then she began to spin within her prison. She screamed as she battered at the spell. Jom's blood stuck to the field, covering it in red. But more importantly than that, the magic was covered in liquid. Dianat spun faster and faster, creating a stronger and stronger pull. The blood on the outside began to flow, pulled along by the strength of Dianat's movement.

The blood moved faster and faster, gaining momentum even as Dianat increased her speed on the inside. Soon, the blood was spinning around the outside of the spell faster than Jom could see. With one last surge, Dianat struck the binding spell. The magic, weakened on both sides by the force of the liquid, cracked ever so slightly. Dianat immediately flowed through the fissure into the blood. The crack exploded from the force and the spell disintegrated with a flash.

With a terrible scream, Dianat launched herself at the Saint. The Saint, taken by surprise by the eruption of his spell, staggered back out of reach of Macar's blade just as the Water Banshee slammed into him. Without realizing it, Jom dropped to his knees as the blood continued to gush from his wound. He watched as the ebony blade of the Shadow Saint danced through the watery essence of the Banshee. The Saint slashed and spun, narrowly avoiding Dianat's claws as she flowed around him like a whirlpool, swimming through the darkness of the assassin's blade. They were a blur of motion as they parried back and forth. Jom shook his head, trying to focus. He still had work to do. The battle between Dianat and the Saint was a stand-off at best. He could not hurt her but neither could she get any serious blows past his defenses.

Jom staggered back up to his feet and cast his eyes around the battlefield. He saw the Mind Harp on the ground. The Saint and Dianat were between him and the Harp though. Grimacing from the pain, he stumbled forward, trying to outflank the combatants. As the battle raged, Macar circled, slashing at the Saint whenever he saw an opportunity. The Shadow Saint easily parried both Macar's blade and Dianat's claws, dancing around them on lithe feet. Pula barked behind him and Jom turned. The Womf was struggling to get out of Nebt's arms and run to him. Jom held up his hand.

"No, Pula. Stay with Nebt. Stay safe. I'll be all right." But even as he spoke, he felt a wave of dizziness roll over him. He steadied his feet and blinked away the tears. He smiled at Pula. Even though the Womf couldn't see Jom, Pula whimpered, encouraging him despite his fear.

Jom turned around and stumbled forward. His vision blurred as he walked. Dianat was a storm of liquid smoke, roiling though the air around her opponent. The Saint's ebony blade and dark cloak swirled around him as he dodged attack after attack. Jom dodged to the side, avoiding an errant slash as the battle rolled towards him. His leg gave out and he tumbled to the hard ground. He barely rolled out of the way. He was near the edge of the light and stopped himself from entering the shadows that surrounded them. He heard scrapes and moans from the darkness beyond. Jom scrambled back from the dark, avoiding the grasping talons and claws from the creatures of the dark. He crawled forward, trying to keep away from both the unseen monsters and the combatants. Danger was on all sides but he blinked again, clearing his vision and kept moving. Then, with effort, he pushed himself a few more steps before collapsing from exhaustion.

Even as he lay there, he felt something under his hand. He looked up and saw the Mind Harp. His fingers curled around the

Harp, bringing it closer to him. The symbols on the Harp swam in his field of vision. He concentrated, turning the Harp over until he found the glyph for Strength. He strummed the chord with bloody fingers. A surge of energy shot through his body and his vision cleared. He strummed again, letting the power of the Harp give him the strength he needed to do what needed to be done. Once more he strummed, feeling almost whole again.

He looked up. Neither the Saint nor Dianat showed any sign of exhaustion. But Macar swung his sword slower and Jom could clearly see him waning. They were running out of time. Jom took a deep breath and got to his feet, cradling the Harp. He wiped the blood off his hands and steadied his nerves. Then, looking at the battle, he strummed the Harp, focusing on the Saint and himself. The energies around him overlaid his vision but he didn't close his eyes this time. He didn't shut out the reality of what was happening. He glanced down at Ravola's body. He looked to NDX's inert form. He saw Macar barely able to hold his sword, yet continuing to fight. He saw Pula shivering from fright in Nebt's arms on the other side of the battlefield. And he saw Dianat desperately fighting for all their lives. He strummed the Harp again, letting the energies flow around him, picking up strength. He formed an image in his mind, an image he had seen in his dreams. He plucked at the Harp, offering up his own body's lifeforce to power the magic of the Harp.

Then, when he couldn't sustain it any longer, he released the energies. They shot forward, grabbing the Shadow Saint in their unbreakable embrace. The Saint yelled in surprise as he was lifted off the ground. Jom felt his body rise in the air as well, moving towards his nemesis. The Saint struggled, slashing at the force that held him. Jom strummed the chords and a rift opened in front of him. Moving quickly, Jom plunged through the rift with the Saint in tow. Once through, Jom willed the rift closed before anyone--not his friends, not the creatures of the dark, not the denizens on the other side—could track it and come through.

: Fighting Shadows :

TOM PUSHED THEM THROUGH the aether, searching for a particular energy. The planes flashed by rapidly as they tumbled through the dimensions. The aether swirled around them in an explosion of color and sound and smell. Lights became stars before exploding into nothing. Time bent, becoming the future before turning into the past and vice versa. He felt his body being torn in a thousand directions. Every movement felt like he was in multiple places at once. Some small part of his brain registered that this was the first time he traveled through the aether without Dianat's help. He wished she was here now. But it was for her, and everyone

else, that he was here now alone. No, not alone. He concentrated on the dark figure behind him. He kept the Shadow Saint tightly held as he searched for a particular tendril of energy among the countless strands of reality. Finally, he saw what he was looking for and they fell through reality, landing in daylight.

They found themselves on the roof of a tall building in the middle of an abandoned city. Great spires of stone rose all around them towards the heavens. The city went as far as the horizon in three directions. In the fourth direction, a tall stone wall stood between the city and the empty landscape beyond, stretching as far as the eye could see. They stood on a circular roof high above the throughways below. A brisk wind whipped across Jom's face and he shivered. The building they were on was tall, rising high into the dim light of day. No birds cried out, despite their height nor did any people move below. As far as Jom could see the city was deserted. And yet he knew they would be found quickly enough by the inhabitants. He had to act quickly. He turned to look at the Shadow Saint.

The Saint slowly stood to his full height. His ebony sword was gripped loosely in one hand. As always, Jom saw little of his features behind his thick cloak and the darkness that clung to him like a fog.

"You hasten your own death," the Saint said matter-of-factly. "Without your friends to protect you, you cannot hope to win against me."

"I've already won," Jom replied, clutching the Harp to his chest.

"Your toy will not protect you from me," the Saint said, nodding to the Harp. "I've already shown you I can beat its power."

"Maybe so. But I didn't bring you here to fight you."

The Shadow Saint stopped. There was something in Jom's voice that made him hesitate. "Where have you brought me?" he asked, peering out over the cityscape.

"Somewhere you can't hurt my friends," Jom replied.

The Saint laughed. "Haven't you been paying attention, boy? I can track anyone across the planes. Once I'm done with you, I will hunt them down and kill them. You only delay the inevitable."

Jom shook his head. "You won't leave here."

The Saint looked around again, his instincts warning him of danger.

"Where are we?" he asked again.

Jom gazed out at the city. Not only were there no citizens in sight, there was no color either. No splashes of fabric or colorful transports. No advertisements. No banners or flags fluttered in the wind. Nothing.

Only grey.

Slowly, realization dawned on the Saint. He stared about, then turned his eyes to Jom.

"You fool!" he hissed. "You utter and complete fool! What have you done?" He took a step towards Jom. Jom backed up. The rooftop they were on was not large, only a dozen or so paces across. He soon reached the edge of the roof. He felt the cold wind blowing up the side of the grey building.

"Take us from here quickly!" the Saint demanded. "Before we are discovered!"

"No." Jom shook his head. He pushed back the sickening bile that rose in his throat as the reality of what he was doing sunk in. He was light-headed from losing so much blood. He forced his legs to not give out. But there was no other option. His friends' lives were at stake. He would do what needed to be done to save them.

"Give me to Harp." The Shadow Saint sheathed his blade and held out a gloved hand. "We can leave together or I will leave alone. But one way or another, I will leave this place."

Jom shook his head again. "No. No you won't."

Then he lifted the Harp above his head and flung it into the empty space next to him. He watched as the Harp tumbled through the air, dropping quickly out of sight into the silent city below.

"NO!" The Saint ran forward, pushing Jom out of the way. But even he wasn't fast enough to catch the Harp before it fell out of view, disappearing into the clouds that clung to the side of the spire. He watched the Harp for a moment, and then whirled to confront Jom. But Jom was already running for the other side of the roof. A ventilation hole was cut into the stone of the building and Jom ran as hard as he could for it, hoping to find somewhere to hide.

He heard a roar of anger behind him. Not daring even a glance over his shoulder, Jom sprinted for the opening. He leapt the last few paces, diving into the hole, hoping for the best. Suddenly, he was falling down a dark shaft. He bounced off hard walls, tumbling into darkness. Jom flailed his arms and legs out, hoping to slow his fall. His leg was painfully twisted as it caught on a wall. His head hit hard. Then his hand grabbed a passing outcropping and his fall was arrested. His fingers slipped and he dropped again but managed to catch himself a little ways further down. Dazed and bruised, he looked up. The opening of the shaft was a small point of light far above

him. He looked down and saw nothing but blackness below. A steady wind blew up past him. The wind was stale but not rotten, giving Jom the smallest glimmer of hope that there was a way out somewhere below.

Cruel laughter drifted down to him from above. "You know you are not safe from me," the Saint's voice floated down. Jom looked up and thought he saw a shadow high above blocking the meager light.

But you're not safe here either, Jom thought. He felt his way further down the shaft, finding small irregularities in the rock to grasp and perch on. The light above got smaller and smaller until he was left in total darkness. He heard movement above him and small pebbles fell on his head. The Saint was pursuing him down the shaft, and moving quickly by the sound of it. Jom began to panic. He scrambled down through the darkness as fast as he could. His fingers were slick with sweat and blood and his feet slipped on the rocks. Pebbles and laughter rained on him from above.

As he climbed, he became aware of a dim light below him

coming from the side of the shaft. He found he could vaguely see his hands and feet again. Moving quickly, he grasped the stones and made his way down to the light. He shifted to the adjacent wall and lowered himself level with the opening, peering through cautiously. Despite the danger from above, he knew the threat of being discovered was worse.

He looked through a heavy grate and saw an empty room. Nothing moved. No one was there. Jom tried to grate and found it was easily removed, held only by thin metal bands. Working as fast as he dared, he took off the grate and set it on the floor of the room. Then, without hesitation, he continued to move down the shaft. Further and further he descended, until the light from the room was well above him. He gripped the wall tightly and waited.

Before long, he watched as a shadow detached itself from the darkness above and slide through the opening into the room. Jom heard furtive rustling and footfalls as the Saint explored the room. Jom held his breath, willing his heart to not beat so loudly in his chest. Only after the sounds had long died away did he move. Cautiously, he lowered himself, continuing his descent through the darkness. Eventually, he found another grate, this one opening into a darkened storage room. Jom peered through the grate but saw nothing but metal containers stacked against walls. Making as little noise as possible, he removed the grate and entered the room.

The room was small and cramped and a thick layer of dust covered everything. Jom allowed himself a small breath of relief. This room, whatever it was, was obviously not used often. He carefully replaced the grate and pushed some heavy containers in front of it, just in case the Saint realized he had been tricked and came down the shaft after him. Taking a few deep

breaths, he then tore off a strip of his tunic and wrapped it around his arm. He dared not shut his eyes, not yet. In the gloom, he looked at the crates. Words were etched into the metal in a strange language.

Curious, he opened one of the crates. Inside was a collection of odd devices. He picked one up and examined it, turning it over and over in his hands. It had a variety of dials, all labeled in the same strange language. It had the look of some sort of communication device. He put it back and opened another container. More of the same devices.

Of course, he thought as he sifted through them. *There's no use for these anymore. Everyone on the planet is of the same mind. Literally.*

He shuddered, thinking of the collective nature of the Swarm and closed the lid to the crate. Then a thought struck him. If the Swarm didn't need communication devices anymore, maybe they didn't need weapons either. After all, what did they need to protect against? Perhaps there was something in the crates he could use to protect himself.

Jom searched the rest of the containers in the room but didn't find anything that resembled a weapon. Cautiously, he stepped to the door to the room. It slid open soundlessly at his approach. Dim light from a hallway flooded the room and he ducked back into the darkness. Only when he was sure there was no one in the corridor did he step out. He found himself in the middle of a long hallway. Doors were set at regular intervals on both sides going off in both directions. He sighed. It would take an eternity to search all these rooms. Trying not to succumb to despair, he stepped up to the next door. Inside was another storeroom filled with containers. He entered the room and let the door slide shut behind him.

As he explored the contents of the containers, Jom heard a shuffling sound in the hallway outside. He froze, straining his ears as he listened to someone walk down the corridor. Carefully, he crouched behind a tall stack of crates and held his breath. The footfalls went past the room and proceeded down the hallway. Jom heard whomever it was moving around in an adjacent room. After several heartbeats, the footsteps retreated back up the hallway and the area was quiet once more. Slowly, Jom let out a breath. All he could hear was the rapid beating of his heart. He took another couple of deep breaths and tried to calm down. He didn't move for a long time, too afraid to continue. Finally, after what seemed like an eternity, he forced himself to his feet.

After searching the contents of the room and finding no weapons, he crawled behind a large stack of crates. Ensuring he was out of sight and safe from discovery, Jom lay down. The enormity of his situation weighed on him. He was truly and utterly alone. He had no weapons, nothing to defend himself with. He was in the middle of a universe filled with creatures that

would steal away his very identity. And he was being hunted by a relentless assassin. He wrapped his arms around his chest and closed his eyes, trying not to cry.

Eventually, exhaustion overtook his nerves and he fell into a restless sleep.

: Dream of the Dark Planet :

JOM WAS RUNNING THROUGH the night. Dark claws reached out, grasping at him as he ran. Through the tears and sweat in his eyes, he saw a light ahead. At first, it blinked in and out of sight as the darkness swirled around him. But as he ran, the light grew stronger. He made for it as fast as his legs could run. He ignored the pain in his side and ducked another set of claws. Laughter followed him through the dark as he sprinted--mocking laughter that taunted him. He tried to ignore that too, concentrating only on reaching the light.

Claws tore at his clothes and skin as he ran. He felt cold blood running down his arms. He stumbled in the dark, tripping from exhaustion. As he fell, he heard the laughter get closer until it was almost on top of him. With a surge of energy, Jom regained his feet and ran on. The light was closer now. Just a little farther. Pushing off the claws, ignoring the pain as they dug into his flesh, he burst through the open doorway of the small cottage that appeared out of the dark forest. He slammed the heavy wooden door shut to keep out the horrors of the night. Jom leaned against the door for a moment, catching his breath, then raised his eyes to the interior of the cottage. A warm, inviting fire burned in the corner. Seated in a large, comfortable-looking chair next to the fire was...

"Abla!"

The tiny man whirled his head around quickly. "Where?"

"You!" Jom cried, rushing forward to the historian. "You're Abla'than'abla! Don't you remember me?"

Abla screwed up his face and studied Jom. "Of course, of course," he muttered. "Of course I don't remember you."

"But.."

"But?"

"But you sent me on this horrible quest!" Jom felt tears threaten to spill from his eyes. "Please tell me you remember."

Abla patted Jom's hand and indicated he sit down on the hard wooden stool next to him. "My dear boy, it's difficult to remember things that haven't happened yet."

"But..."

"I'm sure it was a lovely visit," Abla interrupted. "But we have much to discuss. And very little time to do it." He giggled to himself. "Little time."

Jom sat down and hung his head. "I don't understand."

"What's to understand?" Abla asked. "You're on a quest. Finish the quest!"

Jom looked the old man in the eyes. "How?" he demanded. "How can I do that? I'm alone! I have nothing to defend myself with. I don't even know how to defend myself!"

Abla tutted and shook his head. "You're not alone, boy. You're never alone. Don't ever think otherwise."

"But I am! My village is gone. My Grandmother is gone. My friends are gone..."

"There's always rabbits."

"My....what?"

"Rabbits. They're very friendly. Always good to have a rabbit handy."

"What's a rabbit?"

"What's a rabbit? You don't have rabbits where you come from?"

"I don't think so. Is it like a Stenisiar?"

"What's a Stenisiar?"

"It's a pack animal we use to pull plows."

Abla shook his head. "No. They're nothing like that."

"Oh."

"Rabbits don't like to plow. Lazy things, they are. Just want to hop around all the time, nibbling on a leaf."

"I..."

Abla waved his hand in the air. "Never mind all that now. Have you dreamt of the First Races yet?"

Jom nodded his head. "Yes. I mean, I was told of them. By a Latuip named..."

"Yes, yes. All of them?" Abla leaned forward intently.

"I—I guess so."

"How many Birth Worlds are there?"

"Five?"

Abla shook his head. "No. No. No." He scratched behind one of his large ears. "Of course the Latuips wouldn't know."

"Know what?"

In response, Abla reached over and touched Jom's forehead. His body stiffened, then relaxed and slid off the stool. He was asleep before he hit the floor.

Jom floated through the aether. He saw five worlds spinning around a silver star. One planet was blue. Jom knew this was the water planet Iad. Next in line was the white planet of wind and air. That was Sfo. Then the brown planet of Ord—rock and stone. The fire planet Ewr was next. Finally, a planet of light that shone almost as bright as the star they circled. This was Iah.

Jom watched as time spun by and the planets danced around one another. Great civilizations rose up. Five races took to the stars. Ships of metal and ships of fire clashed above the skies of the Birth Worlds. Jom covered his eyes as great bursts of energy lit up the galaxy. The universe shuddered from the war. But then, just as the war threatened all of existence, the fighting subsided and the First Races went away, leaving their homes behind.

Time passed. Jom slowly became aware of something new. Another planet, this one as dark as the emptiness of space, born from the violence of the Great War, spun around the others, forever in the shadows, forever denied the warmth of the silver star. This dark planet, Cle, spat demons from its uncaring embrace. The dark things of the universe came from this planet. Unnoticed, they spread out, following their brethren into the far reaches of space. Wherever the Five Races went, they followed, tainting the light with darkness, keeping the warmth of the fires from growing too big. They were the Night-bringers, the Dark Ones. The First Five, always looking forward, never thought to look back at what they had left behind and so they never saw the darkness spread over their creations. Instead, they continued on, pushing ever forward.

The Dark Ones whispered into the ears of the First Races from afar, encouraging them to travel further and further from the center silver star, further and further into the darkness. Their birthworlds were left far behind, forgotten. As the First Races spread out across the universe, so too went the Dark Ones, always the shadow behind the light. The Dark Ones followed along, forever encouraging the First Races to travel farther and farther. When the First Races reached the Wall of Eternity, the edge of everything, it was the Dark Ones from Cle who whispered to them to shatter the barrier and see what lay on the other side of forever.

Then, once the First Races were gone, the Dark Ones laughed. The universe was theirs for the taking. The planes were like fruit on the tree now.

Jom blinked and looked up. He was in the cottage. Abla was humming softly to himself. Jom sat up.

"What happened?"

"You were sleeping."

"Oh."

"You seem to sleep a lot," Abla said, clicking his tongue.

"I—I'm sorry. I don't know why I fell asleep."

"Probably because you needed to see something. Sleeping is a good time for that."

Jom shook his head, clearing his thoughts.

"Do you remember your dream?" Abla asked, looking at him with intense eyes.

Jom nodded. "I do. I dreamt of the sixth of the First Races. The Dark Ones."

"Good. Don't forget."

"I don't understand what it means, though."

Abla shrugged his thin shoulders. "You better figure it out quickly."

"Why? What's going on?" Jom looked around the cottage. "I'm so confused. How did I even get here?"

"You're dreaming."

"I thought I just woke up."

Abla giggled. "Everyone does."

Jom began to question the historian but Abla waved a hand at him. "No time for that now. You have to wake up. Again. Don't forget what you've learned."

The cottage grew dimmer and dimmer until Jom was left in darkness. He slowly opened his eyes. A thin light permeated the storage room. He looked around at the crates that surrounded him and sighed.

: The Silent City :

QUESTIONS BOUNCED BACK AND forth across Jom's mind as he cautiously stepped into the corridor. There were no sounds or signs of life in either direction. He carefully stepped to the next door. It slid open silently and, after holding his breath and taking a quick look around the doorway, stepped into another uninhabited room. This room contained no crates. A large window looked out onto the city. There was a dusty interface terminal in the center of the room—a vid monitor perched on a slim stand. Otherwise the room was empty and featureless. Jom tiptoed over to the window and gazed out over the city.

His breath caught in his throat. Unlike when he was on the roof of the building earlier, the city was now full of activity. Thousands of creatures filled the streets and buildings. They were mostly tall beings, with pale grey skin, little or no hair, two legs and four arms. They ebbed and flowed around each other with uncanny precision. Jom then began to understand the power of the hive mind. Jom watched in fascination as the Swarm went about its business. The collective moved in perfect harmony. Transports skimmed the surface in formation, individual crafts turning off down side avenues at full speed with barely a hand's width to spare. Everyone moved in unison, like an immense flock of birds or school of fish. Each individual moved with the group. Everyone was part of something larger. Jom found a latch for the window and cautiously opened it.

Under the wind, there was an utter lack of the noise he was accustomed to. In his village, there was shouting from person to person, yelling at children, haggling over prices. But there was none of that here. Everyone moved about in silence. There was no need to talk. They were one, a billion parts of the same creature. Jom closed the window and shuddered. The eerie quiet of the bustling city was unlike anything he had ever experienced before. The power of the mind that controlled the Swarm was beyond his comprehension. For it was not just this city. The planet…the system…the galaxy. His head spun as he thought of an entire universe moving in silence. This entire plane of existence was one mind, one consciousness. He simply couldn't understand how a single mind could control so much.

He moved out of view of the window and thought about his situation. He needed to find a way back to his plane. He remembered from his dream that the Swarm did not have the means to cross the aether. Thankfully it was stranded to this plane. He just needed to go back through the aether to his home. But the Mind Harp was gone, most likely shattered against the unforgiving stone of the city streets. Or was it? Jom wondered if it was possible that the Harp had survived the fall from the top of the building. After all, he didn't know what the Harp was made of. Perhaps it withstood the fall. Maybe it was strong enough to survive.

Both hope and fear stirred deep in his chest. If the Harp was intact, he needed to find it quickly, before the Swarm or the Shadow Saint found it. If the Saint found it, he would leave Jom to the Swarm and go back to slaughter his friends. And if the Swarm found if it the entire universe—every universe—would fall to the grey. At the very least then, he knew he had to make sure the Harp was destroyed. He couldn't be responsible for unleashing the Swarm into the rest of the universe.

But how? The city was abuzz with activity as the local populace went about its daily business. If he waited until moonrise there would be less chance of being discovered. Jom shook his head. To wait that long...it wasn't an option. The Saint was out there. The Harp was out there. He had to find it first. There was too much at risk. He leaned back against the cold metal wall and thought. His thoughts rapidly spiraled down into despair. His impossible situation had grown worse. After sitting staring blankly at the opposite wall for a few moments, he sighed heavily, shrugged and got to his feet. There was no possible way he could avoid an entire city for long. But he couldn't sit in the dark and hope for the best either. He had to act quickly. The lives of his friends were at stake. The fate of the universe had suddenly fallen onto his shoulders. No. He shook his head. This is my fault. I brought the assassin here. I have to make sure he stays, that the Swarm stays. He took a couple of deep breaths, and then stepped to the door. The sensor activated and the door slid open with a whisper.

The corridor was empty. He looked both ways, and then hurried forward. There was a junction ahead of him. A pale light illuminated the corridor and, as he approached, he realized there was a window to the outside. After making sure he was alone, he scurried to the window and looked out. Instead of concentrating on the people, though, he appraised his situation critically. He counted the windows in the building across from him and saw that he was ten stories up. The city looked similar to what he had seen when he was on the roof but he couldn't be sure he was on the same side as where he had thrown the Harp. So he probably would have to search the base of the building once he reached street-level. Grey citizens moved about below him. Transports whizzed by in perfect formation. There were a number of buildings next to his. It was possible, he thought, that the Harp had landed on the roof of one of the smaller buildings. But that meant sneaking through even more buildings. He shook his head. He had to start with the bottom, he guessed, and then work his way up.

He looked back down the corridor. There were numerous doors. He could only guess where they led. He thought about going back to the ventilation shaft and making his way down that way. But then an idea struck him.

He turned back towards the window and watched the people move about. After a few heartbeats, his idea was confirmed. This may not be impossible after all. He only needed some luck and...

Quickly, he went back up the corridor. Counting under his breath, he found the third storage room he had explored and stepped inside. As the door slid shut, he heard movement in the corridor outside. He ducked behind a stack of crates and listened, holding his breath. A set of footfalls came down the hallway. He realized he was in the same storage room as when he almost got caught the first time. Praying to the gods, he swore he would never set foot in this room again if he survived.

Apparently, the gods were not listening. As he cowered behind the crates, the door slid open and someone entered the room.

He was paralyzed. All he could do was crouch further against the wall and pray he wasn't discovered. He could see a little bit of the area by the door and caught a glimpse of grey fabric enter the room. Then another crate was dropped onto the top of the stack he was hiding behind. A heartbeat later, the door slid shut and he was alone again. He barely heard the footsteps recede down the hallway over the beating of his heart.

He couldn't move for quite some time. His courage had given out. He huddled in the dark, knowing it was only a matter of time before someone else entered the room, found him, and made him part of the Swarm but he couldn't move. His legs wouldn't work. His heart wouldn't stop beating so fast. His eyes kept jumping to the door, expecting it to open and let the Swarm in.

But that didn't happen. Eventually, after some time with no one coming down the corridor, Jom slowly gathered the courage to continue. Breathing deeply, he stood, listening intently for the slightest sound. When he was sure he was safe, he quickly rifled through the storage crates until he found what he needed.

Moving quickly, before his courage disappeared, he stepped into the corridor and went back to the empty room he had found upon waking. The room was as it was before, a simple vid monitor station and a large window overlooking the city. Jom studied the area around the door, looking for a control panel of some sort.

There was nothing he could see that could disable the door and he grunted in frustration. It would be better if he could lock himself in the room but couldn't see any way to do it. After a few moments of searching, he gave it up and went to the window. He couldn't afford spending too much time here. He had to be swift. He went to the window and pushed it open. A hot breeze blew into the room. The silent city was below him.

The thin rope he had found in the crates was quickly tied to the vid monitor post. Walking to the open window, he threw the rope out. Jom watched as it unraveled against the side of the building. Looking out, he saw that it went about as far as the top of the second level of the building. He watched for several tense heartbeats, but no one looked up. He nodded in satisfaction.

There was, after all, no reason for anyone to look up. They were of the same mind. They all saw the same thing. No one was curious. No one randomly glanced skyward. There was no need. Jom was betting that the single entity on the planet had no need to casually look up. It thought it already saw everything.

He took a deep breath, pushed the window further open and, grabbing a firm grip on the rope, climbed out. The wind, although strong, was not enough to swing him about the side of the building. He reached up and closed the window as best he could. Perhaps if someone entered the room, they wouldn't notice the rope. He knew it was a silly idea, yet he had to hold onto any hope he had. He glanced down, and then began to descend. The city, still silent, moved about below him like a hive. Yet there were no cries of alarm, no yelling. He lowered himself, floor by floor, hoping and praying that no one would look up. No one did.

The Swarm moved about all around him, focused on their individual tasks. Never once did someone turn astray, look somewhere they didn't need to. His heart threatened to explode out of his chest as he climbed down. His hands were slick with sweat. He continuously expected to hear a shout of surprise from below. He tried to stay focused, concentrating on moving down the rope as rapidly as he was able. Then, suddenly, he was at the end of it.

He looked down. His feet dangled a good six or seven paces

above the street. There were a few citizens walking to and fro but they all kept their gazes directly in front of them. Jom held his breath as they passed below him, expecting any one of them to look up and expose him. Finally, there was a break in the traffic and the street below him was quiet.

Steeling himself, Jom let go of the rope and fell. He hit the ground hard but rolled with the impact, quickly gaining his feet. He dashed to a shadowed alley before anyone came upon him. Pain flared in his ankle and he leaned back against a wall, nursing it. He looked out at the street, watching the Swarm move past him.

In between winces of pain, he scanned the area. He didn't see any sign of the Harp. He did spot another shadowed alley further up the street and, when the traffic had a lull, he dashed to it as best he could. His ankle almost gave out on him as he reached the alley and he bit his tongue so he wouldn't scream out. Once safe, he caught his breath and looked about. Again, there was no sign of the Harp.

He spent the daylight limping from shadow to shadow around the building, looking for the Harp and avoiding the Swarm. He felt his ankle swell but he tried to ignore it as best he could and hobble along, dashing to the next alley before he was discovered.

Finally, as the shadows lengthened and the sky turned dark, he saw it. His breath caught in his throat as his eyes lit upon the Harp. It was lodged on a small outcropping of the building across the street from him. It was above street-level, unseen by the Swarm and appeared to be intact. The traffic increased and Jom moved back into the shadows of the alley. As he waited, he looked about. His eyes fell on an alley across the street from him.

There, among the shadows of the alley, moved a darker shadow. Even from that distance, Jom could sense the Saint smile.

: Between the Shadow and the Grey :

JOM MOVED BACK INTO the alleyway as one of the Swarm walked past. He looked across the street. The Shadow Saint sat, unmoving among the darkness, like a predator that waits patiently in the dark for its prey, watching, always watching. Jom peered down to the other end of the alley he was in. Perhaps if he could lure the Saint away from the Harp, he could circle back around. There were no doors or windows the length of the alley though. No way to escape except at the end. If the Saint crossed the street while he was still in the alley, there was nothing to stop him from catching Jom and slaughtering him at his leisure. He glanced across the street again, keying in on the Saint's position. Just as his eyes landed on the Saint, Jom saw him crouch down. A large group of Swarm drones walked past. Jom took the opportunity to run down the alley. He looked back just in time to see the Shadow Saint dart across the street into his alley. Suppressing a yell, Jom took off, running as fast as he could for the end of the alley. He heard a soft laugh behind him.

Reaching the far end of the alley, Jom skidded to a halt while still in the shadows. The Saint was on him in an instant. Jom dropped to the ground and rolled out of the way. Talonn's blade struck the ground a heartbeat later. The sound of the ebony blade striking the concrete echoed through the silent city. Jom gained his feet and dashed across the street, dashing from the shadows that threatened to suffocate him. Luckily, the avenue was empty and he gained the next alley without being seen. Without slowing, he sped down the alley, sparing a single glance over his shoulder. The Shadow Saint was forced to wait while another drone walked by and Jom ran harder, trying to put some distance between them.

And so it went. A long night passed as the Shadow Saint relentlessly hunted Jom through the dark alleys of the silent city. Jom could never get more than a block or two away before the assassin found him once more. The lack of drones on the streets was both a blessing and a curse. Jom could move relatively freely through the alleys and avoid detection. But so could the Saint. As he ran, his thoughts kept circling back to the Mind Harp. It was his only means of escape. He needed to get the Harp before the Swarm or the Shadow Saint discovered it. He was

near exhaustion as dawn began to slowly creep over the city, Jom circled back through the city to the building where the Harp was waiting.

With the sun came the Swarm. It became increasingly difficult for either Jom or the Saint to cross streets and Jom's heart beat loudly in his chest. It was only a matter of time before he was found or caught. His legs burned from running since the last dawn. He hunched down in an alley, trying to catch his breath. He looked up and realized he was back in the alley across from the Harp. Risking a glance, he saw the Harp was still on the outcropping across the street from him. He breathed a small sigh of relief. The sigh died in his throat as he looked across the street to see the Saint hiding almost directly underneath the Harp behind some dead, grey bushes. They were almost exactly where they had started the previous night.

A desperate plan formed in his mind. He scanned the alleyway for any sort of rubble. The city was remarkably debris-free. Perhaps not so surprising given the nature of the citizens. Still, after several heartbeats, he found a loose chunk of masonry and pried it out of the wall. Crouching down, he waited until one of the Swarm walked by. Silently, he counted how long it took for the grey drone to pass by. He counted again the next time someone came through. The Swarm moved at a consistent speed; each individual member was locked into the same rhythm. If he timed it out just right...

He waited as another drone walked by, then, after he was sure he wouldn't be seen, lobbed the masonry across the alley. It struck the side of the building. The echo of the impact rang across the silent city. Jom cringed. He hadn't realized how loud it would sound. Suddenly, everything stopped, including Jom's heart. He sank as far as possible into the shadows. He saw the Saint rise up in alarm.

"WHAT WAS THAT NOISE?" a trillion voices across the universe spoke at once. The noise was defening. The drone that had just passed by turned towards the sound. It stared directly at the Saint.

"AN INTRUD..." Before the Swarm could finish, *Talonn* flashed in the half-light of dawn and the drone was a bloody pile at the Saint's feet. The assassin turned towards Jom, his sword ready to strike.

"WHERE DID YOU COME FROM?" the Swarm asked. Suddenly, a dozen drones were crowding in the street, staring at the Shadow Saint.

The Saint leapt into action. Jom watched from the safety of the alley as the assassin became a shadowy blur, tearing into the Swarm. He cut down everyone within reach before Jom could blink. Still more of the Swarm entered the street and soon the Saint was fighting a group, then a

mob, then a horde as the Swarm reacted to his presence. Jom pressed himself against the wall of the alley as more and more of the Swarm converged on the Saint.

"YOU WILL TELL ME HOW YOU GOT HERE," the Swarm said. Jom heard the voices echoing throughout the city. He imagined every living creature in the entire system speaking as one. "YOU WILL TELL ME HOW YOU GOT HERE," it repeated.

The Saint whirled about, striking down drone after drone. Grasping grey hands reached for him. For every two hands he cut off, six more reached in. Soon, even he could not fight them all off and he drowned in a sea of grey.

The Swarm, now over fifty strong, grasped the Saint and immobilized him. Even still, he fought back, throwing drones off him until he was weighed down by sheer numbers.

"I will find you!" the Saint yelled from beneath the grey mass. "I will find you and kill you! This is not over!"

"WHO DO YOU TALK TO?" the Swarm demanded with countless voices. "IS THERE ANOTHER WITH YOU?"

Jom got up and made his way further into the alley, desperately looking for some place to hide. He hugged the shadows as he moved. He scurried away as quickly as he could without making any noise. Jom heard the Saint continue to yell at him from behind. Fear quickened his pace and he reached the far end of the alleyway. Daring a glance into the street, he saw drones moving quickly down the main streets towards the Saint. Jom scrunched down behind an outcropping, waiting for them to pass.

"IF THERE IS ANOTHER, I WILL FIND THEM," the Swarm promised.

Jom cursed under his breath. He needed to find somewhere to hide and quick. The Saint was probably already telling the Swarm his location as a bargaining ploy. He waited until the way was clear, and then dashed into the next alley. Here, there were a number of recesses cut into the stone up the side of the building. Jom crawled up into one then, after making sure no one was around, leapt up. His fingers just caught the edge of the lip of the next one and he quickly hauled himself up into it. He chanced one more leap up, settling into a recess that was well above street-level.

He pushed himself back as far as he could. From here, he

couldn't see anything happening below. But no one could see him either. The opposite building had no windows from which he could be seen. He wrapped his arms around his chest and waited. The Swarm spoke all around him, allowing him to hear at least half of the conversation it was having with the Saint.

"TELL ME NOW. HOW DID YOU ARRIVE HERE?"

"WHERE IS THIS DEVICE?"

"YOU LIE. WHERE IS THIS DEVICE?"

Jom's breath caught in his throat. The Harp was resting on a ledge just above the Saint. If any of the Swarm so much as glanced up, it would see the Harp. But Jom could only hope for the best. There was no way he could retrieve it until the Swarm cleared the area. Once darkness fell, he would retrieve the Harp and leave this plane. His heart beat wildly as he thought of what would happen if the Swarm found the Harp. Tears welled up as he thought of himself as the person that brought about the end of existence.

"YOU WILL TELL ME WHAT YOU KNOW."

As Jom listened to the Swarm, he hunkered down and made himself as comfortable as he could. He calmed down the more he listened to the Swarm. The Harp was still safe. And he was safe as well. He doubted he would be discovered there and the thought calmed him. He closed his eyes and listened to the Swarm interrogate the Saint. The conversation continued all through the day until night fall. As he lay there in the dark, he found his eyes closing more and more often.

Despite the danger, Jom nodded off.

"YOU WILL STAY HERE UNTIL YOU TELL ME WHAT I WANT TO KNOW."

Jom's ears perked up. It had been some time since he gained the recessed shelter. The city was dark; night had descended. He yawned and moved cautiously to the edge of the recess. There were no drones in sight. The fact that he could still easily hear the Swarm though told him he was not as alone as he would have liked. He cursed himself for a fool and looked around again. The Swarm had obviously taken the Saint somewhere. But had the Saint told the Swarm about him? Probably. And that meant going back for the Harp was most likely a trap. He cursed himself again. How could he have fallen asleep?

Taking a deep breath, he carefully lowered himself to the next recess, pausing for some time before descending to the lowest one and reaching the street. From the corner of the alley, he peered in all directions. He waited for the Swarm to speak but the city was silent once more. He tried to shake the feeling of a million eyes watching him.

He had no choice. He had to see if the Harp was still there. It was his only chance for getting home again. And if it wasn't? He sighed. He didn't know how he would fight the Swarm for the Harp. But best leave that thought until necessary.

He sulked back through the alleys, moving slowly and light-footed. Nothing stirred around him but he didn't allow himself any measure of confidence. He eventually reached the alley where he had exposed the Saint. Saying a silent prayer, he peeked around the corner. His eyes landed on a drone and he quickly ducked back into the darkness of the alley. After a moment, his heart jack-hammering in his chest, he dared another look. The drone had its back to Jom, as if it was guarding the entrance to the street. He leaned back out of sight, and then stole a glance up. The Harp was miraculously still on the outcropping just across the street from him. He could see its outline among the night shadows.

He sat back and thought. One sentry that could turn and see him at any moment. The Harp was out of reach. It was only a matter of time before the Saint told the Swarm about him, assuming he hadn't already. He grabbed another chunk of masonry. Hefting it in his hand, he gauged how likely he would be able to knock the Harp off the ledge. If he could do it in one shot, he could run out, grab the Harp and escape before the Swarm could react.

If he missed, though, he would be found out. He dared another look at the drone keeping guard. Or he could use the stone to bash in the head of the sentry. That could possibly buy him a few moments, at least, before reinforcements arrived. But if this was all a trap? Then the Swarm would be on him before he could reach the Harp and he would be tortured and converted, doomed to spend the rest of his days as part of the grey.

As he considered his options, the drone walked past his alley. Jom held his breath and pressed himself against the wall. The sentry walked to the other end of the street and stopped. Jom closed his eyes, listening to the thundering of his heart.

As he stood there in the shadows, he became aware of something peculiar. He saw color. Swirling colors in his field of vision. He concentrated and the colors faded. Thinking he was seeing things, he relaxed and the colors returned. Soft greens and blues swirled around up and to the right. He opened his eyes and realized the colors were coming from the Harp. He looked in wonder at the fingers of energy. After using the Harp, apparently his mind had begun to register those energies even when he wasn't physically in contact with the Harp. He closed his eyes again and reached out with his thoughts. The Harp reacted immediately, the energies intensifying in his mind's eye. Tentatively, he reached out again, gently pulling the energies towards him. The Harp responded, wrapping tendrils of energy around his thoughts. Jom slowly opened his eyes and saw the Harp floating above the ledge, held aloft by the energy that swirled around it. With a quick glance at the sentry, Jom reeled in the Harp. It slowly moved through the night air towards him. Jom thought of Strength and Bravery, picturing the glyphs in his head. The tendrils strengthened. He willed it to come to him. The Harp floated down to him and he reached out.

Just as his hands touched the Harp, the sentry turned. Jom froze. The grey face contorted in rage.

"YOU WILL GIVE ME THE DEVICE."

The sentry ran towards him. Jom wrapped his hands around the Harp and thought of home. Energies swirled around him and he felt his body pass through the membrane of the planes. Then, just as the silent city faded away, a grey hand reached through the aether and clamped down on his arm.

: Not Grey :

JOM TUMBLED THROUGH THE dimensions, spinning around and around as the grey drone of the Swarm grappled with him for possession of the Harp. The creature's four hands were all over Jom, pulling at the Harp, pushing against his face. Even with the roar of the aether around him, Jom heard the Swarm yell.

"YOU WILL GIVE ME THE DEVICE!"

Jom fought back as best he could, but it was impossible to get his bearings as they fell through the aether. He tried to focus on the energies of the planes swirling around him—the strong green energy that surrounded them and protected them from the aether, the bright red that was taking him back to his friends. And the grey tether that reached out behind them, linking the drone to the Swarm that was sure to follow.

Jom concentrated. The grey tendril was stretching ever thinner as they moved between planes. He reached out with his mind, touching the tendril. It recoiled. The drone twitched in its struggles. Jom did not hesitate. Clutching the Harp with one hand, he reached out with the other and grabbed hold of the grey. The drone screamed as Jom twisted and yanked at the link. The drone fought harder, not understanding what Jom was doing but feeling a pain unlike any he had felt before. But Jom couldn't break the tendril with only one hand, no matter how hard he pulled and tugged. He released the rope of energy and held up his hand.

He gathered energy from the Harp and mentally shaped it to his will. Desperate, Jom brought forth as much energy as he could. The Harp responded to his thoughts and his touch and white energy erupted from the Harp. Jom took the energy and stretched it, molding it with his mind. He grasped at the energy with his free hand. It twisted and spun in his hand. Jom directed his thoughts into the pure white energy. It settled as it took on a shape Jom knew. Then, when the shape had solidified, Jom took his newly-formed sword of light and slashed at the grey tendril with all his might.

The tendril snapped. The drone screamed. And then the aether opened and they fell to solid ground.

Jom blinked in the bright light. He held up a hand to shield his eyes. Two bright suns hung in a red sky above him. He blinked again, taking in his surroundings.

He was standing on a rocky plain. Tall mountains loomed in the far distance. Rolling hills covered the space in front of him. Tall pillars of brown and red rock rose from the ground all around them; immense towers of rock that looked like some giant had taken boulders and staked them on top of each other for sport. The tops of the pillars were hidden in wispy clouds. Short yellow grass sprouted between the rocks, covering the land in a blanket of dirty gold. Before him were signs of a fight. Dead carcasses of strange creatures were scattered about the area. Jom recognized them as the monsters that had attacked them in the darkness. It's the same place, Jom thought, looking around, the same place where I left them. Only it's daylight now.

Blood was everywhere too. Lots of it. Jom's heart jumped into his throat. Anxious, he looked among the bodies but did not find any of his friends. The image of Ravola lying on the ground, stabbed in the back by the Shadow Saint, loomed in his mind. But she was not among the dead. Nor were any of the others. He found bits of cloth, possibly from Macar's tunic, and stray bits of gold metal that he assumed came from NDX. Then, almost by accident, he found a strange marking in the rocky ground. A crude arrow had been hastily scratched into the rock, pointing to the mountains in the distance.

He immediately started off in that direction but, after only a few steps, stopped and turned back. Lying face up on the ground behind him was the drone. Cautiously, he approached the creature, picking up a large rock along the way. He did not relish the thought of killing it but he would do what he had to in order to protect his universe from the Swarm.

The drone was still. Unseeing eyes stared up at the sky. It was male, at least two hands taller than Jom, and slim. Its skin was ashen grey, as were its clothes—a simple shirt and pants. Jom stood over it, hefting the rock over his head. The creature didn't move. Cautiously, Jom nudged it with a foot.

It blinked. Once. Jom stepped back and raised the rock higher, ready to smash the creature's head in.

It blinked again and looked at Jom. There was something in his grey eyes. Some look that made Jom hesitate. Like something new was being seen for the first time. Jom slowly lowered the rock. The creature opened his mouth, and then closed it. He swallowed and spoke.

"....not grey...."

Jom cocked his head in confusion.

"What?"

"....not Graaa....not Graaa!"

Suddenly, he got to his feet. Jom stepped further back, holding the rock at the ready. The creature looked around wildly. Seeing the red sky and the yellow grass seemed to frighten him and he jumped about until he was standing on a large rock that stood out from grass.

"Not Graaa!"

"It's all right," Jom said, holding up his palm to the man. "No one is going to hurt you." But he didn't drop the rock. Not just yet.

The man gripped himself with his arms and stared at the world around him. He was obviously terrified. Jom took a step forward.

"I'm Jom. What's your name?"

The man looked at him in bewilderment. He opened and closed his mouth several times before finding the words to reply.

"....Graaa but not Graaa. No more Graaa."

"No more grey? Where's the grey?"

"No Graaa!" He stepped off the rock, saw the yellow grass, and jumped back on. Slowly, Jom began to understand the situation.

"You aren't part of the Swarm anymore, are you? When I cut the tendril, I cut you out of the Swarm completely."

"No Graaa. Am Graaa."

By now, tears were freely rolling down the man's face. He kept his head down, not looking at the suns or the sky, trying not to look at the grass, looking only at the grey rock under his feet. Slowly, Jom extended his hand.

"You're not alone. Let me help."

The man looked at Jom with eyes that couldn't see past the pain.

"No Graaa," he whispered.

"I'm sorry. I had to. I couldn't let the Swarm into this dimension."

"I? What is...I?"

Jom was taken back. This man had no concept of the individual at all. Even when he was in the Silent City, Jom thought there had to be some sense of individual among the millions of drones that made up the Swarm. But there wasn't. For the first time in this man's life, he was alone. He was a man cut off from everything he had known. Jom realized now that he had forced upon this man the ultimate horror; he had taken his entire world from him, had marooned him in a world he would probably never understand. He stepped closer, the rock falling out of his hand as he approached the man.

He touched his chest. "I. I am Jom. You." He pointed to the man. "You are not Jom."

"Not Jom?"

"No." Jom shook his head. "I am Jom." Again, he touched his chest.

The man pointed to himself. "Not Jom. Not Graaa."

Jom nodded. "That's right."

Anxious to go after his friends yet unable to stop feeling responsible for the man, Jom glanced up at the suns. He scanned the area, finding his beaten and battered pack. He took a quick inventory and was pleased to see he still had a few dried fruits and a half skin of water. He stuffed the Harp into the pack and pulled out a small bit of food. He offered a piece of fruit to the man, indicating he should eat it. The man slowly took the fruit but didn't eat until Jom put a piece in his mouth.

"I'm sorry. I truly am. But I have to find my friends. You are welcome to travel with me. I wouldn't mind the company, to be honest. I've been alone for a while now."

The man looked at Jom, still not understanding the new existence he found himself in.

After a moment, Jom offered his hand. "Come with me."

The man looked down at the yellow grass. He pointed with one of his hands. "Not Graaa."

Jom shook his head. "No. It's not. But it won't hurt you. See? I'm walking on it." To demonstrate, he walked around the man.

Tentatively, the man stepped off his rock onto the grass. He lifted his feet several times but eventually got used to it.

Jom began walking in the direction of the arrow. "Come on! We have to find my friends!"

It took several moments, but Jom finally got the man to walk with him.

"You need a name," Jom said as they set off. "What are you called?"

"Graaa. Not Graaa."

"Right. How about if I just call you Not Grey for now? We'll come up with something better later."

"Not Graaa," he said, hitting his chest.

Jom nodded. "Exactly."

As they walked, Jom kept a constant lookout for signs of his friends. Every once in a while, there would be another arrow scratched into a rock, or a bit of cloth. Disturbingly, once he found a tuft of dark fur from Pula. His heart leapt into his throat. He hurried forward, Not Grey trailing behind. He scanned the horizon but couldn't see any sign of his friends. They walked until the suns were low in the sky.

Despite his worry, Jom found himself trying to help Not Grey acclimate to his new situation. The man would point to a mountain or a cloud and say "Not Graaa." Jom would have to tell him what it was called besides that. To him, the universe was simple; everything was either part of the Swarm or it wasn't. And everything had been part of the Swarm. Now though, he had an entire universe to learn.

Near dusk, they saw a thin column of smoke ahead among the foothills of the mountains. Jom and Not Grey hurried to some large scrub bushes and peered out. From that distance, they couldn't see much. But it was obvious someone was camping there for the night. Jom knew in his gut that it was his friends. But were they alone? Had they been captured by someone?

Jom turned to Not Grey and pointed to the camp in the distance. "I think my friends are there. But they may be in trouble. We need to be quiet and sneak up to the camp." He put a finger to his lips, trying to get the ex-drone to understand.

Not Grey looked at the camp intently and nodded. "Not Graaa," he agreed. Jom sighed and nodded back.

Carefully, they moved from bush to bush, slowly coming closer to the camp. By the time he saw movement in the camp, it was too late and rough hands were grabbing him. He was forced to his feet by black-clad men and, along with Not Grey, hustled into the camp. His pack was taken from him and he was pushed to the ground. Looking up, he saw his friends, bound and gagged, in a huddle near him. His elation at finding them quickly turned sour though when a figure stepped from the underbrush and stood before him.

"It's about time you showed up," Kala Azar said in his metallic voice.

: Battle's End :

J OM STRUGGLED AGAINST HIS bonds. With a wave of his hand, Kala Azar kept his men at bay and allowed Jom to regain his feet.

"What do you want? Let us go!" Jom demanded.

"What do I want?" Kala Azar laughed. "I want what I've wanted all along." One of his men handed him Jom's pack. The fallen prince reached in and pulled out the Mind Harp. "I want the means to regain my throne."

"Take it then!" Jom spat at the man's feet. "Take it and leave us. We don't care about your little rebellion."

"Choose your words carefully, boy," the bandit hissed. "I hold all your lives in my hands."

"I'm tired of fighting," Jom replied. "I have been on the verge of death for cycles now. I'm tired. If you're going to kill me, then kill me. If not, let us go."

"Kill you? Oh no. I can't do that. Not yet at least. I need you to show me how this works." He turned the Harp over in his hands, studying the strange symbols carved into it.

"I won't."

Kala Azar stopped and looked at Jom.

"I think you will."

"I will not!"

"If you don't, your friends will die. Slowly." At a look from the cyborg, one of the bandits struck Macar with his weapon. Macar grunted in pain but did not cry out.

Jom looked over to them. Ravola was lying on the ground. Her wound had been bandaged but the binding was red with blood. Her eyes were closed and her chest rose and fell quick and shallow. NDX was inert, not moving. There was no light in its eyes. Macar, Nebt and Pula seemed battered but otherwise all right. Pula whined, sensing Jom's presence. Nebt held him tight, lest he try to run to Jom. Dianat was at not in sight. Jom hoped she was all right and somewhere close by. But he dared not mention her. If she was hiding, waiting for an opportunity to strike, he didn't want to tip the bandits off to her presence. He was on his own.

After a moment, Jom sighed and looked at Kala Azar. "Fine. Release them and I'll help you."

The prince laughed. "I think not. You will help me regain my throne. Only then will I permit your friends to live."

"You lie. Once you have your precious throne, you'll kill us all. Release them or I destroy the Harp and you'll never get the throne."

"Now who lies? You are bound at my feet. What can you do?"

In response, Jom reached out with his thoughts, feeling for the energies of the Harp. He found them instantly, swirling around the Mind Harp, waiting for Jom's touch. He pushed them, speeding them up around the prince. Kala Azar looked at the Harp in alarm as it grew warm in his hands.

"What are you doing?" he demanded.

"I will destroy it. Let my friends go."

At a signal from Kala Azar, men rushed forward and put blades to his friends.

"Stop at once or your friends die!"

With barely a thought, Jom directed a snap of energy. It lashed out, knocking the men off their feet and away from the group. As he touched the energy of the Harp, his confidence grew. With another thought, a bubble of emerald energy enveloped his friends, protecting them from weapons fire. The power of the Mind Harp was swirling around him now. He let the energies flow in and through him.

"Stop!" Kala Azar dropped the red-hot Harp. It stopped before it hit the ground and remained suspended in midair by the energies Jom was controlling. Kala Azar pulled a pistol from his belt and leveled it at Jom. Instinctively, Jom threw up another forceshield and the blast bounced harmlessly off it. Jom heard Kala Azar raging. The cyborg blasted at the shield, spittle flying from his mouth as he demanded Jom stop.

Jom closed his eyes. It was obvious that the prince would never give up until he controlled the Harp. In his mind, it was the only thing that would help him regain his lost throne. He would continue to hunt Jom and his friends until he got what he wanted. But Jom couldn't bring himself to kill the man. There had to be another way, something he could do to get Kala Azar to leave them alone. Then, with sudden clarity, he knew what he had to do. With a heavy sigh, Jom turned the energies of the Harp inward.

The Harp began to spin in the air, buffeted by the energies being taken from it and turned back against it. It began to glow, pulsating as it filled with more and more energy. The Harp emptied its vast potential into the air, only to have it directed right back into it. With a final push, Jom sent every last bit of power into the Harp. The casing split with a loud crack. Kala Azar yelled in despair as the crack grew. Then the Mind Harp exploded.

Shards of stone flew in every direction. With a sudden thought, Jom grabbed some of the energy that flew outward from the center of the explosion and brought it back to him. He felt the cells of his body absorb the energy. It filled the empty niches of his mind and infused his muscles and organs. He felt the Harp enter him, albeit in a greatly reduced way. The explosion knocked Kala Azar and his men off their feet. Jom's forceshield could not withstand the force of the blast and collapsed. Everything was silent in the aftermath of the explosion. Bandits got dizzily to their feet. Kala Azar, his hands still smoking, roared with fury and raised his pistol.

Jom shook his head to clear the stars and, seeing Kala Azar point his weapon, instinctively wrapped the energy of the Harp around him. The first blasts from Kala Azar's gun ricocheted off the forceshield. Jom took the energy that was now raging within him. With a flicker of his mind, he cut the ropes binding his hands.

He held out a hand and formed a brilliant sword of white energy. Kala Azar's eyes grew wide. He fired again. Jom slashed with his sword, deflecting the blasts with white fire. The prince threw his blaster away and drew a long, thin rapier. Thumbing a button on the hilt, the blade sparked with electricity, powered by his cyborg body.

With a snarl, he leapt at Jom. Jom got his sword up just in time to block a killing blow. Using the Harp-energy to augment his strength, he pushed Kala Azar back. The prince immediately came at him and they traded a series of blows. The white fire of Jom's sword and Kala Azar's electric blade clanged as they met time and time again. Jom, outmatched in skill, speed and strength, relied on the energy that flowed through him to balance the odds. His muscles burned. His eyesight was sharpened. He parried and ducked the electric blade with a grace he had never known before. The cyborg hissed and snarled as he pressed his attack, trying to break through Jom's defenses. Jom knew it was only a matter of time before Kala Azar would succeed in killing him. He could already feel the Harp-energy draining away.

In the midst of the battle, a part of his brain drifted off, remembering his dreams. Jom huffed in frustration. He had always felt like he was half-walking in another world, even in the best of times. Here, now, in a life-and-death battle with a crazed cyborg prince, he still couldn't fully concentrate. Part of his mind touched on the dream conversation with Abla and the lesson he was supposed to have learned.

Then, with a click, as the swords collided again and his white fire dimmed a little, it all fell into place. The First Races had been pushed to war with each other by The Dark Ones from the hidden planet. After the strife and destruction, though, they were motivated to explore the universe and seed the worlds in part to atone for their violence. Then they were again influenced by The Dark Ones to push further and further into the unknown until they eventually reached the Wall of Eternity. They never would have gone so far without that shadowy influence. It was that push and pull of light and dark that had defined the universe.

Jom needed to embrace both the light and the dark if he were to succeed. He needed to balance the opposing forces in order to master them.

Suddenly, his mind realigned. The white fire of his sword shuddered and a tinge of black snaked through it. Kala Azar stepped back, uncertain at the change. Jom's sword swirled with black and white, light and shadow. His eyes sparkled with the colors of a thousand emotions. The wind picked up and spiraled around him, prompted by the echoes of the music of the Mind Harp.

Jom swung. Kala Azar parried and took another step back. Jom pressed forward, letting the energy flow from his mind to his hand to his blade. The prince was forced to retreat under the ferocity of Jom's attack. Jom thought of his friends' suffering, of his village, of his Grandmother. He thought of all the abuse he had endured and all the wonders he had seen. Love and hatred, pity and remorse; all these emotions ran through his body. The sword in his hand blazed a brilliant light and consumed itself with its own shadow, flickering back and forth between the two. The cyborg screamed as Jom took his arm from his body. Sparks of electricity jumped from his body as the implants overloaded. With a final metallic scream, Kala Azar collapsed and did not move.

Jom looked down at his opponent. He hated him, he felt sorry for him. He hated himself for what he had done. He had to atone. With a flick of his mind, his sword disappeared and he bent down, cradling the cyborg's head in his hands. There was a tiny spark of life still left in him; Jom saw the energy still there. Just a little bit, but it would be enough. He carefully nurtured it, allowing it to grow just strong enough to ensure he would survive, and then dropped Kala Azar's head back to the cold ground and walked away.

: The Spark of Life :

PULA LEAPT INTO JOM'S arms with a yip of joy and licked his face while wiggling around in his hands. The others grinned as they rubbed chafed wrists and ankles. Jom bent down over Ravola. Her red fabric was torn and shredded, revealing bits of pale pink skin underneath. Her eyes fluttered open and she managed a smile at Jom.

"You've come back to us," she said weakly.

"You're safe now," Jom responded, gently adjusting her bandages.

She slowly shook her head. "I am past harm, I think."

"We'll get you some help. Just hold on."

She patted his cheek. Her many tentacles writhed about around them slowly, dropping one by one to the ground and remaining still. "It's all right. It is time for me to join the Sky Hunt."

"Can't you do anything?" Macar asked from behind him. Jom heard a note in the man's voice he had not heard before and it made his heart break.

"I—I don't know."

"Try. Please."

Jom closed his eyes and concentrated. Just like with Kala Azar, he saw the weak life energy of his friend. It slowly spilled from her body, leaving less and less behind with every passing moment. Without asking, everyone stepped closer. Jom opened his eyes and looked to his friends; Macar, his face distraught, Nebt and Not Grey looking on curiously, Pula on his shoulder, and Dianat hovering in the air protectively over the inert body of NDX.

"I'll need your help," he said to them. "I'll need...part of you." As one, they nodded their assent, understanding what he was asking without questioning.

Jom closed his eyes again, feeling for the spark that barely clung to Ravola. He touched it with his mind, cradling it and whispering for it to stay just a little longer. The spark flickered at his touch, responding as if to an old friend. He gently moved his mind around it, encouraging it to hold on, cradling it in his thoughts like a mother would her child. Then he reached out, touching each of his friends in turn, taking from them just a little of their spark. He gently brought the pieces of their sparks to her, whispering to them. They swirled around Ravola's body, then touched her faint spark, adding their light to hers. He reached into his own spark, taking a large chunk, enough to keep hers going. He felt his body shudder he did so, but the Harp energy that now flowed through him kept him alive. He blew his spark into her with a gentle push of his mind. He gathered all the pieces of his friends that floated above her still. With one last soft but urgent push, he gave all those pieces of life to her.

The others gasped as a piece of their life flowed into her. Jom directed the energies gently, letting the sparks mingle quietly, helping them become one. A wave of dizziness washed over Jom as the life left him but he managed to hang on to consciousness. Pula squeaked in concern and he absently scratched behind the Womf's ears as he steadied himself. Ravola moaned as her spark joined with the others. Her body shuddered with new life. Her eyes fluttered then opened and, after a few heartbeats, focused on Jom.

"How?"

Jom gently touched her lips with a finger. "Time enough for that later." He looked to Macar who quickly sat down, taking Ravola's head in his lap. "Rest now."

Jom stood and looked around, gratefully petting Pula who was wriggling around his shoulders.

"Not Graaa," Not Grey said, pointing to NDX.

Jom walked over to the clock-work boy. "Is there anything we can do?"

"The Master can!" Dianat said, trying to modulate her scream so it didn't hurt their ears.

"Take him then," Jom decided. "Take him back to Abla. We will follow as we can."

"Won't leave you!" she protested.

Jom looked around. The bandits had scattered when Kala Azar had been defeated. The cyborg, alive but just, lay alone among the rocks. Nothing else moved within sight.

"I think we're safe enough now," Jom replied.

Dianat screamed in frustration but Jom was firm. He looked around at the group before him.

"We can't continue," he said. "We're hurt. We're tired. We need help."

"We're not finished yet," Macar responded but Jom held up his hand to stop the man.

"We can't continue. But I can. Dianat, take NDX to Abla and get him fixed up. Macar, stay here with Ravola and the others. She needs you."

Macar looked down at Ravola, softly stroking her head as she flittered in and out of consciousness.

"Nebt and Not Grey, you stay here too. Help keep her safe."

"Not Graaa."

"What about you?" Dianat cried as she circled around them in agitation.

"I'll take Pula and find the Chair."

"You can't do this alone!" Macar protested.

Jom nodded. "I still have some of the Harp's energy in me. I can feel it. But it's fading. If I don't go now, I'll lose it." He looked at each of them. "This is how is has to be."

Macar grunted but held his tongue. The others looked at each other but nodded in agreement. Not Grey, confused and scared, came over to Jom.

"Not Graaa," he said earnestly.

"You have to stay here," Jom said gently. "I'll be back. I promise." Pula squeaked in agreement. Jom bent down by Ravola and took one of her hands into his.

"You rest. Stay strong."

Her eyes fluttered open and Jom saw a small smile beneath her fabric. Then she was out again. Jom gave Macar a pat on the shoulder.

"Keep her safe."

Macar nodded. Jom turned to Nebt.

"You stay safe too." The Latuip waved at Jom and shuffled over to Macar and Ravola. Jom sighed, rubbed his eyes and took Pula from his shoulders.

"Are you ready to finish this?" he asked the Womf. Pula licked his hand and barked. Taking a deep breath, Jom felt around for the energy of the Phobetor Chair. He saw a thin tendril of the sickly green energy come off Pula and disappear into the aether. With one more glance at the others, Jom concentrated on the tendril and let himself slide onto a different plane of existence.

: The Here :

THE GREEN TENDRIL QUICKLY grew stronger, leading them to an abandoned ship orbiting a dead planet. They had been so close before the Shadow Saint's attack. Jom pulled them to the source of the energy. Pula squirmed as he felt the influence of the Chair grow stronger and Jom held him tightly, reassuring him that it would be over soon. They stepped through the aether into a large open bay on the ship. A weak force field kept the vacuum of space out to their right. Small emergency lights flickered weakly at regular intervals around the bay. There were no ships in the bay. No people. Nothing except an object in the middle of the bay: The Phobetor Chair.

"we are here"

Jom whirled around. The whisper felt near. But no one was around. He turned and studied the device, keeping his distance. He saw the sickly energy swirl around the chair. It had an overpowering aura of evil lingering about it. Jom gagged and took a step back. Pula whined and scrambled up to Jom's shoulder, keeping close and shivering. Jom reached up and stroked the Womf's thick fur.

"It's all right," he reassured him, wishing he believed the words. As he studied the swirling energy, he became aware of something else; a murmuring of voices whispered to them. Jom looked around. They were alone in the bay. But there were definitely voices. He could hear them better now. They sounded like they were coming from far away yet still close by. And they sounded like they were in pain. Anguished screams and angry shouts echoed around them. Jom whirled around, trying to pinpoint the source of the voices. Then he heard something else. He heard laughter.

The energy that swirled around the chair coalesced into a figure. The features were indistinct and hazy but somehow familiar. His laughter floated around them, mocking them, teasing them. Pula whimpered and hid behind Jom's head, clinging desperately to Jom's shirt. Jom reached around and gently pried the Womf from his clothing and held him tight. Pula barked at the figure before them, provoking more laughter.

"How interesting!" a voice said. "My first subject has come back!"

Pula barked again and Jom felt his chest tighten as he realized who was standing in front of them.

"The Shield of Ku'baba!"

The figure bowed. "At your service."

"we are here" Again, Jom heard voices whispering in the darkness. Sparing a quick look around, he saw nothing but an empty cargo bay. He tried to block out the voices and studied the apparition before him.

"But how?"

Even though the image was hazy, Jom could see the cold sneer crawl across the face of the Shield. "I cannot be destroyed. I am eternal."

"As am I!"

The energy swirled around the other side of the chair, coalescing into a large muscular figure in armor.

"The Sword of Ku'baba!"

Pula barked again. Jom felt the energy shudder as it concentrated into the two figures flanking the chair. The Shield lifted an arm and gestured. Jom felt Pula tremble and let out a cry of pain. He looked down. The thin tendril of energy that connected Pula to the chair was pulling at him, bringing him back to the source of all his pain. The Shield smiled as Pula cried out in terror.

"No!" Concentrating, Jom called forth his sword of energy. A brilliant white sword laced with the darkest black formed in his hand. With a cry, he brought the sword down, slicing through the green tendril. Energy connected with energy and the tendril that had kept the Womf chained for so many cycles was severed forever. Pula cried out once then was quiet. The Shield staggered back.

"How did you do this?" the apparition demanded. The Sword of Ku'baba stepped forward menacingly.

But Jom ignored them, looking down at the Womf cradled in his arm. Pula nuzzled against him. He was still shaking from shock but did not seem, finally, to be in any pain. Pula managed a growl at the spirits in front of them. For the first time in a very long time, the small creature was not in horrible torment. Jom could already feel Pula's energy grow as the effects of the Chair finally began to fade away.

"We are here"

"No more," Jom said, looking up at the figures. "No more! The Chair will never hurt anyone ever again!"

"How will you stop us?" The Sword asked, lifting a massive battle axe that materialized from the cloud of evil that surrounded it.

The Shield laughed "How will you stop us?" he echoed.

"We Are Here."

Jom focused his mind, looking for the source of the whispering that had continued nonstop since they arrived. Then, he saw who was whispering to him and he allowed a small smile creep onto his face.

"I won't stop you," he said to the figures before him.

"Of course you won't," the Sword boasted.

"I won't stop you," Jom repeated, "but they will."

"What do you mean?"

"We. Are. Here."

Jom closed his eyes and concentrated. The whispers were now stronger and growing in intensity. Jom reached out with his mind, using the power of the Mind Harp to touch the whispering entities that circled around the Chair. He pictured Justice and Sacrifice. He lent Stength and Bravery. He allowed the little Mercy he felt be tempered with Wisdom and Loyalty. He brought the diffused energies that swirled around the chair together, strengthening them, encouraging them to grow. As the mists gathered, their voices grew in strength as well. They were heard again, perhaps for the first time in thousands of cycles.

"We. Are. Here."

The Shield and the Sword looked around, hunting for these new voices.

"Who is that?" The Sword demanded, hefting his battle axe.

"Show yourselves!" The Shield yelled at the darkness. Jom poured more energy into the mists, bringing the voices into the light.

Slowly, figures began to take shape all around them. Shadowy outlines of all manner of creatures--tall, squat, four-legged and two-legged, amorphous blobs and razor-sharp exoskeletons—shimmered into view. The bay filled with the memories of a hundred, a thousand victims of the Chair. The light from the uncounted apparitions flooded the bay and Jom squinted. As they manifested, they turned towards the Shield and the Sword. They all stared at the Shield and the Sword. They all pointed to the figures flanking the Chair. And they all spoke the same words:

WE ARE HERE

"What is this? Who are these cretins?"

"These are all your subjects," Jom told The Shield. "These are all the souls you tortured. These are your victims."

"Impossible!"

"It's your fault. Your chair kept their souls chained to it. Just like the chair kept you two. It never let go of you and it never let go of them. They are here. They've always been here. They've suffered for so very, very long. And now they're free. And they're not happy with you."

The horde of creatures surrounded them like a sea. The Here moved towards the two figures slowly at first, then quicker as they found they now had an outlet for all their suffering. The Sword swung his great axe. Its misty shape cut through the shadowy apparitions that advanced on him. The Here reached out, grasping at him. The Sword roared and swung again, trying to cut them down. But there were too many for the Sword to fight off. The Here fell on him, their hands and claws and teeth digging into the ectoplasm that was all that remained of the great Sword of Ku'baba. They tore into him and he fought back but he was powerless against the immense pain and agony that propelled the Here. They ripped him apart. The Sword roared in anger as his essence was shredded and dispersed.

The Shield, seeing the great warrior fall to the mass of apparitions, begged and pleaded but his pleas went unheeded. The Here tore into him as well. They flung pieces of him off into the aether, destroying every last bit of the architect of their suffering. His screams echoed around the bay long after he was finally destroyed. As he perished, the energy of the Chair dimmed. Jom watched as the last bits of sickly green energy faded away. Without the Shield's evil to keep it contained, the energy of the Chair dispersed into the universe. Once the Chair was finally powerless, the Here, strengthened by the power of the Mind Harp, turned to it and pulled it apart. They burned it away with their hatred and suffering. They melted it down to nothing and scattered the fumes to the winds of the aether. Pula barked in encouragement as the Here dismantled the Chair piece by piece until there was nothing left. The evil that was the Phobetor Chair was gone forever.

Finally, the Here turned to Jom and Pula. They crowded around, pressing in closer and closer.

"We are Here," they said, a thousand voices echoing off the walls of the bay.

"But you don't have to stay here any longer," Jom replied. "You're free now."

The apparition nearest to Jom reached out a hand. Steeling his heart, Jom took it and smiled. "You're free," he repeated. But it slowly shook its head.

"We are held here no longer. But we cannot pass on." Jom looked at them in confusion.

"You can't?"

It shook its head. "Too much time. Too much damage."

"I'm so sorry."

"We wish to help," it said, its voice echoed by the rest.

Jom looked out over the sea of creatures standing before him. As one, they nodded in agreement. Jom could see their energies pressing forward towards him, eager to be part of something once again after so long of drifting in pain. After being lost in the dark for an eternity, they now could bask in the light. They looked to Jom to give them the opportunity to give some meaning to their existence now, instead of wandering forever in the aether.

"If you're sure." Again they nodded. Pula yipped in agreement.

Jom took a deep breath and reached deep inside himself. There was still a little of the Mind Harp's energy in him. He took that energy and flung it out over the Here like a net. They leapt up, entangling their essences with Jom's. Jom pulled, bringing the Here into him, bringing their energies, their souls, their stories into him. He felt his body fill with the lives of a thousand creatures, each giving him something precious, something unique. He looked down at his hands. They glimmered with life. The Here whispered to him, telling him their stories, giving him knowledge. His mind exploded with voices. It was overwhelming and Jom fell to his knees, unable to process so many images and songs and smells all at once. But the Here, sensing his distress, quieted down. Softly, they spoke to him. It would take time, but, they assured him, he would learn, they would learn, how to work together. Pula licked his face and Jom smiled an unsteady smile.

"Let's go get the others."

: Return :

JOM THOUGHT ABOUT HIS friends and searched the aether for signs of them. Like a favorite note from an old song or hearing your child cry in a crowd, he was able to pick out a familiar strand among the countless tendrils of energy that made up the universe. He reached out with his mind, bolstered by the Here, encouraged by Pula in his arms, and grabbed hold. Clutching Pula tightly to his chest, he pulled on the tendril and stepped through the veil that separates worlds.

Bright light streamed in from windows high above their heads. The massive library of Abla'than'abla was warm and cheery. The great fire in the center of the room blazed high into the air, warming Jom and Pula as they stepped through the aether. His friends looked up and were instantly on their feet, surrounding Jom and checking him for wounds. Pula yipped in delight as Nebt took him from Jom's arms, licking the Latuip's face amid excited yelps. Jom breathed a heavy sigh of relief when NDX and Ravola stood to greet him. Ravola, still weak from her wound, gave him a mighty hug that lifted him off his feet and he admonished her, pleading to be set down again. The clock-work boy, wound up again and functioning, was in the process of reattaching its arm. Jom laughed in delight and gave the automaton a hug.

Psedjet had food and drink waiting and they settled down near the fire. Abla, in between burning the present, kept close to them so he wouldn't miss any details about their adventure.

"Not Graaa," Not Grey said, unsure. Jom placed a hand on the drone's shoulder and nodded.

"Don't worry. We'll help you adjust."

NDX studied Not Grey for several heartbeats. "Are you positive there is no connection to the Swarm?" it asked. Jom concentrated and peered through the veil.

"I don't see any, no. I know I cut through the energy that connected him to the grey while we were traveling the aether."

"Not Graaa," Not Grey agreed, his face lonely yet hopeful.

"Interesting," NDX replied. "Perhaps we will be able to come up with some defense by studying him."

"He's not an experiment," Jom protested. "He's just now able to be his own person and live his own life. I won't let anyone take that from him."

NDX held up its hand. "I did not mean to suggest otherwise."

"I know. I know." Jom sighed. "I just..I just don't want anyone to suffer anymore because of me. There's been so much pain lately."

"Life is painful," Ravola said, wincing as she settled onto some cushions next to Macar. "Do not fear the hurting."

"I don't fear it. Not for me. For him," he stroked Pula's head, "hurting for so long. For the Here. They suffered so much. And for...." Jom looked around wildly. "Where's Dianat? Is she all right?"

In response, NDX opened the compartment in its side and withdrew a crystal vial. Jom took the vial and looked at it closely. Inside, he could see a face swirling around amid the dark liquid.

"Are you hurt? The Phobetor Chair is destroyed. It was the only way."

Dianat opened her mouth in a scream that Jom couldn't hear, protected from her voice by the crystal.

"She says she is fine. When the connection was severed, she went into shock but has since recovered," NDX said.

"I'm so sorry. I never meant to hurt you," Jom told the Water Banshee.

"She says do not worry. She is finally free of the Chair's pull. You have released her from its evil."

Pula scrambled down Jom's arm and licked the vial, telling the Water Banshee he knew what she was going through.

"Dianat thanks you. You have done something she never thought possible."

"Which is why you must continue your quest," Abla said from behind them. He casually threw a scroll into the fire and joined them. "You must become the next Technomage and make the universe a better place."

"I don't know if I can. There's so much evil out there. It's all so...so much bigger than I am."

"You will rise. You will become as big. If you imagine yourself to be bigger than the evil, that is."

Jom shook his head. "I doubt I can do that."

Abla laughed. "Doubt? Don't be silly. It's already history. It just hasn't happened yet."

"I really don't understand how that works," Macar muttered.

Abla studied the man for a moment.

"What's to understand? He will be a Technomage. You will be a hero. And I will grow younger."

Macar shook his head at the historian. "If you say so."

"Meh."

"Not Graaa."

A soft wind stirred the dust at his feet. Jom stood on a hill, Pula on his shoulder. They looked into the distance. Past the fields, nearly to the horizon, lay a small village. They could see the fire burning in the center of the small huts that served as homes for the handful of people scraping a living on this small planet. Dusk was settling over the land and Jom could hear the mothers calling in the children that roamed the area. A thin creek ran along the edge of the fields. Its black waters murmured quietly as they ran over hidden rocks and concealed predators. Jom moved lightly across the hard dirt towards the river. He saw a dead bush along the river's edge and picked his way towards it. Reaching down, he pushed the dead branches aside and peered into the small hole carved into the hillside. Memories stirred within him and he fought back tears. It looked so tiny now, although he doubted he had grown any since he had last been in it. At least physically.

Once, this had been his only refuge. Here he had dreamed of walking among the stars and meeting gods. Here he had hidden from the blows and punches and words of those bigger than him. Here he had told himself the stories his Grandmother had told him.

But now he had his own stories. And more. The Here whispered in his head, eager to tell him their histories, their tales. He quieted them, letting his own story replay in his mind's eye. He looked up, staring at his village in the distance and smiled. One day, he would return to the village. He would let Grandmother hear his tale.

But not yet. He had too much to do yet.

Scratching Pula behind the ear, he whispered to the falling darkness.

"Let me tell you a story..."

ABOUT THE AUTHOR

Armed with little more than a lifted eyebrow and a sarcastic quip, Jeff Monday wanders the space between what you didn't say and what you sorta meant, listening to your tall tales and scribbling them down the backs of cocktail napkins.

Look for him on the interweb. He's around. Or buy him a drink at the pub. He's thirsty.

Made in the USA
Charleston, SC
01 August 2015